THE BROTHERHOOD OF MAN

THE
BROTHERHOOD
OF MAN

KIMANI KINYUA

SBI

STREBOR BOOKS

NEW YORK LONDON TORONTO SYDNEY

Strebor Books
P.O. Box 6505
Largo, MD 20792
http://www.streborbooks.com

Cover design: www.mariondesigns.com

ISBN-13 978-1-59309-064-7
ISBN-10   1-59309-064-1
LCCN 2006923552

First printing August 2006
Manufactured and Printed in the United States of America

10   9   8   7   6   5   4   3   2   1

For information regarding special discounts for bulk purchases,
please contact Simon & Schuster Special Sales at 1-800-456-6798
or business@simonandschuster.com

ACKNOWLEDGMENTS

I would first like to thank God for blessing me with the strength, perseverance, patience, talent, and flat-out common sense needed to complete this book. I would like to thank my mother, Nancy Brown; father, Tommy Brown; and my sister, Susie Brown, for your support, ideas, and inspiration.

To my daughter, Solana Silas, and my niece Jaylla Brown, though you're too young to read this right now, thank you for going to bed on time, which gave me time to write every night. Oh, and thanks for testing my patience. What are kids for, right? I love you guys.

Thanks to Siria Silas for being a great role model and mother to our beautiful daughter who is the inspiration for my next book. Oh yeah, thank you for the years of support and that painfully unique inspiration you provide. It pushes me to be great beyond my own expectations.

Special thanks to my good friends Maricruz Lopez, Cheryl Butler, Stacy Robinson, Lucy Shafner, and Susan Parrish. The support and words of encouragement are greatly appreciated.

Lastly, a very special thanks to my literary agent, Maxine Thompson, and to Strebor Books. Thanks for all of your help and thanks for giving me this opportunity.

To the crew: Vic, Steve, and Kenny—enjoy this one 'cause those ol' skool Fridays are what made this thing happen.

PROLOGUE

Now this is a hypothetical case, but I wonder. Why is it if a man kills another man in the heat of a battle, he's considered a hero, but if he kills someone in the heat of passion, he's considered a murderer? I stood on my balcony that rainy Saturday morning briefly pondering over that little brain-teaser, smiling to myself over the irony of how much it applied to me. It was indeed an interesting way to begin my thirty-first birthday.

Although I was comfortable distancing myself from the concepts of remorse or a guilty conscience, I found myself uncomfortable with my current status as a fugitive. It was insulting. As I saw it, I was a free man; free of the past, so to speak.

Still, I was probably fooling myself. For about a year or so, I kept my life as stress-free as possible, choosing simply to go through the motions of participating in the life of a natural introvert. I seemed to be waiting for something—I just wasn't sure what. Many could say that I'd been on the run for a year, but that wasn't the case. I simply wasn't an easy man to find. Or so I thought.

With all of the choices I've ever faced, the last one I expected to be making at this juncture in my life was that of prison time, a mental institution, or death. Instead of moving forward from a fairly decent life with its share of anguish, toward one full of new possibilities, I was now in some strange kind of ghetto purgatory with no sensible way out.

ALEX

etective Anthony Games slowly found his way from Chicago, Illinois to my bachelor's apartment in Southwest Washington, D.C. I lived on the thirteenth floor of what was probably the worst high-rise apartment in the District—the only one in the city with thirteen floors. For me, it was perfect. I enjoyed an inspiring view of the Potomac River, the building's shitty plumbing, broken elevators, faulty heat and air-conditioning. Therefore, constant police presence was a reasonable trade-off. Truthfully, I never took much time to enjoy it. Actually, I hadn't been able to enjoy much of anything over the past year.

Detective Anthony Games arrived at my place that afternoon to pay me an unexpected visit. The knock at my door wasn't as surprising as I'd assumed it would've been, considering my place had never seen a visitor in the ten months that I resided here.

"Nice suit." I snickered, staring at him as he stood in the doorway.

"Thanks." Games nodded, a calm smile playing at his lips, knowing I had a reason to jest considering the fact that you'd catch Games in a suit about as often as you'd catch Al Sharpton at a KKK meeting.

"Pick that out yourself?"

"You go'n let me in or what?" Games' smile left his face as if it had no business being there in the first place.

I opened the door, fully inviting him into a less-than-inviting apartment. I studied his suit and continued to laugh to myself. Time had eaten away at my taste for any degree of decorative class as far as my home was concerned. As a result, Games was greeted by a well-buffed, empty, hard-wood floor living room. I chose to throw caution to the wind and live without the luxuries of those who entertain company so 99% of my home was well, like I said before…empty; no chairs, tables, stools, couches, love seats, cute little lamps, plants, flowers and the like. Walls and floor was fine with me.

And unlike common folk, who decorate their living rooms with paintings, family pictures, and the like, I chose to fill the walls of that empty space with my past. Black and white 8 ½-by-11 photos of everyone who was ever important to me were pasted on all four walls from top to bottom. It was obvious from Detective Games expression as he looked around that he felt justified in paying me a visit. Considering the fact that the detective and I had known each other for over twenty years, I felt the whole thing with him dropping by to be rather "poetic justice," for the lack of a better word. What better scenario than to send a wanted murderer's best friend to retrieve him, especially considering that the best friend is one of Chicago's top cops.

"Wanna drink?" I asked as I headed to the kitchen. I grabbed a bottle and two shot glasses and placed them on my kitchen counter, which I loved because it was like a little mini bar separating the kitchen from the area that was supposed to be the dining room.

"Yeah, looks like I'll need one." Games stood in the middle of an empty living room staring at the walls. He focused his attention on the pictures of himself along with so many others close to both of us. For the most part, Games stayed true to that old "not on duty" thing when it came to drinking, but under some circumstances, like the company of dear friends, he made exceptions. Truthfully, it didn't matter since he could almost certainly shit on the White House lawn and nobody would care as long as he was takin' out the bad guys.

I prepared a shot of aged whiskey for the both of us, eyeing Games the whole time. "You come alone?" I held onto the bottle, knowing the first shot would definitely not be the last.

"What do you think?" Games heaved a deep sigh before downing his shot.

"What's wrong? You seem tense. That should be me from what I hear," I poured another shot for him and myself.

"Really, so what have you heard, Alex?" Games finished his second shot.

"What do you want, Games?" I asked, returning the same icy stare, remembering how much I missed the fact that Games was the only one who called me "Alex" or "Alexander," rather than the commonly used moniker "Blue"—short for my last name Bluesen. Given the fact that you don't run into many black men with last names like my own, I was comfortable with my nickname.

"Fuck you. What you mean, 'what I want'?"

"I mean…what is it that you want? Why are you here, Games?"

"I want to help you, Alex. I'm here to keep you from fuckin' up anymore than you already have."

I don't know if it was the whiskey or his genuine concern, but his tone changed as he appeared to be more interested in talking to me rather than at me.

"I appreciate the offer but I'm not in need of anyone's assistance in my life right now."

"To the contrary, old friend," Games whispered in a deep voice, glancing at his watch. He took a minute to assess my humble apartment with a complete once-over before walking over to the sliding glass doors leading to my balcony. "You're in a bad spot—one you can't get out of without my assistance."

I walked over and stood next him. "Shit is tight, ain't it? Step outside. You get a better view when you're on the balcony."

We stepped out on the balcony and enjoyed a quick moment of silence. We casually took a minute to savor my view of the District of Columbia and all of its politically influenced glory. Ordinarily, that picture of the nation's capital is a peaceful one and not even the yelling, screaming, cussing, loud music, or gun shots from below are distractions to the…wait a minute…now that's interesting. Ordinarily, I would've been glancing at all of the loud police sirens, crazy traffic and overall commotion below as if I were any of the other tenants, simply thinking "what in the hell is going on now?" It appears that I'd spoken too soon because the helicopter and unannounced six police patrol cars and SWAT van buzzing below my balcony was a huge distraction.

"What are you gonna do, Alex?" Games glared at me, before placing his hands in his pockets. He'd stepped inside at this point and was watching me as I stood on my balcony witnessing the fact that his visit was not solely that of a good friend.

"You brought all that for me." I laughed. It was all I could do to cover my surprise.

"I had no choice…"

"Don't worry about it," I interrupted before he could explain. "I wouldn't expect anything less, considering my actions."

"What you did was wrong man. I understand why but…"

"You know," I stopped him again, and thought quietly to myself, "I haven't really thought about it much really, especially the repercussions and all."

As I waived to the cavalry below, stepped back in, and made my way back over to the bottle of whiskey to pour us another shot, I wondered if this would be the last time I would talk to my old friend. A year ago things were so different, but now…well, now is now and I had another decision to make, another choice.

"How's Dali and Cyprus?" I poured the shot.

"Worried about you."

"You think?"

"Alex?" Games asked, his confidence at this point appeared more like concern. I looked at him in reply.

"I'm running out of time dog."

"It's probably best you go now, Games." I choked down my shot.

"Alex."

"I can't leave with you, man."

"What are you gonna do?"

"I don't know, maybe nothing at all, maybe something special. Either way you can't be here. I love you, Dali, and Cyprus like brothers, but I fucked things up…"

"Alex, you talking crazy, dog. Look, man, let me take you back home. Shit'll work out, trust me…"

"You gotta go, Games."

"Alex? *Are you crazy?*" Games' eyes widened as he stared as if I was deranged. I believe he truly didn't know what else to say. If he did, he didn't know how to say it.

"Take care of yourself, Games. Take care of my friends." We stood there for a second or two staring into each other's eyes perhaps speaking to each other in a fashion that was beyond words. I noticed tears finding their way from Games' generous heart to those serious eyes of his and I assume he felt them coming because he suddenly stepped to me and hugged me. Returning his embrace and his sentiment, I felt just as calm and relaxed as ever. I only wished I could've helped Games feel the same.

"Everything's going to be okay, big man. You gotta go now." I smiled and squeezed him like the big brother that he unknowingly was through being true to himself and to me as a friend.

I damn near had to push him out of the door, but it was best for both of us. I'd been a one-man show for a while and I wanted to keep it that way. Maybe I was crazy, but it really didn't matter now. Games was right about one thing though. The clock was ticking. I'd soon have unexpected and unfriendly company. Oddly enough, all I could think about was Games, Cyprus, Dali, and Avida and how life used to be.

I walked down the short hallway to my linen closet and grabbed the shotgun that liberated me a year ago. I felt just as empowered as I did the first time I held it. I could hear the police radios and hard footsteps from the boots of the police stampeding outside in the hallways. I could never have imagined that there would come a time where I would be walking with both God and the devil simultaneously. This was that time, and my fate was inevitable and unknown.

A YEAR EARLIER...
FRIDAY NIGHTS

Sooner or later, we all get to a point in our lives where a serious break is needed. It's just natural. Regardless of age, sex, race, religious or cultural backgrounds, everyone, to some degree, deals with issues concerning relationships, children, money, love, loss and well...simply maintaining a sane and secure grip on reality. In all honesty, *living* takes a lot of work. On occasion, we look for a little fun to off set all that work. My friends and I chose Friday evenings.

Fridays were literally sacred for us. We thought of them as holidays. Even though Sunday through Thursday wasn't exactly hell for us, it was always reassuring to know that even if it was there was at least one day out of that week that we knew would go right. Fridays were a ritual and under many circumstances, they frequently tended to be the only thing that kept us sane and secure, some of us at least.

I suppose it would be easy to label our Friday gatherings as the typical "boys night out."

To the outside eye—especially those of girlfriends and others looking to be—it was just a night where the fellas would get together, drink and lie about their sexual escapades and anything else they could think of. For men like us, however, Friday night was a necessity. We needed it. It was the one day of the week that evened the scales of the responsibilities of being a black man.

During the week, we concerned ourselves with finances, the well-being and safety of our families, our jobs, the needs of our "significant other" or "others" and well, the list goes on. Bottom line for getting together on Fridays was this, "When everything around us seemed to be falling apart, we felt relaxed and re-energized. When everything around us was right, we felt perfect." We were our own spiritual counselors, priests, and psychologists.

Ironically, not a whole lot happened when my friends and I were together aside from the typical testosterone-driven chit chat and enough alcohol and marijuana consumption to keep the local liquor stores and corner weed hustlers happier than kids on Christmas Day.

Still, every weekend, Lorenzo Dali, Anthony Games, Cyprus Kane and myself would get together, get fucked up and discuss every thing from pussy to politics, crime to civil rights, old days to nowadays. It was not only a time to hang out, it was a time to forget about living and simply think about life.

In thinking about life, sometimes you really can't help but realize that hey, shit happens; bullshit, dumb shit, real shit, you name it. When it does, some people are prepared for it and already have contingency plans in the works. Others simply stand there, astonished and confused as to how shit happened and why is it that it smelled so bad.

The fellas and I all had our ways of dealing with shit. Some ways were more effective than others. Still, our individual approaches to both life and shit enabled us to appreciate each other's differences.

My partner, Cyprus, for example, had a pretty simple way of looking at things. He saw life in the same fashion soldiers saw war; capture or kill the enemy, take his shit, come home alive and be prepared to do it all over again tomorrow. His style wasn't too surprising considering he was a predator by nature. He always had been.

I'd known Cyprus since I was ten years old. He was two years older than Dali and I and by far the craziest of the four of us. Cyprus was one of those rare kids who was a bad ass from birth. Though he fell into that typical category of the young black male missing the strong father figure, Cyprus indulged in criminal activities because he wanted to. He had the same choices in life of any other middle class kid. His mother and his aunt had raised him, and oddly enough, he fared quite well in school.

While cartoons, candy, and kickball entertained the rest of us in our youth, Cyprus was always instinctively drawn to darker pleasures. When he was thirteen, he started working as muscle for a small-time local drug dealer named

Honey. At that age, Cyprus wasn't pressed for money or struggling to put food on the table and he actually wasn't what you'd consider a big kid, but it was at that time that he began to master the art of criminal intimidation. Three years later, he killed Honey. Aside from wanting to "move up," I recall the reason for his ruthless behavior to be that he was simply tired of working for a nigga who called himself "Honey."

Suffice to say, he was a damned dangerous individual when he wanted to be, and that was more often than not. At six feet even and around two-hundred pounds, he spent his free time, which was basically all day, with weights in his hands. Though he'd never been to jail, you couldn't tell by looking at him. With the exception of a skin tone as healthy and chocolate as an African model, you would swear that he'd been at Riker's Island for years. His arms were draped in tattoos, mostly of symbols and words representing his lifestyle. He boasted the acronym hidden in the picture of a gun on his forearm which read, M.P.R., the familiar street formula for longevity and success, Money, Power and Respect.

In person, Cyprus was a true menace to those who didn't know him, sometimes even to those who did. He made it a habit to look directly and intently in your eyes during a conversation, giving the impression that he would know if you were lying to him even if you were thinking about it. And I always thought it was strange how in many instances he was like an experienced soldier at war, invariably edgy but with almost a dead-like calm—ready for anything. As kids, we when ran into trouble, he was generally the first to both start and finish a situation with his foot in someone's ass. As a result of his approach to solving problems, he suffered only one injury, which was at the time a nasty scar that ran from his from his eyebrow to the top of his cheek on the left side of his face. The young man holding the knife that cut him hasn't been seen since. We were all in our teens at the time—around fifteen years ago. As far as the scar is concerned these days, women find it sexy. Go figure.

Cyprus runs with a crew that serves as "business associates," more so than friends. He is both a professional thief and murderer, but not one of those average nickel-and-dime, stick-up-kid types. Cyprus is one of those patient, methodical criminals you always root for in the movies. Constantly scheming, and unlike so many others in his line of work, he is never too greedy. For some reason, he had a problem with doing honest, legitimate work.

Actually, he viewed stealing and killing for money as if it were a job—his job. To him, it was honest, legitimate work. I think that if Cyprus wanted to he could write a book on the dos and don'ts of being a bad guy. The fact that he admittedly kept an open mind and was always learning, in regards to the street, made him even more intriguing to those in the same line of work. In addition to his academic attitude and approach to his work, he stayed busy perfecting his skills. When he wasn't being "contracted," he used his spare time *practicing*.

He spoke rather highly of his last little piece of work. Cyprus had a thing about high profile hustlers with their fancy diamond rings, expensive clothes, and overrated cars. He didn't like them very much. I don't think it was the way they flaunted their stuff that bothered him as much as it was their careless attitude. Cyprus felt that the streets were like a jungle and that all creatures should be aware of the predators.

CYPRUS

Blue's a trip. I ain't never thought of myself like he does. I'm just a regular mufucka tryin' to get paid like everybody else. I guess I just gotta different way of doin' it. It's cool though. Blue's my man. He's the only one out of the four of us who really listens to a nigga when he got some shit on his mind. I dig the way he gets into the shit I be tellin' him about. Nigga be askin' questions and shit…makes you feel like you always got somebody to tell that story to that no one else would ever believe.

On my last shit, I was wit' my usual crew: Big Mo', Pete Quest a.k.a PQ, Mink, and Ron. We spent the whole damn night combing the streets for "prey." Coming up short, we headed to a party that an old girlfriend of mine was throwing in a high-class neighborhood in the 'burbs right outside of Chicago. It was a block away from the party where we found what we were looking for.

"White BMW." I nodded, pointing to these three dudes.

"You like that?" asked Mink.

"Definitely." I turned off the car lights and parked my old Ford station wagon a half-block away and sat for a couple of minutes.

"What's with this waitin' shit, man?" Big Mo' bitched and lit his third cigarette.

"Give 'em a minute. I wanna see how many and if they plan on gettin' out any time soon."

I gotta funny habit of rubbin' my goatee when I get irritated. "What's your fuckin' rush, anyway?"

"I told my girl I'd be back kinda early tonight. You know a nigga gotta get his shit on."

"Shit, I don't know what's worse…these niggas we 'bout to get, or yo' bitch ass." PQ laughed.

"Aiight, let's go," I told 'em.

"Hey, 'C,' what we doin' wit' these mufuckas, man?" Mo' asked.

"Fuck it....I ain't in the mood for any heavy shit tonight. Let's get 'em for what they got and roll."

We got out and I motioned for them to split up and spread out. I told Mink to check the BMW to make sure no one else was in the car and PQ to walk a yard or two behind him on the left side of the street. Me and Big Mo' would approach on the right side.

Them mufuckas were basically standing around, and waiting for what would be the inevitable that evening. I walked up and one of 'em turned to me. He had perfect timing. It was after two a.m. and the streets were deserted and quiet. Probably a bit too quiet, but I ain't never had no problem taking a little bad with the good.

"'Sup, nigga, what you need?" Dude asked. I figured he thought I was looking for drugs or some shit.

"Rent, muthafucka, and I think you bitches can cover it." My 380's were like magic wands. They moved from the small of my back to my hands in less than a second.

Before them bitches knew it, they were surrounded by that infamous criminal element that you hear so much about in movies and music. Guns and extremely nasty attitudes suddenly popped out of the street's shadows.

"Come up off all ya' shit, bitch, right now. I'm in a fuckin' hurry." Mo' said.

"In the bag, muthafucka—coke, weed, cash, all that iced-out shit and the keys to that bitch-ass ride. If the shit's worth somethin', yo ass is leavin' without it!" announced PQ.

And so, we got 'em for what I'm guessing was damn near everything they owned at that moment; I'd guess worth around thirty to forty grand including the car. Not a bad night for a few of minutes of work. We made 'em run back to where ever they came from on foot. Me and the crew headed to the party.

Now, don't get me wrong. I ain't the fuckin' the steal-from-the-rich, give-to-the-poor type. I just know how to catch people who ain't being all that careful. With me and jobs like that, it wasn't so much the money as it was the business of gettin' the money.

GAMES

The time was about ten forty-five p.m. Friday. Blue and I were at Dali's place. These nights usually began with a barrage of phone calls amongst the four of us, checking to see if everyone was still coming. It really served no purpose aside from reassurance. We were all quite busy during the week, so by this time, we were like teenage girls on prom night. Anxious and ready.

We met at Dali's place, more often than not, for a number of reasons. His place was top of the line. That was Dali's style: imported Sasaki kitchenware, custom-made contemporary living room furniture from American Leather, rare paintings, antiques, and crystal. All of it was carefully placed and positioned in his high-rise, three-bedroom condo with the help of one of those high-priced, home decorator consultants. He was the only brother I knew with a subscription to *Metropolitan Home*.

Dali, Blue and I sat with drinks, cigarettes, and cigars in hand talking and laughing about the good, the bad, and the ugly. We were talking about the women we had dated and slept with as we casually flipped through an old photo album, the pictures had gone back almost twenty years. There was always some sort of music being played, usually something old 'cause I'm an ol' school kinda guy. Al Green's "Love and Happiness," War's "Slippin' into Darkness," and Parliament's "Flashlight" were some of my favorites. They reminded me of times when things seemed easier. I generally like to think of the entire mood of the evening as therapy, especially considering my line of work. Not too many black folk I know can afford shit like those two-hundred-dollars-an-hour, psychological atonement sessions. The four of us could give a fuck about those so-called doctors who could never truly understand and treat what we'd been through. So the alternative—good friends—was how we survived. We looked to one another for some sort of mutual guarantee that life could only get better. If reality could imitate that sentiment, we'd all be better off.

"Shit." I burped, finishing off the last of my Jack Daniel's and Coke. "It's fuckin' nine-thirty. Hey 'D.' Hit Cyprus on his cell again," I told Dali, as he glanced at his watch.

According to Blue and Dali, I got this undying and constant preoccupation with Cyprus' whereabouts. What can I say? The shit comes with the territory. Blue with his cerebral ass thinks it's 'cause of some mutual concern that we all shared for one another. The truth of it is, I'm a cop. Cyprus, though he's my dog, also served as my fuckin' nemesis at times. Hell, I think he does some of the shit he does just to fuck wit' me.

"Why?" Dali laughed. "What's ya hurry? What? You itchin' to roll and go twist out that white girl?"

"Fuck you!" I shouted jokingly.

"Ooohhh shiiit, he went low on that shit," Blue added. "Hey 'D,' she ain't bad for a white girl though...blonde hair, blue eyes, and cleavage bangin' like L.A. gangs, ol' girl on some fuckin'...Playboy bunny shit, you ask me."

"No doubt, but ain't nobody ask you." I pushed Blue on the shoulder before grabbing my crotch with both hands indicating that his comment was right on point, "Bullshit aside though, ya'll know I represent sistas 'til the day I die. But it's hard to fight temptation when it's constantly thrown at a mufucka."

A loud banging at the door interrupted us.

"Who is it?!!" we barked in unison.

"Me, muthafuckas," Cyprus returned, opening the door.

Dali always kept the door unlocked on the evenings we hung out. "S'up, niggas, I got smoke, some Hennessy XO, and the drop on five of the wildest freaks in the city." He was clearly feeling good about something because he was yanking bottles, weed, and rolling papers out of the bags. He displayed them to us like we were on a game show and hadn't had a good time in months.

"They betta not be like them thieves you brought over here last time," Dali reached for the VSOP. He immediately poured a glass for all of us. I guess Cyprus' excitement was a bit catching.

"I ain't hear you complainin' when they was here." Cyprus reached out his glass for a toast.

"Yeah, but I woke up in the morning to find two bottles of wine, a fifth of Belvedere, five CD's, a bag of weed, and three DVDs missing," Dali added, as we all raised our glasses and shared a toast and a laugh.

"Where you been?" I asked Cyprus.

"Out and about, my brother. Why?"

"Just curious."

Dali chose to finish that little conversation with a simple, "Fellas, save it for some other day, some other time."

We finished the rest of the night with drinks, jokes, and overall "cool" attitudes. Anyone could see, however, that drama filled the air as much as the smoke did. This "crew" of ours operated on a premise similar to that of a business. Although many things seemed perfect on the surface, there were internal complications. There is a common belief that all good friendships come with a degree of differences. Over the years I could see that some of our "differences" were far from ordinary.

Cyprus and I are like a two-headed monster that's kept alive by struggling with itself. Cyprus is, well, a professional bad guy. He possesses all the qualities it takes to be very good at his job: intelligence, patience, preparedness, and just plain evil at times—a criminal's criminal.

Me, I'm just a good ol' fashioned cop. Not your common, pain-in-the-ass, racial-profilin', fuckin'-with-you-for-no-reason-at-all cop. I'm one of those brothers who became a cop because I really believed that I could make a difference. It didn't take long for me to find out that that shit was easier said than done. To be real though, I take my shit seriously. Go to Marion Penitentiary and ask about me. I've been behind the arrests of a lot of niggas who thought they'd be hustlin', stealin', and killin' forever.

I mean ,shit, I ain't as swole up as Cyprus but I don't need to be. I make up for muscular fitness with raw doggedness. The only weights I like to lift are the ones that require loaded clips. That attitude of mine is what drew the comparisons to Cyprus. It didn't matter though, 'cause in my heart I knew that we were very different in a lot of ways. Even as kids, the main difference between he and I could be found in our motivations.

While Cyprus was content with knockin' guys out, my thing was helping them up and bringing them back. Shit didn't always work, though. That's the frustrating part about my job…dealin' wit' knuckleheads who just don't get it. Me, I figured it out a long time ago. I've been on my own since I was thirteen.

Granted, I've seen as many altercations as Cyprus over the years, but I was generally kickin' someone's ass to defend a woman's honor, to teach a dead-beat dad a lesson in responsibility, or to educate some youngster on earning respect. I became a cop simply because for me it was the right thing to do. The fellas weren't the least bit surprised.

The three of 'em still clown me about lookin' like a cop. I don't mind, though. Hey, sue me. I'm a plain, jeans, work boots, T-shirts and sweatshirts guy and that's when a muthafucka's casual. At around six feet two and two hundred-thirty pounds, there really ain't much special about me as far as appearances are concerned. And fuck what you think, I like it that way. I could care less about shit like shaving and spending one hundred dollars on colognes to impress women. I leave that to Dali. Actually, I try to keep my distance from extremely attractive women, 'cause I don't do the high-main-tenance thing.

I keep my lifestyle simple by spending my free time with my five-year-old son, Christopher. He means the world to me. I spend time in front of the TV where I dedicate myself to ESPN. Simplicity with me, however, ends there. When it comes to the job, I'm as committed as anyone, especially Cyprus.

He and I live on the flip side of the other's coin and work opposite sides of the streets. We fight to maintain our friendship. It was difficult. His associates know his best friend is one of the roughest detectives in the city. My colleagues know my best friend is one of the most well-known contract killers and pro-fessional thieves in the city.

No bullshit, though, I seem to get it the worse. My cop cronies have diffi-culty following the cat-and-mouse game that Cyprus and I have been involved in over the past fifteen years. It is a very dangerous game of chess between two good friends.

I think I struggle more with the situation to be honest. If you ask Blue, it's because he can see a side of Cyprus in me. Personally, I think it's because I have a conscience and morals. Cyprus has no idea what those words mean. I got my son, too. He keeps my grounded. He helps me put all of the vile shit I see in perspective. Guys who do jobs like me need kids. We need someone to fill a void that neither a woman nor even a good friend can. We need someone to look at what we say, what we do, and who we are as if there is nothing else more important in existence. We need someone to give our lives some kind of value. We might have problems doing that alone.

That is something people don't understand about the present situation of black men. You hear so much about black kids being without guidance and positive role models, which causes them to become killers, thieves, and drug dealers. Still, there seems to be no real recognition, let alone respect, for those black men who actually put forth a concerted effort to make some kind of change. At times, I think African-American communities are the worst. I mean, hell, we get a little surface praise here and there, but nothing truly substantial. For the most part, black men catch shit from all directions—mothers, fathers, brothers, sisters, girlfriends, wives, churches, community leaders, politicians, the media, and sometimes friends. Respect and power generally goes out to the brothers who take lives rather than the one's who nourish and protect them.

Anyway, let me get off my soapbox and get to the get-on. Kickin' it on Friday is always on some crazy act-a-fool shit; Saturday is when I got to cool out and be grown. The shitty part about my job is that there are times I'd have to leave because I got a call from work. This Saturday, I hoped that wouldn't be the case. I arrived early and was later joined by Blue and his girl to see Dali play at this popular jazz club in downtown Chicago. It's called The First Set, where all the uppity Negroes go to hang out.

DALI

Chicago has always been a city with a rich jazz scene and, from what some folk thought, I was slowly becoming a revolutionary. My band and I worked a number of the popular local spots like Andy's Jazz Club on East Hubbard, the Jazz Showcase, and the Hothouse over the years. Those spots elevated me to more than just the typical local player. I got started with small gigs workin' to create a solid fan base in the same fashion that popular go-go bands did in Washington, D.C. That fan base followed me all the way to The First Set where I headlined.

This is my thang. I'm the best at it and I put in a lot of time to get to this point. The fellas have always been behind me, supportin' me, lookin' out for me even. They like to joke about how rare it is that a thug, a cop, and a photographer find a best friend in a musician. We were about as odd a group as you could get. We worked it as best we could.

I wasn't like the rest of the fellas as far as background. Unlike Blue, Games, and Cyprus, I wasn't local. I'm a Louisiana boy. I'm an old-fashioned, Momma/Grandmomma-raised gentleman type. I ain't much into cursin' and I still prefer to use "ma'am," and "sir" with my elders. I spent the first six years of my life in one of the worst neighborhoods in New Orleans. My father, a struggling jazz musician, introduced me to music before I could walk. Though Momma didn't approve too much, he had me practicing wit' him. I had my own lil' toy horn and everything.

I don't know why Mom had a problem. Pop's band only drew small crowds of fifteen to twenty people at a small bar no more than three blocks from home. It didn't matter 'cause I loved every minute of it. It tore me up pretty good when Pops died from cancer. I was five years old but I dealt wit' it. Pop's dyin' only motivated me to be great at what I do and never give up.

I met the fellas when me and Momma moved here a couple of years after Pop died. A lotta schools thought I was like this child prodigy or somethin' 'cause of my talent. We were all around seven or eight at the time. They kinda dug it 'cause nobody in the neighborhood was like me. They used to listen to me practice my tenor sax outside our apartment. They rolled up on me one day. We started talking and they been my dogs ever since. We been through a whole lot together and that's one thing that ain't never changed.

What has changed, however, is my style. When we were younger, I would sometimes surrender to peer pressure, in an attempt to fit in. Over time, though, I realized I didn't have to "play down" who I really was, especially with the fellas. By the time we were in our teens, our individual personalities and tastes were quite clear.

I wanted to be a professional jazz musician—one of the best in the Midwest. So I did everything possible to make that happen. I didn't take long. In a short period of time, I made my talent pay off for me. The effort showed up in my bank account. I know I'm country, but a lil' money and the jazz scene in Chicago helped a brotha get sharp as I don't know what. Though Cyprus and Games like to poke fun. I always tell 'em… "Hey dog, it's good fo' bizness. Feel me?" I gotta look the part. I am not the one to be caught slippin' as far as the appearance is concerned. It's about the perfectly tapered haircut, tightly trimmed goatee and a wardrobe that makes NBA players ask, "Hey dog, where you get that at?" Many may not like me, but you can't hate me. Momma would throw a fit if she heard me stroke my ego as I do in my social circles. She always said that she raised me better.

Back to jazz. The band and I hit at The First Set pretty much every Saturday. Games, Cyprus, Blue, and his girl come all the time. I see Blue more than Games and Cypus 'cause those two work nights more often than the rest of us, if you know what I mean. I was happy to see Games, Blue, and his girl this particular evening. I got 'em some of the nicest seats in the house and headed over to join 'em when I finished the second set.

"'Sup, what ya'll think of the new set?" I pulled up a seat next to Games and across from Blue and his girl.

I like to check in wit' Blue about what he thought about how I did. He always thought that was kind of strange since he didn't know enough about jazz to notice if I made any mistakes. I just like to ask him 'cause he is always honest. It really doesn't matter because he tells me the same thing every time I ask.

"You was all right."

"You trippin,' I got this joint locked."

"Here you go." Blue laughed, shaking his head. "No doubt, you hit your shit this evenin'."

"And believe I got mo' where that came from."

We passed the time wit' small talk over a couple a drinks. At times, I was a bit distracted by somethin' behind him. I figure Blue and Games thought I was trippin' until they figured out that it was a woman.

What can I say? I gotta weakness. The average brotha sees women as women (tits, big ass, attitude, etc., etc.). To me, women are artistic creations of Almighty God, made of beauty, class, style, and grace. I love women.

"Who's that?" I leaned and whispered to Games.

"No idea."

"I'm feelin' that dress she's wearin'. Nice manicure, too."

"What? How can you see that shit from here?"

I countered with a double jerk of my eyebrows, excused myself, and headed for the empty seat next to the young woman who had caught my fancy. I guess that I was distracted to the point that I didn't notice the brother at the bar. He was also interested in this woman. The jealous-punk-ass-ex-boyfriend-to-be type interested.

"This club tends to get boring really quick when you're by yourself," I said as I sat down next to her.

"Oh, I'd have to disagree," she replied.

"Is this your first time here?"

"No, I've dropped by a few times actually. My girlfriends and I heard you play a couple of weeks ago," she said, smiling, reaching for her drink.

"What did you think of tonight's performance?" I asked, taking note of her French manicure while she sipped her drink.

"You make it look easy."

"Really?"

"Yes, really." She smiled.

"My name is Lorenzo Dali, and yours?"

"Her name is Allura."

The voice came of nowhere. It was much deeper hers and nowhere near as pleasant.

Like so many things in our lives, she was too damn good to be true. Up steps this cocky brotha, a pretty, red-boned, collegiate-boy type. The kind we never really liked all that much.

"And this is?" I pointed up to dude.

"This is my friend." Allura gestured with a bored flair of her hand. Her eyes and her attention were focused on me and I don't think her "friend" liked that too much. Not that I really cared.

"S' happ'nin,' playa." I extended my hand.

Mr. friend's hands remained on his drink and in his pocket. "Yeah, whatever, nigga."

"What's with your friend?" I raised an eyebrow to Allura.

"You bitch," he fired back, sitting his drink on the table between Allura and me.

I had to stand up on that one. An insult like that didn't need me to answer with words. I figured an ass beatin' would be more appropriate.

I mean, c'mon. I'm pretty much as cool as a Jacksonville fall breeze, nine times outta ten. But I just can't stand for outright disrespect. And I'm in my club on top of that. Go'n call me a bitch. Naw, I don't think so, dog.

Before anything could jump off, a good eight or nine brothas, including Games, Blue, and myself were standing around a small table in a big jazz club ready to let loose. Then the bouncers showed up and that was that. No problems. I suppose it was for the best, but I still thought they needed they asses kicked. No big deal. There was always next weekend.

BLUE

With things winding down for all of us after the near brawl at The First Set she and I headed home. It was nights like those when I really appreciated having someone to go home with. Avida and I had been together for a little over a year. She was materialistic, we had nothing in common, yet I was in love with her to a degree that I didn't fully understand.

At that time, the intricacies of our relationship didn't matter much to me. We had fun, great sex, and we couldn't get enough of each other.

"Tired?" I asked.

"Not really," she replied, looking at me from across her living room with the most evil and yet most beautiful eyes I had ever seen. "You?"

"A bit, but I'll manage."

She walked slowly over to me as she unbuttoned her blouse and began to take off her shoes.

"Wait," I told her, "those two hundred-fifty dollars pumps stay on."

She laughed as she now stood before me, about five feet seven inches of goddess. An open silk shirt complimented by a Victoria's Secret lace bra, a short black skirt, and black thigh-high pantyhose. Just looking at her had me breathing like a chain smoker after running the 200.

"Lose the skirt," my mouth whispered in response to my thoughts.

Her skin was bronze, soft, and flawless. I used to think her name, Avida, meant just that. It was literally impossible for me not to look at her at times. She was beautiful. And getting myself between her legs, as often as I did, would end up costing me more than dinners and material items. Nonetheless, my soul was stubborn, so we played throughout the night.

We woke up about two p.m. that afternoon which wasn't bad considering we didn't fall asleep until about seven a.m. that morning. Those were the good times. No arguments about money, who's spending time with who, or what ever else we could think of.

✠ ✠ ✠

"Blue, I'm hungry."

"What you want?" I asked, yawning as I looked up at the clock.

"You cookin'?"

"Uh, naaah, let's go out and get something."

She agreed to that idea, and I followed her for another small piece of last night's activities as she went to the bathroom to take a shower. We enjoyed the rest of the day with a late lunch, early movie, and overall appreciation of each other's company. I remember thinking to myself that I wish every day we spent together could be like this one. Unfortunately, they were not.

I left late that evening, happy with my weekend. However, I was beginning to get depressed thinking about the upcoming week. Still, driving home I also thought of the evening I'd spent with this woman. This glorious, yet at many times, deceitful woman. I tried my best to concentrate on the best in the relationship.

My love for her was unlike any other. Many feel that hate that causes so much of the destruction and chaos that you see in the world today. However, I believe that love can be just as dangerous. True love is consuming, controlling, and in its extreme, destructive. In retrospect, I remember my constant yet futile struggle to maintain some kind of control in regards to Avida. Sadly, it was a battle I could never win.

Anyway, not but two or three minutes after I stepped into my apartment, I got a phone call from Cyprus.

"Whassup, nigga!" he shouted into the phone. This was followed by laughter, then coughing. He was probably puffing on a blunt.

"Not too much, I just got in about a minute ago."

"Back from Avida's?" he asked.

"Yeah."

"I see you chose not to take my advice."

"Yeah nigga, whatever."

"I'm just fuckin' wit' you, dog...anyway, I heard you niggas was 'bout to get in some shit at D's gig last night. Tryin' to be me and shit."

"Please, we'd a tossed yo' ass, too, if you'd came wrong."

"Here you go. You know you can't fuck wit' me, dog, especially when I'm 'bout ta get put on."

"What you talkin' 'bout?" I asked, sitting back for a second. I frowned thinking of what he'd gotten into now.

"Man, you know Fat 'Chicago' Tone, right?" He coughed again.

"Yeah, kingpin gangsta mufucka, got like half the city locked down."

"And he wants me to help him lock down the other half," he returned.

"No bullshit."

"Nope, no bullshit. I got a meeting with him this week."

Now this is the thing; Cyprus was one of the best at his trade. However, he was still seen in certain big league circles as nothing more than a talented freelancer. A street thug, who though made some of the biggest scores in the city, was viewed as lacking "direction." I mean if he truly got caught out there he would have no one to keep his ass out of jail. Cyprus needed a family. A support group to protect him from some aspects of the game. That's where Fat Tone or Chicago, as he was also called, came in.

Chicago seemed to be something snatched right out of a movie script...a true-to-life mafia kingpin with all the trimmings. He had everything—money, cars, businesses, real estate, women, and, most important, power. He lived up to a very nasty, self-created reputation of being the "wrong nigga to fuck with."

When Fat Chicago Tone sneezed, a whole lot of people jumped and searched for Kleenex boxes. He was a very cool character. People could never anticipate his moves and I suppose that was what made him untouchable. It was a quality Cyprus hoped to acquire as a result of meeting him.

"Oh yeah, and I picked up some DVD players this weekend. Want one?" Cyprus asked.

"Yeah, I'll put it in the bedroom," I replied. I glanced around my house and grinned. Half of the nice stuff in my apartment was boosted from Cyprus.

"Cool, see you in a few."

CYPRUS

The meeting between me and Chicago was the following Wednesday night. Chicago was what Blue calls eccentric and what I call just flat out fuckin' strange. Whenever he needed to discuss business with clients, or in my case potential "employees," he always picked different places. Occasionally in his home and his nightclubs or restaurants because of surveillance, wiretaps, and the like. I feel that...kinda. Tonight, me and my crew waited at a junior high school playground on a bench overlookin' a dimly lit, empty basketball court.

"Man, I hope this ain't no fuckin' setup."

"Setup? Nigga, shut up. I don't know why you'd be worried anyway...you ain't done shit to nobody. All you do is drive, that's it." I gritted at my man Lil' Whip. I called him that 'cause he could handle a getaway car with the best of 'em. "Only mufuckas that a set yo' ass up is the fuckin' Department of Motor Vehicles on some ol' traffic violations shit."

"Cyprus," a voice called me from the darkness.

"Chicago, what's goin' on, player?" I answered, acknowledging Chicago's arrival from directly behind the bench.

"Ain't shit. C'mon, let's talk."

"Cool."

I always roll with a real tight clique of four or five. Fat Chicago Tone, on the other hand, generally traveled with somewhere in the neighborhood of eight to twelve guys. If it had been a setup, I would've had some problems. But it was cool. Chicago's intentions were as legitimate as they could be.

"Word is you makin' a lot of moves on the streets these days. Got ya name on the walls and shit," Chicago said as we walked toward the basketball court.

"I'm tryin,' man, you know, I likes to be the first nigga on the block and the last one to leave..."

"I hear that shit. Fellas all got good things to say about you, dog, and folk tell me that just meetin' with you is worth my time. Still, with all due respect, my brotha, you working some small-time shit."

"I just made ten grand last week. How you figure 'small time'?" I asked, truly curious.

"Man, *searchin'* for scores in itself is small time. Maximum risk with minimum returns ain't go'n work out for you in the long run."

"I wouldn't call my returns 'minimum,' questionable at times maybe, but..." I replied while rubbing my head.

"Questionable ain't much better."

I continued to rub my head.

"I mean shit, dog, there's a lot more niggas dead or locked up than there are out here making money. If you want a healthy bank account instead of a cell or a grave, you gotta keep your shit tight."

"That's how you roll?" I asked.

"Hey dog, I'm like high class, low profile, dig?" Fat Chicago Tone grinned as he lit a cigar.

"You call three clubs, and two restaurants low profile?"

"The spots are all legit, Cyprus. They ain't got shit to do with street business. The Feds and IRS would just love to catch me slippin' on my taxes, but that shit ain't go'n happen."

"So why you talking to me?" I asked, rubbing my goatee.

"My business got clogged arteries, dog. Needs a transfusion, know what I mean...new blood," Chicago answered. He continued to puff on his cigar, generally keeping it clenched in his teeth and hanging out of the left side of his mouth. Occasionally he took it out with his index and middle finger, when he spoke.

"New blood, huh?"

"New blood, dog. Clean, useful help to perhaps help flush out' my system." Chicago stared into my eyes.

I returned his stare, only nodding my head to show that I knew where he was comin' from.

"Tell you what...you alright from what I've heard and seen. Shoot by my club downtown on Saturday night. I'll introduce you to anybody you don't already know. We'll talk more details, numbers, some other shit."

"No problem. I'll be there."

And that was that. The beginning of a very dangerous and yet lucrative friendship. This had the potential of being very right or very wrong. I knew that sooner or later I could eventually fall prey to cops. Without "protection," Chicago worried about being hit from the inside. That's where and when he would really need someone like me. The bottom line was that Fat Chicago Tone may have owned the streets, but I knew 'em better than anyone.

Still, my homie, Detective Games, was a force to be dealt with. He just happened to be watching me during the whole meeting through one of those high-powered scopes they use for surveillance. I wouldn't have noticed him if he would've taken my advice from way back when. He needed to stop using those big-ass cop vans for stake-outs. The big, plain, white vans stick out like presidential motorcades.

It don't matter. This little thing with me and Chicago was something that was a problem for Games. I know that nigga. He would wait and see what came of it. He was unhappy with the whole situation. It made sense, I guess.

GAMES

I needed somebody to talk to after what I'd just seen. I caught up with Dali early Thursday afternoon, before we all got together the following evening.

Dali needed some ties. I had to join him on a quick trip to the mall. Granted, this is an event you don't often catch guys doing together, but when Dali goes looking for clothes it's a perfect time to talk. He shops like a woman. It takes him fuckin' hours.

"Whatcha think?" he asked me as he held up a tie to a pair of dress slacks.

"It's alright, I guess. I don't know. I don't wear shit like that."

"Yeah... I suppose you got a point there."

"Anyway, this whole thing with Cyprus and Fat Chicago Tone got me worried."

"And that's always been a big problem of yours. You worry too much. They probably got together to feel each other out, Chicago especially. You already got 'em makin' deals and what not." He continued to match ties with slacks and shirts.

"Ah, man, bullshit. Niggas like them don't get together to just fuckin' chat."

"Look, all I'm sayin' is that this is a situation where you gotta show a little patience."

"Yeah I know, but I ain't tryin' to be too late when it comes to Cyprus."

"I hear that. How you like these?" Dali held up two more ties.

"Those are alright."

"They better be, for seventy-five dollars a pop." He looked at them and the other two he decided to buy. "Alright cool, we done here. I gotta grab a couple of pair of shoes now."

"I guess we should go ahead and get our hair and nails done once you're finished with that."

"Well, if you're not going to appreciate my efforts to get all dolled up for you, then maybe you should just take me home."

We walked through the mall discussing life, women, and whatever else we could think of. Then all of a sudden, there she was. Now, I'm not really big on fate, destiny, and all that kinda shit. But I had to admit this was a bit too much to be just blind coincidence. We were about to walk into a men's shoe store, when Dali happened to glance to his left. There they were—a familiar pair of eyes that he thought he'd never see again.

"Whoa," he said.

"What?"

"It's her."

"Who?"

"Honey from the club. Allura."

"Who?"

"Hang back for a second, I'll be right back."

"Alright, but I ain't holdin' your fuckin' bags."

DALI

W hile Games may not have been a believer in fate, destiny, and things like that, I was. I walked into one of those African art and culture stores where uppity negroes like to buy stuff like post cards, calendars, paintings, books, etc. Anyway, she was there alone, and it was like she was waiting for me. She was without a doubt, one of the sweetest-lookin' women I'd ever seen. I mean sweet like homemade molasses ya grandma used to have when you were kids and never heard of Aunt Jemima's syrup. She was wearing this long black skirt, which fell to her ankles and had a slit that went up to about the middle of her left thigh. Her shirt, also black, matched the skirt. Her skin was smooth and clear. She had these big brown eyes that looked like they'd make you dizzy if you looked at 'em too long. Ah man, she was definitely the type that could get a man in a lot of trouble. That was a risk I considered and felt had to be taken.

"Nice place," I told her as I looked around the shop.

"You like it?"

"Yeah."

"I opened it about six months ago."

"Wait a minute. You own all this?"

"Yep."

"Impressive."

"Thanks."

"So, I'm curious. What are the chances that you remember my name?"

"What are the chances that I would forget a name like Lorenzo Dali."

"I'm wondering…is your friend going to interrupt me again?" I joked, looking over my shoulders.

"No, not this time."

"Good. You know ordinarily I'd be thinking of some kind of sharp and witty line to run." I looked into those big brown eyes of hers and began to get a little lightheaded.

"Really."

"Yeah, but I reckon you heard it all and the last thing I want to do is be… you know, like anybody else."

"I don't think that's a problem for you Mr. Dali."

"Please, call me Lorenzo." I gestured for her to step from behind the cashier's counter.

"Lorenzo it is. So, Lorenzo, why am I standing here in front of you?"

"Ah just wanna look at you when I talk to you, that's all," I answered politely.

"And what are we talking about?"

"How 'bout us?"

"That might take some time."

"I have plenty to spare this evening. How 'bout dinner?"

"Sounds good to me."

By this time we were standin' less than a foot away from each other. I mean I didn't wanna keep Games waitin' outside too long, but I wasn't in a hurry to leave. It was cool. As I saw it, I'd have plenty of time to get to know her later. We talked for a couple more minutes before I left.

BLUE

I've known Dali for years, many years. Something about his approach toward Allura was special. At first I thought it was just me but, I began to wonder. For the most part, every woman he has had considered him the consummate player. And given the opportunity, those women would probably tell Allura that she is going to end up just like they did—replaced. Dali talked to talk to her as if he was trying not to live up to his reputation. Then again, maybe he'd come up with a new approach to get women to fall in love with him. Who knows? At this point, it was too soon to tell.

The whole situation made me think. Dali's love for life always seemed to be more colorful and rewarding than my own. It was strange when I thought of my relationship with Avida. I knew without a doubt what love was, and what it should be. I knew and understood that what I have felt and still feel is not mere infatuation or even lust for that matter. It is the kind of true love that will allow a man to give two hundred percent of himself without condition, question or hesitation. Still, it hurts sometimes not to receive the same in return and that made me think of relationships in general.

I've often questioned the motives of black women regarding what they truly want in life and in a man. I understand their desire to be loved, cared for, trusted, admired, and respected like the precious queens that they are. I'm familiar with their relentless quest to no longer be seen as the vindictive, materialistic, greedy, money-hungry, conniving, and promiscuous bitches and whores which they have so frequently been portrayed. I'm also aware of their objections to being abused, neglected, and exchanged by the next nice set of tits, ass, and legs that floats by. My guess would be that I'm not the only black man in the world who knows that black women are constantly being mistreated and have been since the beginning of time. I can both comprehend and work with those issues.

I have trouble with women like my beloved Avida. They get what they want and need in a man, and still fuck it all up. This is not just a personal thing. I have seen a number of men's hearts shattered by many a confused sister. I realize that this may be due to black women being so mistreated by fools in the past. Still, the past is the past. When a man gives freely and sincerely of himself he shouldn't be taken advantage of. The respect black women think so highly of is a two-way street. It must be *earned* on both sides.

Avida's name alone tends to get me wound up at times. The thought of my heavenly, yet selfish, goddess drove me to pay her a surprise visit.

"Who is it?" she shouted in response to my knock at her door.

"It's me."

"Oh, hey baby. I didn't expect you."

"What you yellin' at the door like that for, anyway?"

"I don't know...shit, I thought it might have been somebody I ain't want to be bothered with."

"I hope I don't fall into that category."

"Nah, you aiight."

"Thanks," I said sarcastically, looking at her as she strolled into her kitchen wearing a pair of very short cut-off jeans and an old T-shirt she acquired from me some time ago. I found myself truly mystified at her ability to be so elegant at any given point and time—even when she was unaware.

"What are you staring at?" she asked.

"You," I replied as her cell phone phone rang.

"Hello," she answered. "Who's this?...Oh hey, how you doin'?...I'm alright, a bit busy, though...I got company...lemme call you back...aiight, bye."

During this conversation, she had a certain body language that I'd seen before. I was pissed with it then, and this afternoon was no different.

"So I'm 'company' now?" I interrogated.

"Don't start with me tonight, Blue," she snapped as she lit a cigarette. She walked out of the kitchen and sat down at her dining room table.

"Don't start with you...what the fuck?"

"Don't cuss at me, either."

"Fuck that. With some of the shit you pull, me cussin' at you should be the least of your worries."

"What shit?" she asked, confused.

"Who was on the muthafuckin' phone?"

"Baby, it was just some dude Charlotte and I bumped in to when we went out a couple of weekends ago. So please stop cussin' at me." Her voice got softer. "I don't know why you get so jealous. I would never do anything to hurt you so please stop looking at me like that." She walked toward me while taking off that old T-shirt. As I sat there rather tense on her couch, she straddled my lap.

She, like so many women, somehow had the ability to manipulate hostility. Suddenly, her kisses felt like shackles—controlling, powerful, and draining. They moved from my lips to my neck and made me unaware that my belt and jeans had somehow become unbuckled, unbuttoned, and unzipped.

I had made a mistake by telling her of my weakness for her well-manicured nails. I'll be damned if she didn't use them against me. They caressed my face and chest. With my mind now distracted, both nails and hands held "all" of me tight. She somehow managed to get my shirt off. My head went back and hers went down. I don't care what any man says—when the woman you love blesses your manhood with her mouth, you've just lost the battle, no matter who started it.

I left later that evening realizing that I had little control in this relationship of ours.

It was cool. Maybe these bittersweet moments were just the growing pains of a strong relationship. Looking back, I don't feel that I was naive, or "whipped," as they say. I felt blinded because my heart wouldn't allow me to see anything outside of Avida. It happens to the best of us at times.

Dali was lucky. He didn't have to worry about these types of problems. Everything seemed to be working out fine for him and his new friend. For the first time, he didn't seem overly concerned with the sexual aspect of his initial contact with a woman. That's a step in another direction for Dali.

Friday arrived again and I was the first through Dali's door. I had a lot on my mind and I wanted to get the evening and my intoxication started early.

We had chosen Dali's apartment as our Friday meeting place. It served as a neutral safe haven of sorts. Don't ask me why. Maybe it was because the rest of our apartments were pigstys. Whatever, I always felt very comfortable in the brother's home. We all did.

"'Sup, Blue? Whatcha' want?" Dali asked, looking through a part of his kitchen, which he had made into a mini bar.

"Patron," I mumbled from across his kitchen counter. I must've looked like George Foreman after his lost to Ali in Zaire-exhausted and confused.

"Patron? Must be somethin' heavy on ya mind, or Avida's got you twisted up again, or...both."

"How you figure that?"

"Well, you see I've known you since we were kids and you've always been a bit too complicated for my taste."

"Too complicated?"

"Blue, you were impossible to read until we all starting drinkin', smokin', and gettin' into all types of other craziness. See, alcohol gives tell-tale signs of your emotions, dog," he said, lifting up the glass of tequila, and passing it to me.

"Here *you* go," I returned.

"I'm serious," he said, sipping his Absolut and cranberry juice. "With you, hard liquor's for depression. Beer...that's for hanging out and wine is for when you *think* you gettin' some sex."

"Man, I don't ever *think* I'm gettin' some sex."

"Please, I seen you kinda unsure many a night."

"You full a shit." I laughed, sipping my drink thinking that the fool may be right.

"What's goin' on with Allura? Games had you pegged as gettin' all new and shit."

"Oh, it's cool, man...can't stop thinkin' 'bout her for some reason. I mean, I feel pressed, and you know Dali ain't never pressed."

A loud rapping sounded at the door, almost making the door jump from the hinges.

"It's open," Dali said irritably, pausing a second before sipping his drink again.

"S'appnin', fellas?" Games walked in with a six-pack tucked under his arm and about three bags of pork skins in his free hand. "Whassup wit' this dark-ass mood lightin'?"

"Anybody seen Cyprus?" I asked.

"Yeah, he came with me. Nigga downstairs talkin' to some broad in the lobby," said Games.

"Cool...How's your son, man?" Dali asked.

"Oh, he's cool. I'll take him out to that circus on Sunday if the weather's straight and I don't get any shit out of his mother."

Two loud knocks resounded at the door.

"'Sup?!" Cyprus said coming in.

"S'goin' on, partner?" I replied.

"Ain't shit. Pimpin'. Fuck's up with the lights in this bitch?"

Games busted out laughing—loud. Hell, it *was* funny so I joined him.

"Alright, alright, lemme turn on some lights for you pork skin-eatin', un-cultured, no ambiance-knowin' fools man," Dali said, turning the lights up, and chuckling.

We talked, laughed, drank, and smoked. Although there were more important issues bouncing around in our minds, we took this short time to simply unwind. Games and Cyprus put their differences aside. Dali stopped thinking of Allura. For a while, well, let's just say the only love I concentrated on that night was in that apartment. Like I *used* to always say, "These were the good times."

CYPRUS

Saturday night we had our personal business to handle. Much to Blue's surprise, I wanted to include him in mine. When I asked, he told me the same thing he always tells me when I try to pull him into my little excursions—no. I can be a persuasive SOB. I wouldn't take no for an answer. I pointed out that he needed to get his mind and body away from Avida. He said I might have had a point.

I had a meeting with Fat Chicago Tone. We headed to Chicago's club uptown, 24/7. All the rich folk, both black and white, went there to play. Chicago had spots in every corner of the city. He made money everywhere, from ghetto sewers to corporate boardrooms. So, I had to get dressed up for the shit. I wasn't too big on the idea. but we gotta do what we gotta do.

Me, Blue, PQ, and Mink got to the spot a little after ten that night. The door was virtually hidden by two bodyguards who looked like trucks with arms. I knew 'em from back in the days, though. They recognized me immediately and let us in. Blue said he felt like a *60 Minutes* journalist accompanying a Third-World dictator as he prepared to slaughter a couple of hundred revolutionaries. What the fuck is that supposed to mean?

24/7 was big and packed wall to wall, but it wasn't one of those dance-till-you-sweat, get-somebody's-phone-number-type spots. It was the kind of club where Chicago could entertain politicians, lawyers, judges, and the like. It was the kind of place where big boys played. A location where the large paper was spent and gangsters like Fat Chicago Tone secured their future. And as far as my ass was concerned, it was a nice place to be.

Chicago went out on a limb with the club's décor and mood, though. It had a gothic, vampire theme like one of those medieval castles. He even had a few of them gargoyle sculptures. I thought it was a bit over the top, but no one else seemed to have a problem with it.

People from all walks of life walked around drinkin' shit with names I can't pronounce. The men all had on these Italian tailored suits, fancy; diamond-laced Rolex watches, and what not. The women were off the chain and outta my fuckin' league. It didn't bother me 'cause I don't fuck wit' bitches like that, anyway. Besides, it wasn't the kind of place where you *just* walk up to some-one with a "baby-can-I-call-you-sometime" attitude.

Dali would've liked the first floor. It had a live jazz band with candles all over the place and this strange blue lighting. The second floor bumped reggae music. The third floor had the Top 40 R&B to the oldies-type groove.

Chicago was on the third floor sitting at the bar with his entourage. The bar was the big three-sided, five to six bartender type. Chicago took a whole side for himself. Blue and my crew took seats while I headed over to speak to Chicago.

"Cyprus, what's hap'nin'?" Chicago leaned against the bar as one of the three women standing next to him lit his cigar.

"Ain't shit, just checkin' out ya spot. This place is a fuckin' trip."

"Legit enough for ya?" Chicago grinned a platinum-tooth smile.

"Oh, most definitely," I said taking a long glance over the floor.

"C'mon, let's talk upstairs with some of the fellas."

"Okay."

"Cigar?" Chicago asked.

"Yeah."

"Cyprus, I believe that we have a lot to offer each other. You give me the assurance that shit is done right, no offense to my boys or anything. It's just that a lot of them lack... experience. Something that *you* have a great deal of. In return, I have comfort to offer. In other words, you won't have to worry about cops bitin' you in the ass whenever you happen to toss some nigga off a twenty-story building for me. Cool?"

"Makes sense," I said, shrugging my shoulders as we walked into his office.

"True. That's the thing about the shit we do. It's usually very simple, and everything generally works out, if you do it right. And my friend, it is for that reason that I want to put you through a bit of a trial run. Just to see how you work out with the fellas."

"Trial run?"

"You know, test the chemistry and shit. I want you to go out on a couple of runs with the boys before we can look at getting you into the big circle."

I paused for a minute, then nodded my head. "Shit, that's cool with me, just let me know when and where."

"Cool...in a couple of days I want you to take some of the boys here and pay someone a visit. I want you to play bill collector for me." With that shit, I guess he noticed a lack of enthusiasm in my body language. "Listen, I know you've done this type of thing before and it seems a bit...let's say, below your standards. But, shit, you got to start somewhere if you want to impress the brass dig."

"Yeah, I feel you."

"This ain't your ordinary debt, anyway. The gentleman I want you to visit is one hundred grand in the hole. Ain't interest a bitch? I don't want him dead. I'm beyond that settin' an example shit." Chicago gave a belly laugh, which resounded throughout the room. "I just want what he owes, and I know he has it. See, I don't think he knows me all that well and I want to get acquainted without me having to see his sorry ass."

I chuckled and let him know that I'd be more than happy to oblige for stakes as high as one hundred thousand dollars. We talked details and made our way back downstairs.

When I was walkin' across the dance floor, two women stopped me and introduced themselves. Chicago sent 'em, no doubt. They didn't look like groupies. Instead of the tight pants, cleavage revealing tops with the six-inch stiletto high-heel look, these girls was on some high-end, designer skirt-suits with matching Prada pumps type shit. They also had the disposition to match. I mean, shit, if I rolled up on either one of these women on the street, they'd probably call the police.

It was obvious that men whose primary concern was getting paid, impressed them. OK, maybe they *were* groupies. They bought me a drink and sat with me at a table by the bar. They asked me all kinds of questions about what I did, but I'm pretty sure they had some idea. We kept talkin' and drinkin' 'til I spotted a familiar face at the bar. I excused myself and let 'em know that I'd be right back.

"This is one bad-ass fuckin' club."

"What you doin' here?" I asked. My homie the cop had just strolled in. It was the last place on earth I wanted him to.

"Havin' a drink, muthafucka, what *you* doin' here? Better yet, what you and Blue doin' here? What, ya'll just go'n leave me out of all the fun?" Games asked.

"Don't bring me in this shit," said Blue.

"Here we go." I shook my head.

"I don't know, dog. This don't look like your kinda spot. Hangin' out wit' folk wit' real jobs and shit. And them fine-ass broads of yours, goddamn! They definitely don't look like your type," Games added.

"Yeah, well let's just say that I've broadened my horizons."

"Really," Games said, staring coldly me.

"You like dead set on fuckin' my shit up around here."

"Nah nigga, I'm just lookin' out and shit, makin' sure everything's cool."

"Man, you a funny muthafucka. We rollin' downtown tomorrow night to hear 'D.' You comin' ?"

"Yeah, that's cool."

I grinned and put my arm around Games' shoulder. "We'll talk *there* if that's alright with you."

"Alright, man, I get the hint. I was on my way out, anyway. Shit, maybe I'll find me one of these fancy bitches to take home."

"Shiiit, good luck."

Games finished his drink and smacked me on the back of my head before shaking Blue's hand and mine. "I'll holla, nigga. And Blue, don't let this mufucka get you in trouble."

He made his way to the entrance of the floor and down the spiral staircase. I watched as he left and thought of the potential problems that this cop, who happened to be a dear friend, might cause. I let that go and returned to the girls.

"Who was that?" one of them asked.

"Just a friend of mine."

"Cyprus!" Chicago called from the bar. I hesitated for a second before walking over, concerned that perhaps Chicago may have recognized Games from somewhere. "Excuse me again for a second," I told the girls.

"S'up?" I asked, approaching Chicago.

"Hey, don't you got a partner that hits at that jazz club downtown? Real good from what I hear. Keeps the place packed."

"Yeah, my man Dali. Best in the city." I relaxed a bit in reaction to his easy question.

"Think he needs some more work, better yet, more money?"

"I wouldn't doubt it. I'll talk to him tomorrow and see whassup."

"Do that if you could."

"I'll holla at 'em."

"Cool."

The following night I dropped by Blue's place to pick up him and Games. We went downtown to The First Set to hear Dali play. We typically didn't do Sundays but this was my call. Tonight was more like a business meeting with an agenda. On the way, I told 'em about how last night went with the girls. It was cool and all, but Games and I knew that things would serious later that night.

I parked and we made our way to the club. Our silhouettes displayed authority as we crossed the street, walking in front of on-coming traffic as if to say, I wish you would.

We roamed the grounds of Dali's spot so often that we were well known by everyone. I eventually spotted Dali talking to this white girl. Her name was Serenity. She was from New York and spent the majority of her life around black folk. She wanted to be Dali's manager. She felt that his talent was being wasted on the small club scene and that he should set his sights on the bigger picture. Dali always reminded her that the smaller clubs were his roots. The two of them stood above us on the balcony, arguing or discussing his career, depending on how you heard it.

DALI

"I don't know what you're afraid of. You're one of the most, if not *the* most, talented player in the city. You're also one of the most underpaid. I don't know why you continue to fuck around with these guys," she said with both fire and confidence. She may have been quite pleasing to the eye, but in regards to business, she was as no-nonsense as they come and knew exactly what she wanted.

"First of all, I ain't afraid of nothin'. I only concern myself with my music. All this other garbage is unnecessary drama," I shot back.

"They're using you, Dali."

"And you're looking out for my best interest, right?" I questioned sarcastically.

"I'd like to."

I shook my head. I couldn't help but admire ol' girl's persistence. I just simply couldn't find out what angle she was coming from. I weighed the pros and cons of the whole thing. My band and I were paid well for our performances, but we were worth more. The bottom line was that we're the best in the city, hell, the state, and this region of the country for that matter. Serenity continuously pointed that out to me. Perhaps, she *was* looking out for my best interest. Her reputation had preceded her as being one crude, business-minded woman who could put anyone on top who had the desire and drive to be there. In addition to that, she was damn attractive. She was one of those white women that sistas even had to admit looked good. She and her proposals seemed right—too right. I would simply trust my instincts. I chose to wait a while.

"Hey 'D'!" Cyprus yelled to me from where he and the fellas were sitting.

"Jesus. Who's that?" Serenity asked.

"Cyprus, Blue, and Games," I said.

"Oh, the troublemakers."

"Them? Naaah." I flashed a guilty smile.

"Hell, last week you guys damn near got half the men in the club thrown out."

"Hey, that wasn't my fault."

She just looked at me.

"It wasn't...anyway, lemme holla at these fools, and I'll get at you later."

"Fine, Dali." She smiled as she brushed her hand down the tie that I'd just purchased a few days ago. There was something special about her. Something that I should stay away from.

Games, Cyprus, and Blue took a seat at their favorite booth near the back of the club. I always looked out for 'em when they came through and set 'em up with a comfortable VIP spot, no matter how many people were there. They needed it that night 'cause the club was damn near standing room only. You almost couldn't see from one end of the club to the other. There was a lot of cigars and cigarette smoke, and bodies around the room. We had a good crowd that evening with a lot of big-name players outta New York.

Games, Cyprus, and Blue didn't seem to care much. They were more concerned with drinking and lookin' at women. Well, 'cept for Blue. He was straight though workin' on his second Hennessy. Detective Tony Games enjoyed orange juice and gin, and Cyprus went through Heinekens like they were water.

"'Sup," I said as I slid into the booth.

"Ain't shit," Games said, finishing his drink in one swallow. "I see you still at it wit' that white girl."

"Yeah, she still wants to put me on. I guess she thinks she can make a nigga the next Branford Marsalis or somethin'."

"Can she?" Cyprus asked.

"I don't know, maybe."

"Well, if you're lookin' for other gigs or more money, Chicago told me that he needs someone at some of his spots. He'll probably pay you two, three times as much what you makin' here," Cyprus added.

"Shit, here you go. Tryin' to get this nigga hooked up with them muthafuckas, too." Games huffed, shaking his head in dissatisfaction. After his statement, he stared at Cyprus with a look of disgust.

Cyprus chuckled a bit and sighed. "I'm sorry, dog, but you don't play any musical instruments do you? I didn't think so. This ain't got shit to do with you. I'm simply relayin' some information to my partner here."

"It's alright, man," I interrupted. "The offer sounds good, but I'd like to stick with what I got for now. Besides, gigs like that tend to take away my creative control."

Cyprus finished his drink and motioned for the waitress to bring him another one. "It's all good. I can understand that. It's an open offer just in case you change your mind."

"That's cool." Suddenly, one of the more flamboyant door hosts walked over and whispered something in my ear about a problem with the bouncers. There was also someone who'd come to see me.

When the hostess sashayed away, Games broke out with a laugh that came from the depths of his stomach. "Damn, I thought that muthafucka was gonna kiss you on the neck for a second. Sneakin' up on a mufucka and shit."

"You know Dali get 'em in all shapes, sizes, and colors," Blue added. Both Cyprus and Games looked at Blue. Then the three of them looked at me and picked up where Games left off...laughing...hard and loud.

"Don't trip, all they do up in here is ask how ya'll fools niggas doin'," I responded.

"Fuck that," Cyprus said.

"Especially you, Cyprus," I said, smiling before taking a drink. "They love thugs."

We all had to laugh at that.

13

SO MANY THINGS AT ONCE

BLUE

Something told me I just should've stayed home. I ordered another glass of cognac and watched Dali excuse himself to take care of the bouncer/guest situation. Seconds later, Games and Cyprus began what was a long overdue discussion. To be honest, not too much is ever accomplished by conversations like these. It's all basically a smoke screen, a method to feel the other out and express one's personal views. I found this a very good time and reason to make my way to the bar for another drink. I had a small feeling that this conversation was one that I didn't need to be a part of.

Unfortunately, when you have a cop and a professional killer as two of your best friends, it's difficult to leave when they don't want you to. I attempted to get up but both Cyprus and Games stopped me. I think they wanted me there to prevent the talk from becoming a fight. As a result, I ignored their wishes. I found a spot not too far away where I could watch the two of them and glance over at Dali to see what happened to him.

CYPRUS & GAMES

"Whassup with you, man?" I asked Games. "All up in my business, fuckin' with my shit and all. I mean before it was cool, but now you playin' a bit too close for my taste. Shit, we go back a long way, but you need to slow that shit down a bit, man."

Games sat back and glanced around the immediate area just to make sure that no one was being nosier than they should be. "You know you're right, we do go back a long way. For that reason alone, you should know that no one tells me what I *need* to do. You got all these muthafuckas out here all scared of you and shit, but I knew you before all of the robbin' and killin' shit and I still ain't impressed."

"Then don't concern yourself with my business."

"Muthfucka, I'm paid to concern myself with your business."

"Ah Jesus."

"That's how it's gotta be, player."

I switched from Heinekens to drinking Remy Martin by this time and damn near emptied the glass before the waitress placed it on the table. I looked at Games with concern. How much was at stake: friendship, trust, loyalty, power. Both of us were a bit drunk at this point, so we stopped biting tongues.

"So, you like fuck me on this one." That statement dipped out of my mouth like the tongue from a cobra. It was weird...like controlled fire from a blowtorch. I was pissed.

"I gotta do my fuckin' job, man."

"Aiight man, long as you know that I gotta do mine," I returned.

"What's that shit supposed to mean?" he asked.

"Don't fuck with me on this, dog. You know what I do and you definitely know what happens to those who try to prevent me from gettin' it done. I been buryin' muthafuckas throughout this city for years and wasn't shit anybody could do about it, still ain't. No bullshit. I'm God out here, player. I love you and all, but I can't have you all up in my shit."

"You must be out of your fuckin' mind," Games snapped, eyes flashing. Now I could see why they wanted me to hang around. Still, why would anyone in their right mind want to get in the middle of a dogfight. "You fuck up this time and that's your ass—bottom line. Like I told you before I ain't these fools you used to dealin' with. I ain't scared of your crazy ass. It's just gonna be what it has to be."

"Fair enough," I said with confidence, "fair enough."

DALI

It looked like Allura was having some difficulties entering the club on my word. I had had problems in the past with letting women in for free. There would be four or five ladies sitting around with attitudes because they were under the impression that they had some kind of "I'm with him" VIP pass. As a result, I chose to slow down on inviting any and every woman I knew to my shows. Nonetheless, I'd forgotten all about those previous problems when I invited Allura to come that evening, so I ended up having to straighten it out with both the bouncers and her.

"I'm sorry about that."

"Mmm-hmm," she replied coldly.

"No, really, sometimes security can get a little overzealous about their jobs. I mean, what do you expect, they're bouncers. The size and authority goes to their head sometimes," I said, sitting with her at a table close to the stage.

"That's not what bothered me."

"What did?"

"The fact that it seems that you have a lot of 'guests' here to see you. No, I take that back. You're a very talented and attractive brother, so I'm not surprised that you have your share of fans. What bothers me, I suppose, is a fear that I am going to end up drowning in this sea of admiration or infatuation that appears to surround you. I really have neither the time nor patience for that."

I was caught off guard. Granted, I had dealt with a number of very intelligent women who would not stand for my "ways." I was always prepared and I almost always knew how to deal with it. Strange enough though, at that moment I felt kind of funny. My heart was beating a bit faster than usual.

Then, it hit me that this was a familiar feeling. A reminder perhaps of the first time I was with a woman so many, many years ago. I was nervous. I was feeling the same way I did back then. *I really don't want to mess this up.*

"Look," I said softly, taking a deep breath. "I apologize for the mix-up at the door. I promise you it won't ever happen again. And you're right about me having a lot of guests coming to see me."

I paused for a second trying to find the right words. I reached out and gently grabbed her hand. "I can't take back anything that I've done in the past and I know you don't expect me to. You got me feelin' all funny, trippin' over my own words like some high school kid. I just want the chance to convince you that I feel you're different from everyone else. All I'll need is some of that valuable time and patience of yours, to show you where I'm comin' from."

She glanced up at me from our hands that rested between us on the table. What went through her mind at that time may have resembled fear, confidence, hesitation, attraction. She, like any well-grounded woman, most likely thought of all the tired men she had been involved with in the past. She possibly wondered if I would join them in the history books. I just hoped she believed me and saw the sincerity in my eyes.

"So what are you going to play for me tonight?" she asked, smiling at me and holding my hand.

"It's a surprise."

BLUE

I made my way back to the booth after a very frustrating and unproductive cell phone conversation with Avida. I found Cyprus and Games laughing at each other as they looked back at the days when Games donned a Jheri Curl and Cyprus sported thick laces in his suede Pumas. I laughed and reminisced along with them, thinking of how simple things were at that time. I compared how happy I felt then to how fucked up I'd been feeling.

Dali made his way to the stage. As he played, I relaxed a bit and forgot about my problems. I frequently did that when listening to music. They chose to go with more of a contemporary sound tonight. The beats were uptempo, almost pulling the audience out of their seats to dance. He dedicated the last set to Allura. She remembered her telling him on a previous date that the song playing on the radio as he drove her home was one of her favorites. He played his version of it tonight. She later told him that she liked his better than the original.

Looking at the two of them as I sat down at the booth, reminded me of the early days of my relationship with Avida. Everything seemed easier back then. Things were different now—more games, more doubt, less easy. When I looked at Dali, I knew that his most difficult times with Allura could never compare to what I went through to maintain a relationship with Avida. He was blessed, and like so many of those who are, he had no idea.

BLUE

The drive home was a long, quiet one for some reason. It enabled me to concentrate on...well, me. That was something I generally tried not to do because I feared what I knew to be true. My friends were generally happy and satisfied with who they were and where their lives were taking them. I simply mirrored any emotions they felt. At the same time, I believe my introverted nature allowed them to treat me as their soundingboard, without realizing it. Since childhood, I was always the one they talked to in confidence simply because they knew I was too closed to tell anyone. As a result, I always knew each and every detailed experience, fear, concern, and motivation of my three friends. It was a heavy load to carry, but I loved them like brothers so I kept it to myself.

I was a mess. I found myself on numerous occasions struggling to find focus in my life, wandering about like one of the city's derelicts. Distractions were my albatross. The biggest one was my relationship with Avida.

Things were beginning to change for me. I felt like I was watching a tornado as it destroyed everything it came in contact with, slowly making its way toward me. You can't stop the inevitable, you can only prepare for it. I would work hard to keep my conscience clear and my mind focused. I felt other elements creeping into the picture. Elements like obsession. While life prior to Avida was emotionally predictable and uneventful for the most part, life with Avida was all consuming. She was all I ever thought about, all I ever wanted to think about. Over the past few months, I found that I was forcing myself to work or hang out, just to take my mind off of her. My thoughts of her weren't just how much I loved her but also not being able to live without her. It was a sickening concern, to say the least.

As I continued to travel with no real destination, I couldn't help but compare myself to those around me. When I did, I thought how much different I was from the others. In recent years, many new emotions found a home in me: self-doubt, dissatisfaction, frustration, sadness, and pain. As time passed, I began to feel negative energy fill and fuel my body to the point that it almost felt natural. I simply could not understand why. Perhaps I spent too much time thinking, but I couldn't help it. That's the kind of person I am.

All of the introspective blah had my heart beating so fast that my brain was probably under the impression that my body had just run a marathon. Why? Maybe it was the result of this evening's previous conversation with Avida. That might account for the fact that I'd driven past my home three times in the past half-hour. I was beginning to worry for those around me: Dali, Games, Cyprus, and Avida.

Avida...I feared that her lack of consideration for my feelings might bring about something very unpleasant. I'd been subdued and submissive for so very long. My tolerance and patience were getting shorter as I got older. Perhaps for someone like me, it was already too late. I just didn't know at this point. I didn't know anything.

It was getting late, and I'd run out of places to both drive and think. Though it would've been in my best interest to simply go home and go to bed, I didn't too much feel like being alone. I was quite sure Avida wouldn't mind the company.

Then again, I wasn't up for the risk.

THE BEGINNING OF
THE BEGINNING

CYPRUS

"What time you got?"

"'Bout a quarter to one. It's gettin' late, Cyprus," Mink said as he puffed on a cigarette.

"Patience, partner, patience," I told him. I looked out of the passenger side window of my old station wagon. Me and my team parked next to a broken streetlight about a half-block away with full view of the apartment complex and its parking garage.

There were five of us—me, Mink, PQ, and two of Chicago's men, Eddie Barnes and Joe Maxey. Eddie's primary duty was to report back to Chicago with the results of the evening's event. This night was kind of a bullshit initiation for me. I didn't trip on it really. It was what it was and that was business as usual.

What had taken place in this situation was basically insubordination. Fat Chicago Tone explained it as someone just owing him a large sum of money. However, large debts to Chicago really didn't even exist at this point in his life. Muthafuckas in the past found themselves in early graves when they bit off a bit more than they could chew.

No, this shit came up 'cause somebody chose to say in so many words "fuck Fat Chicago Tone and his money." Basically, dude grew some balls 'cause he recently made connections with some high-rollers from out of the area. They told him that he would be protected. Unfortunately, our friend was too dumb to know that professional gangsters network like corporate CEO's. They all know each other and owe each other favors. Chicago chose to call in one of his to prove a point.

DALI

"So where you from, Lorenzo?" Allura asked while we sat on the steps of her condo after dinner and a midnight walk. I was one of the few brothers in the world who had enough self-control to "not" invite myself up on the first date.

"Down South originally," I said, taking in the surroundings. Allura lived in a very nice suburban neighborhood about fifteen to twenty minutes outside Chicago.

"You seem content here," she continued.

"Oh, without a doubt. I take it you don't share my sentiments."

"Well, I've been a lot of places and I can't honestly say that this one is a favorite." My heart started to race a bit when she subtly scooted closer to me.

"I thought you'd be used to all the fast-paced hustle and bustle, being a Brooklyn girl and all."

"I guess that's the point. I'm so used to it that I've grown a bit tired of it, in a way. Maybe, that's why I find you so interesting."

"Why's that?"

"'Cause you're kinda different. You know, country." She laughed.

I laughed with her. I was enchanted by Allura's laugh. It was full, deep, and real. It was the kind based in her heart, powered by her stomach, and completed with one of the biggest smiles I'd ever seen.

"What? I like country. It works for you," she said, looking in my eyes

I felt dizzy.

What was probably only somewhere between two and five seconds seemed like an eternity to me as we looked into each other's eyes, wondering what we were getting into. I could smell her perfume. It was Moschino, and although I was familiar with the fragrance, she wore it like it was made for her. For those few seconds, I was lost. The scent of her perfume increased its intensity. I heard the slightest whisper in my ear. "Kiss me," it said. So I did.

CYPRUS

Me and the crew continued to wait in the dark for this nigga to arrive at the high-rise apartments. Unlike Mink, I was used to waiting. It came with the territory. It gave me time to carefully think through exactly what I wanted to do. The main problem facing thieves is the "unexpected." It was the reason the majority of them ended in up jail. And that shit ain't happenin' to me.

"Here he comes." I pointed out a vanilla Lexus with twenty-inch chrome, five-point dubs, the spinnin' kind, which I hate. The car had smoked windows. They drove down into the underground parking lot of the high-rise. Rent for a one bedroom in that bitch was at least a grand.

"You sure...shit, you can't even see in that muthafucka with those tinted windows," replied Eddie Barnes, who was nervous through the whole ordeal.

"Yeah, that's him. Chicago said he just bought that ugly piece a shit 'bout three weeks ago. Sticks out like a sore thumb. Shit, you could spot his ass in a rush-hour traffic jam," I mumbled in disgust. I checked the clip of one of my guns.

I knew the building well 'cause I used to have a lil' honey in here that I hung out wit' when things got hot, so I had a heads-up on how to get in and out with little or no detection.

"Alright, listen," I said, turning to look at everyone in the car. "I got some rules on this shit, feel me? First, as you can guess, what I say goes. You got any questions 'bout what goes on, ask me now or when this shit is over. Second, only speak when I ask you something. Last, don't fuck up. I hate mistakes. We give 'em ten minutes, then we move."

After the ten-minute wait, we made good use of a security camera's blind spot, slipped through a side door and up eight floors. With four sharp, solid knocks on apartment 816, a dude who looked to be in his mid-twenties fucked up and opened the door to the apartment, a bit too wide. Wide enough to feel a sawed-off, double-barrel shotgun pressed intensely against his chest. As he tried to speak, a whisper came from the shadow of men.

"Keep your mouth shut, and move back...now."

He quickly, yet carefully stepped back into the apartment very aware of the shotgun being held by Mink. He now also noticed the .45 aimed at his head as PQ motioned him to stop. We filed in and branched out to cover every view of the apartment.

I was the last man in. I gestured for PQ's .45 and looked at the young man.

"On your knees," I calmly ordered, taking note of the panic in his eyes. Panic always made me a bit uncomfortable.

In my line of work panic is the extreme side of fear. People who are scared to that degree are unpredictable. The unpredictable can turn into the unexpected.

"Where is he?" I asked.

The kid hesitated for a second. I looked at Mink who pressed the shotgun to his head.

"He's in the bathroom in the back...uh...probably in the shower."

With a quick movement of my hand, I motioned for Joe Maxey and PQ to bring out whoever was in the bathroom. They returned, man-handling a tall, fair-skinned, kinda model-lookin' guy. He was a bit older than I expected. He was dressed in a white terrycloth robe with matching house slippers. He was "pretty," so to speak. *Shit*, I thought. *I might end up enjoying this little job after all*. I hate anything one would consider "pretty," especially men.

Joe and Mink brought him to stand in front of me.

"Have a seat," I said, pointing to his black leather couch.

"Who's this?" I asked, tapping the .45 on top of the head of the kid still on his knees.

"Never mind him. Who the fuck are you, and what do you want?"

A bit irritated, I took a deep breath before sharply whackin' him in his mouth with the gun. "See, now...we're getting off to an unhealthy start. Let's try again and I'll make it simple for you. First, I ask, you answer. Second, you work with me and we're gone as quickly as we came. Third, fuck with me, I'll kill you." I turned to the young man. "Who is this?" I asked again.

He wiped blood from his lip and sighed. "He's just a friend."

"What kind of friend?"

"What? Man, what difference does it make?"

"I ask, you answer." I hit the man in the mouth again and aimed my gun at him.

"I don't know what kind of answers you want," he said humbly as he sat back into his couch.

"Wait a minute...ain't this some shit...*you niggas gay*?" I asked, smirking as I waved my gun back and forth between him and his young friend.

He took a deep breath. "What?"

I told this muthafucka. I shook my head and fired a shot into the couch approximately an inch away from his ear. "Are you *tryin'* to make this shit difficult?"

"No, no," he answered.

"Fuck it, ain't no thing. I was just curious since I'd heard some things and all, and wit' dude on his knees here, well...anyway lemme cut to the chase. You know what we here for?" I asked, lowering my gun.

"I have no idea."

"Ah, c'mon now, I know you can do better than that."

"Chicago sent you," he said, now working to make his question seem more like a statement.

"Who sent us is not important. What *is* important is paying what you owe, all of what you owe."

"Look...," he began to explain.

"Look shit," I interrupted. "Don't even think about tryin' to sweet-dick your way outta this shit. We really don't have the time."

"I don't have all of it right now. Just tell Chicago that I'll personally bring every cent to him next week. Tone and I go way back."

"Muthafucka tried me, anyway," I said, speaking to Mink, who still had the shotgun aimed at the kid's face.

I gave Mink a subtle nod. Mink then passed the shotgun to Joe Maxey, grabbed the kid by the back of his head and neck, and roughly brought him over to me.

"Gimme his right hand," I instructed Mink. Mink stood behind him and wrapped an arm around his throat and placed the kid's right hand to where it reached in front of me.

"Damn, that's a nice watch, kid...Bulova, right?" I asked before firing a hole the size of a quarter into his hand.

For the next fifteen minutes me and the crew did what had to be done until we finally got what we'd come for. On our way out the door, I remembered what Chicago told me. "If it's possible, get the money, but leave our mutual friend untouched. I want that muthafucka to feel spared, as if the only reason he's around is because of me." And so it was.

BLUE

Dali drove home after his night out with Allura thinking of her, thinking only of her. It was the first time in a while that he thought of something other than his music. Ordinarily, when he didn't sleep with a woman right away, he would simply plot and scheme harder. He felt this was necessary with difficult women. He believed that since they were probably hurt in the past by an insensitive brother or a lousy one-night-stand lover, they kept their guards up. His feelings for Allura were different.

Ordinarily, when he would go out with a lady friend he would have a back-up woman in case he came up empty. With Allura, the thought never crossed his mind. The rest of the fellas and I thought the brother was losing his edge. Instead of making his way to another woman's apartment for a midnight visit, tonight he chose to simply drive slowly around the city, listening to John Coltrane.

I suppose that he and I were on the same psychological page that night. I called him on his cell phone.

"Hello?" The way he answered gave me the impression that he was probably grinning when he picked up. He probably thought it was Allura, which made me feel kind of stupid for calling in the first place.

"Whassup, playa? It's me."

"Hey, what's goin' on, man? What you doing up so late?"

"You know me man," I returned with a heavy sigh as I rubbed my hand over my face. "Always got somethin' on my mind."

"What's up, dog?"

"It's nothin'. Fucked up, I guess...tired. Fuck, man, I don't know. I'll holla at you later."

"Whassup, Blue? Talk to me, man."

My mind was shooting in twenty different directions at once-some parts of me believing that I should've never called Dali, and others feeling that I might die if I didn't. Self-control was relative for me.

"Don't worry about it, playa, everything's cool. I'm just trippin', that's all." I tried to leave the conversation by simply laughing it off, but my voice was too shaky to control and Dali picked up on it.

"Whatever man, I'm comin' through," he said. His concern made me feel like a bitch. It basically fed my inadequacy and low self-esteem.

This was a debate, or war of wills, that he and I had been involved in on several occasions in the past. I presume it was because though I loved them all equally, Dali was the only one with the patience and emotional depth to deal with someone in the condition that I frequently found myself in. It might have also been due to the fact that though Cyprus, Games, and Dali all secretly thought I was a bit "unstable" at times, Dali was the only one who really wanted to know why.

He managed to make his way into my apartment with little resistance. It was for my own good. We talked about his immense attraction to Allura and how he felt that it was changing his life. He spoke in detail about how the evening went with her, everything from their conversations to her laugh to where she lived. I chose to listen simply because he needed someone to talk to just as much as I did. I never got much out of talking about my relationship with Avida anyway. We continued our debate on the state of my mind and questions of life and death. I've always felt the fear of death quite interesting. It's not necessarily an end. There really isn't anything to be afraid of. My thoughts of Avida seemed to fortify my continuing struggle to live from one day to the next. I occasionally wondered if my life would be more appreciated in death. Dali never liked to hear me talk like that—for fear of a loss, I suppose. Still, nothing is forever. He was always puzzled by the way he saw me change from a young man who seemed to be doing something with his life to an old man indifferent to his own future. I would try to make him understand that men such as myself seek comfort wherever we can find it. He just didn't get it. Maybe he didn't want to. At times, I couldn't really say that

I blamed him. He would always fall back on my parents. I considered it a cheap shot, but it didn't bother me because I knew he meant well. Still, when I got down or depressed, he would always advise me to visit my parents. I used to see them a few times a year, but recently I just haven't been able to motivate myself.

Looking at Dali as he slowly began to fade on me, I thought back of my last visit to Mom and Dad was back in late October. I like the cemetery better when it's cold or raining. For some reason, it just seems more appropriate. Then again, maybe I just watch too many movies. I usually brought my mother flowers and shared a half-pint of Jack Daniels with Dad. I'd spend hours there reminiscing about birthdays, holidays, and other good times in the past. I was twelve when they died, so I remember a lot. I suppose with many people who have lost loved ones taking a trip to their final resting place is bittersweet. I love my parents immensely, and I know their departure was no fault of their own. It was just fate. It took a lot out of me that I haven't been able to replace, but I that's how things go sometimes.

Still, thinking about what Dali said about going out to see them again reminded me of another part of that last visit in October. I remember mentioning to them that I had met a lovely young lady named Avida. I spoke very highly of my new girlfriend pointing out every positive aspect. Near the end of my visit I felt cold. It was odd because it wasn't the fall breeze I was used to but that ice cold you feel in the winter that makes your nose run. That feeling was immediately followed by rain. I left with an uncomfortable sentiment that I haven't been able to shake.

Dali ended up passing out on my couch after the long conversation and late-night drinks. I spent that evening and the majority of that morning sitting on my balcony. Thinking of Games, Cyprus, Dali, and Avida. Thinking of all of us. Thinking of me. Thinking.

GAMES

It didn't take long for me to find out that something was abuzz in the streets. I had a nose for it. I wish I could say that information just fell in my lap, but that was rarely the case. I usually had to work for the real good stuff—the going-ons of Cyprus, for instance. The other night's episode was no different.

Before dealing with that, I wanted to hang out with my boy, Julian. I needed that. It's helpful to me to a degree that he could never understand. Before I hit the streets, I decided to watch the boy play his third Little League baseball game at a small park not too far away from my home. I can't stand the presence of my ex-wife. The only thing positive that ever resulted from my short marriage was Julian.

I love him to death. He's not the best baseball player in the world. He struck out twice that day and was eventually benched for the rest of the game. Ball games really didn't matter much to me. I was happy just to see my boy out there enjoying himself. Besides, I want the kid to be a doctor.

After the game, I took him for ice cream at Ben & Jerry's. One of my partners, Big Tiny, who looked like a building with arms, met me there to discuss our plans for that evening. I raised my son to be very well behaved in public, so when I told his lil' ass to sit in the car and eat his ice cream, he did just that.

"So what you got?" I asked Tiny.

"Shit," was his response as he looked at me as if to say sorry. Big Tiny has been my loyal dirty work assistant for years. I call on him for assistance on the jobs where the police force and the judicial system find their hands tied behind their backs. Tiny was a cop at one time, but ended up gettin' kicked off for the same reason I used him. Specifically, he tossed a drug dealer out of a twenty-story building because the kid raped a cop's daughter and beat the case on a technicality. Cops hate that type of shit. Big Tiny was one who I could count on to take care of that type of shit.

"Shit? Nothin'?" I asked irritably.

"Nothin.' Muthafuckas out here got lock-jaw or somethin'. I mean moves were made last night, but don't nobody know shit. And if they do know, they ain't talkin' to me."

"Well, somebody's talkin' to me. I know Cyprus ran a shake on somebody for Chicago last night."

"Probably. Guess we just got to look harder."

"Naaah, not harder, smarter." I looked back at my son to find him very content with his ice cream and somewhat interested in my conversation.

"So what's next then, boss?"

"You remember that junkie I booked a couple of months ago?"

"Which one?"

"You know, the mufucka walked up in McDonald's, fucked up and ass naked."

"Dreamer?"

"Yeah. He'll know somethin'."

"You think?"

I paused a minute to absorb everything around me. My streets, my neighborhood, my world. "Yeah, he can be a bit funny with information at times. I'm really not in the mood for bullshit today. I'm fuckin' tired of shit goin' down right under my nose and feelin' like I can't do shit about it. I'll drop Julian off at his mother's. Follow me and we'll go from there."

After the quick stop, me and Big Tiny headed back to his place to leave his car. We drove over to one of the city's many rundown neighborhoods to look for Dreamer. After a fifteen-minute drive and following some well-thought-out and careful driving maneuvers to avoid being spotted by corner hustlers, I found just what I was looking for. A thin, frail young man in his mid twenties dressed simply in a black T-shirt and black jeans. They called him Dreamer 'cause he wove the most incredible fantasies when he was high off of who knows what. Dreamer was chatting with fellow friends of the pipe in front of an abandoned, burned-out church that was now a crackhouse.

I watched patiently from across the street as Dreamer laughed, played around, and skated back and forth in a pair of rollerblades he had stolen along with a Nissan Maxima from some white guy he caught "slippin'" at a gas station just outside of the projects.

"Wanna take him now?" Big Tiny asked.

"Uh-uh. Too many folk around, and I damn sure ain't tryin' to chase his ass up and down these streets when he got them fuckin' skates on."

So we waited. It wasn't long before Dreamer was on his way down the avenue toward the liquor store, about four blocks away.

"Alright, let's roll. Sounded like he said he was headed for the store, so I'm figurin' he's headed for the one on Fifth and Alannis. There's an alley cuttin' through the middle of the block before you get to the store. Shit, at least I think I remember one bein' there. Anyway, cut in there, we'll park, and wait for him," I said as Tiny made his way down Fourth Street.

I was right about the alley. We parked behind a Dumpster, got out and waited at the opening of the alley. I took a look up Fifth Street and there was Dreamer with his Walkman blasting, unaware that I was only twenty yards ahead of him.

It was times like this made me happy to be a cop. It was times like this when I knew that I could really do this job and release stress in the process. It was times like this when *I* was not the one to be fucked with.

Dreamer crossed the opening of the alley. I quickly stepped in front of him, snatched him off his feet, spun him in a complete three-hundred-sixty-degree turn and slammed him hard into a wall.

"Fuck!" Dreamer gasped, not noticing that his rollerblades dangled a foot above the ground. "What the fuck is this shit?!"

"What's hap'nin', sweetheart?" I asked.

I signaled for Big Tiny to remove Dreamer's sunglasses and the Walkman.

"Ah shit, Games, you scared the hell out of me, man. Whassup? What's been goin' on, big dog?"

"You tell me."

"Shit, let's talk. No need for muthafuckas to get uncivilized and shit."

I put him down, straightened his shirt, and stepped back, making room for Tiny to step up.

"Look, I'll make this short and sweet 'cause I got no time for games..."

"No time for games, that's funny. You know, you bein' Games and all." Dreamer cautiously patted me on the shoulder as if we were buddies.

I looked at Big Tiny. Tiny pulled out a huge customized knife and placed the blade to Dreamer's throat. "Stop bullshittin, Dreamer."

"Whoa, shit, easy with that mufucka, cuz. What? That's one a them Jeff Dahmer collectible shits, huh...some ol' limited-edition shits. You had to like special order that shit huh?" Dreamer took a big gulp and smiled. "Aiight, aiight, chill. It's all good, player. What you wanna know?" He whimpered as Tiny began to apply a little pressure.

"Last night, you heard about what happened to that rich muthafucka uptown? The one that pissed off Fat Chicago Tone?" I inquired.

"Yeah, Chicago put Cyprus on him. Talk about a dynamic duo. Seems like he was tryin' to get a real point across."

"How you figure?"

"Shit, niggas out here know the type of shit Cyprus do, straight-up wild shit.... outta the movies and all. And that nigga Chicago ain't no bullshit, either."

"I understand all that. What did Cyprus do last night?"

"Well, you know how dude is in the hole to Chicago for like a mufuckin' brick on this business deal that they did. And check this out, right, he got this little boyfriend and shit?"

"Uh-huh."

"Well, uh...look, could you tell Black the Ripper here to ease back with the knife."

I nodded at Big Tiny.

"Thanks. Anyway, according to unnamed sources, your boy Cyprus was like bustin' shots one at a time in the boyfriend dude like fuckin' until dude gave him what he needed. Used a silencer and shit to muffle the sound. I tell you man, Cyprus is a mufuckin' trip. I mean niggas 'round these ways don't do shit like that, man. Anyways, they say youngster was in the emergency room for a while, then dude took him somewhere. Ain't nobody seen or heard from cuz since."

I looked down the alley and focused on the street. Cars and people passed by, totally unaware of my business in the alley. I was both satisfied and worried. I knew I had a major problem in the making.

"Dreamer, how you come across all this shit?" I asked, while lighting a cigarette.

"Hell man, I ain't the only junkie out here. Feel me? And Fat Chicago's peoples ain't like choirboys and shit."

"Ain't that a bitch. Alright, man, roll, and watch ya ass."

"I always do, player. Shit, I wouldn't have too many worries if there wasn't muthafuckas like you out here snatchin' niggas whenever they please."

"Man, get outta here."

"I'm gone."

AVIDA & ME

The following day, I woke up on the couch in my living room. I was in a bit of a daze from the combination of a couple of joints and half a bottle of Scotch. It seemed to be the perfect time to relax and watch a movie. I had considered taking a trip to Avida's, but quickly changed my mind when I remembered our heated phone conversation.

Things these days with us were pretty much black and white. We were basically at each other's throats, or down each other's throats. Rarely was there a gray area. I could never seem to figure out why. The sad part about it was that our relationship started out perfectly. I met her a year ago, the old-fashioned way…at a bar. I was looking over some work for the following day when she caught my eye.

We spent the next twenty minutes staring at each other. I spent more money buying her drinks that evening than I did on myself. It was tough, because she had her triflin' ass, don't-need-a-man friends polluting her mind for the majority of the evening. The alcohol I paid for persuaded her to introduce herself. The rest as they say is history.

Since then, my love for her has grown into this unsettling possessiveness that I dare not even mention to her. I can't even explain it myself. As a result, I've been caught up in this constant struggle to preserve some sense of normalcy.

I dozed off around four that afternoon after watching *The Godfather II* for what was probably the ninth time. The trilogy was a favorite of mine. I was in one of those comatose-type nods when the telephone's ring brought me back to reality. It was times like these when I let my answering machine take my calls. This time, I had a feeling that Avida was on the line.

"Hello?" I answered, almost dropping the phone in my half-awake haze.

"Hey, Blue," whispered her soft and familiar voice.

What had only been a day or two since I had last spoken with her felt like weeks. My heart jumped into my chest and I couldn't do shit about it. I was pressed and I hated it.

"Hey, sweetheart, what's up?" I asked, putting on the most calm and relaxed of voices.

"I keep thinkin' about what happened the other night. Even though I still don't think you were right, I don't want it to be like this with us."

"Neither do I, baby girl...neither do I."

When she called me or came to me, I felt that perhaps this relationship wasn't so one-sided. Hell, even our violent little tiffs didn't seem all that bad. I was most likely fooling myself, but hey, fuck it.

We talked for another hour about her and me and us. Laughing over how things used to be and trying not to concentrate on how things were. Her voice was so sweet. I totally forgot about how she could be at times. I felt better, but nowhere near as good as I felt when she *really* began to talk to me.

"I miss you baby...all of you," she said, beginning to warm up. "I'm tired. Tired of layin' here alone. I feel like bein' tied up....I feel like beggin' for it," she continued, almost purring. Each sentence gradually became a moan. I could faintly hear Jimi Hendrix's "All Along the Watch Tower" playing in the background. I was getting a picture of what she was doing and I figured it wouldn't be long. Nonetheless, I let her continue. I loved to hear her talk about it. I always knew she appreciated our sexual relationship as much as I did, but a little positive reinforcement never hurt.

"You wanna be bad, I see." I actually think my voice got deeper at that moment. It complemented the growing bulge in my pants and grin on my face. I was giddy, to say the least.

"Very," she whispered. "I tell you what. How 'bout you and I play a little game?"

"What kind of game?"

"Well..." She giggled. "Right now I'm kinda half dressed and you're about a ten-minute drive from here. I'll give you fifteen minutes. Five minutes for each article of clothing I'm wearing, and ten minutes for my shower. You make it here in fifteen minutes or less, the door will be open and I'll be in the bedroom waitin.' If you're as much as two seconds late I'll bring tears to your eyes from all of the beggin' *you'll* be doin.' Deal?'

"Deal." I made it there in ten minutes.

Three hours later, I found myself drifting to sleep with her tucked up under me. *Her hair smells good*, I thought to myself. She always managed to be flawless from head to toe. Her perfection was usually at my expense. Tonight I didn't mind. I tried not to concentrate on anything that didn't make me feel good.

I began to think about all that took place, and I wondered about sex...sex, men and women. I began to think about Avida and myself. To be quite honest, our relationship was about seventy percent sexual, thirty percent everything else. I've always heard that sexual relationships can be pretty tumultuous.

Ours was no different, very intense on both ends. I figured one of the problems in my relationship had to do with the perception of sex. I was one of the few men on earth who allowed his emotions to mix with sex. Avida was one of the few women on earth who looked at sex the way the majority of men do—as a physical release. So, what we had was me dating a woman because I'd fallen in love and Avida dating a man because she was getting the best sex she'd ever had.

This matter opened me up to an interesting obstacle. One, which was unfolding right now. As I see it, one's appetite for sex can be compared to that of food. One who loves to eat has a favorite restaurant. That person, however, may still dine out elsewhere for any number of reasons: convenience, variety, curiosity, etc., etc. The same is true for sex. In other words, this queen lying next to me may be dining elsewhere.

✠✠✠

I woke up the next morning and headed home to develop some negatives that I should have done last night. I arrived to find Cyprus parked in front of my place. He was seated on the hood of his car, a black '71 Cadillac that he took much pride in. I parked in front of him, got out, and saw that he wasn't too happy. I was unaware of what was going on with Games, Fat Chicago Tone, and the mystery man with the bullet-filled lover.

"What's goin' on, partner?" He appeared to be upset. He looked me up and down, all frowned up when he spoke.

"Ain't shit, just came from over Avida's."

"Uh," he replied, looking up and down my block and just around, in general.

"Uh...uh what?" I made my way inside ignoring his attempt to get a rise out of me.

He followed.

"Nothin' man, forget it."

"'Sup wit' you?" I asked.

"'Sup wit' ya boy?"

"Who you talkin' 'bout?"

"Games, man," Cyprus said, beginning to laugh and shake his head.

"Oh noo, I wants no parts of that shit."

"Fuck all that. You or Dali, or both of ya'll gotta talk to that nigga and have him raise up off my shit."

"Look at you, all edgy and shit. You and Games go through this same shit at least once a year," I returned.

"Fuck that shit, Blue. This ain't no fuckin' joke. We gots serious problems. This ain't about robbin' hustlers no mo', man. I got Fat Chicago Tone over my shoulders, and Games up my ass."

"Aiight, man, relax, and don't be snappin' at a mufucka," I told him, attempting to calm him down a bit. "C'mon, get ya ass inside."

We did, and he broke down the details of his job for Chicago and his prospects for becoming part of his family. He said he got word that Games had been shakin' down "everybody and they mama" on information about his connection with Chicago. He was pretty pissed about the whole situation.

He rambled on about how long we had all been friends, like I didn't know. He ranted about how Games could potentially screw up everything with him and Fat Chicago Tone. He didn't appreciate me joking about the fact that screwing up his relationship with Chicago was Games' job, despite the friendship. Nevertheless, Cyprus really just wanted to bitch to someone whom he knew would listen. So I did. I still encouraged him to talk rather than argue with Games, maybe they could come to a mutual understanding of boundaries. At least I think that's how I put it.

I figured I'd get some work done during his little tirade since I'd heard it all before. I gave him a Heineken, and he continued on as we made our way to the den, which I had recently transformed into a darkroom. I began to get tired of the nine-to-five grind at *The Chicago Tribune*, so I decided I'd had enough last year. I made a successful transition to an independent contractor working from home. The fellas liked to tease me about the fact that I had one of the most non-black jobs ever. I'm one of a handful of black freelance photographers in the area. I kept things in perspective by reminding myself that I had a college degree in taking pictures, and I preferred to take pictures to pay off my exorbitant college loans over doing anything else. So, even with the jokes, the fellas never seemed to mind hanging out in my darkroom. Personally, I think they appreciated my work more than they would admit.

"Hol' up, what you doin'?" I asked Cyprus, as he attempted to light a cigarette.

"What?" He had a confused look on his face as he stood in front of me with his lighter ignited and smoke flowing from his mouth.

"Ain't no smokin' in here, man. I got all kinds of chemicals and shit up in here."

"Ah, damn...my fault, dog."

"Y'all come over here and keep doin' that shit."

"Well, damn, muthafucka, put up a sign or somethin'."

"Why? You muthafuckas'll look right at that bitch and light up, anyway."

"I guess you got a point there." He laughed, before really beginning to pay close attention to the pictures of various people, places, and my shots of Avida.

He scanned the room slowly. "These are pretty damn good, dog," he said, studying some of the shots of himself and Games at a party we attended some time ago.

"One thing, though, try not to make a habit of catchin' Games and me on film. Hell, I don't know who you might have in here," he noted. "I like the flicks and all...I mean shit, we had fun like a muthafucka that night. I guess the shit just makes me kinda nervous."

"Nervous?" I inquired.

"Think about it," he continued, looking on at the back wall filled from left to right and top to bottom with shots of Avida, "I can't too much afford to be slippin' and shit...and trust, man, I can't fuck wit' it these days."

"I hope that ain't some shit I'm supposed to take personally."

"I don't know man," he said, squatting down to stare at my more "revealing" pictures of Avida, which I felt was some of my best work. "Damn, you got a lot of shit on this girl."

"Pass me those two rolls of film to the right of you."

"She *is* fine. It'll be the death of you yet." He laughed.

"Here *you* go. It's gonna be a bit difficult for you to do the sleepin' with one eye open. You usually pass out every night and all," I said, glancing at some of my more recent negatives.

"What you talkin' 'bout?"

"I'm saying,...you, me, Dali, and Games been rollin' tight since we was in diapers. You bound to come up short tryin' to close everyone out. I mean hell, that shit ain't gonna help yo' ass in the long run, and you the main one talkin' 'bout us layin' back like goodfellas five, ten years from now. We all you got. Despite all that drama between you and Games. Both you mutha-fuckas know that we run thicker than that."

"No doubt," he said, now sitting and listening. Unfortunately, he still didn't see things exactly how I saw them.

"I hear where you comin' from, Blue, but it ain't that simple. We've always looked out for each other, but now it's a new day, new time. I gotta cover my ass, and get paid in the process. Ain't shit changed as far as being tight is concerned, but still business is business. I don't do shit to get in ya'll way and I expect the same in return. Games ain't playin' by the rules."

"What...you expect Games to look the other way while you handle yo' shit. You know that ain't gonna happen. He prob'ly sees it as business is business, too. Shit, back in the days, you used to appreciate a little competition," I contended.

"This ain't back in the days, though, and Fat Chicago Tone ain't competition."

"What the fuck you trippin' over Chicago for? Half his fuckin' crew is scared of gettin' on your bad side, anyway."

"That's right—*my* bad side. They don't give a fuck about Games. Hell, they don't give a fuck about cops in general. I mean, shit, a nigga ain't got time to be keepin' my shit right and makin' sure Games don't get hemmed up 'cause he so pressed to slow me down. That's all I fuckin' need."

Listening to Cyprus, I began to realize that maybe he wasn't just bitchin' because he couldn't have his cake and eat it, too. He had a very good grasp on all that was going on around him. Perhaps he needed to talk it out for it all to make sense. He was smarter and sharper in his thinking. His concern for Games was truly unselfish and more mature than he led on. I was under the false impression that Cyprus' dilemma with Games was strictly personal, influenced by Chicago's offerings of security and money. Maybe Cyprus wasn't as self-seeking as I'd always assumed.

After I finished separating the negatives I wanted to use from the shots that I wasn't all that impressed by, I shut everything down in my darkroom. Cyprus and I ended up just hangin' out and bullshittin' in my living room. Initially, I figured he had only intended on staying a couple of minutes to get my angle on this situation with Games. Men are like women sometimes when it comes to talking. Though we don't like to recognize it, guys can frequently get tied up in idle banter for hours. All that's needed is a strong bond, one that generally takes years. Fortunately for my clique, we pledged both life and death for each other sometime ago.

DALI

"What's this? A security deposit?" I asked, counting the band's earnings from this past weekend's gig.

Easy Pete, the club manager for my regular gig at The First Set, was a degenerate gambler who had a bad habit of finding himself in debt to virtually every loan shark in Chicago. I was growin' very impatient with Pete's excuses for not having all of what he owed us. I decided to go to the club to try and "persuade" him to cease with all the blah-blah and find the money. Cyprus offered his assistance, but I declined. I knew that Pete was familiar with Cyprus' methods. I also knew that the club was owned by Italians, and I didn't want anything too heavy going down over a couple of dollars.

"C'mon, Dali. I told you that I pay bills first, then you," said Pete, flipping through some papers on his desk.

I looked around Pete's office. "Lights is on, bar's full, rent's paid, and I know the water's runnin' 'cause I just came from the bathroom."

"Daaaliiii," returned Easy Pete.

"Dali nothin', Pete. I mean you been short before and you always come quick with the difference plus interest, but this right here man...this is—"

"Dali, man, listen...I got some shit I gotta take care of wit' the peoples that run this joint, man. I got myself into some financial problems."

"What that gotta do wit' me and the band? I mean we can't afford to be without rent money every time you start placin' bets on the Cubs and the Bulls. Hell, the Michael Jordanless Bulls at that. I mean damn, Pete, nobody in Chicago does that."

"Dali, don't act like I ain't looked out for you in the past."

"That ain't the point, all I'm trying to say is"

"Who is it?!" Pete asked angrily at a knock at the door.

Serenity gracefully strolled in as if she owned the club. "Dali...Pete."

"Sweetheart, who the fuck let you up here?" Pete snapped.

"I let myself up, and don't call me sweetheart."

"Whatever. Look, what do ya want? I'm busy here."

"Not busy enough from what I hear."

"What's that supposed to mean?"

"Never mind. I need to speak to Dali."

"What's up, hon'?"

"Lemme talk to you for a second, baby."

"Cool."

"Wait, hold up, Dali," Pete said.

"Pete, concentrate yo' attention on paper."

I ended the discussion on that note. Serenity and I ended up at the bar. Drinks were on the house. It was the least ol' Easy could offer.

"I see you're still having problems getting paid all that you're worth," she said.

"You know, you somethin' else."

"Dali, you should really consider making your business, *our* business."

"Alright, why?"

"I'll give you two reasons. More high-profile gigs and a lot more money," Serenity answered, looking and feeling very confident.

"And why do I get all of this attention?" Would it hurt to explore options? I was tired of chasing down my money.

"Why? Please! Dali, honey, you're the first local horn player I've seen pack this club on *weekdays*. Shit, I know people who would pay top dollar just to hear you sit in with someone else's band. "

"Good point," I said, wondering what I might be gettin' myself into. A white woman managing my career. The idea alone was insane. Not to mention the fact that I found her attractive. It truly was quite hard not to. She got style for a white woman, more than any I'd seen. I liked her professional Donna Karan suits, her evening skirts with slits that rose up the side of her legs, her impeccable taste in everything. She also was just interested in my career. Still, she was a woman, and not as yet to be trusted, especially with money. Man, Pops would turn over in his grave. Then again, he might say, "Boy, if she's good with money and you trust her, then go for it." I just didn't know about the latter.

"Why don't we get together later to talk specifics?"

"Works for me," was her response, as she straightened my collar, brushed her hand down the lapel of my suit, and smiled. "You still have my number?"

"You've given it to me twice."

"Cute. Look, I'll talk to you later. I'm on my way uptown for an early dinner with some friends. They'll be interested to know that you and I *may* soon be working together."

"Alright, I'll talk to you."

"Bye," she said, leaving just minutes before Allura walked up behind me and put her hands over my eyes.

"Guess who?" Allura invited.

"Ooh, uh...Sharon, no...uh, Sharon's mom, Cherelle!"

"You need to stop."

"Hey, baby." I turned around to greet her with a big hug and soft kiss on the neck.

"You're early."

"I figured I'd surprise you. How'd I do?"

"Eh, I've seen better, but hey, you tried."

"Shut up." Allura chuckled. "Are you ready?"

"Waitin' on you."

We were on our way to dinner like we'd been doing for the past couple of weeks. I was proud of myself. I didn't stress 'bout spending time and money on a woman without getting something "tangible" in return. Allura wasn't one of those women who didn't mind giving themselves away for a free meal or money for hair and nails. Besides, she probably made just as much—if not more—money than I did.

I felt no pressure, no worries and no need to put on false faces to impress her. She made me feel comfortable. For the first time in my life, I was in no rush for physical intimacy. I kinda liked that.

I took her to one of my favorite steakhouse joints rememberin' just as I looked at the menu that she was a vegetarian. *Damn*, I thought, *nice move, man*. I may be country, but I'm quick on my feet. I excused myself and tracked down the manager so I could explain my situation. I simply requested that he have our server recommend the best meatless dish the chef had to offer. I returned to the table and gritted out a few minutes of awkward silence before the server arrived and saved me. We ordered and everything was okay. She loved her dish. I definitely enjoyed mine 'cause you can never go wrong wit' a Porterhouse steak.

"Why are you looking at me like that?" I asked after finishing the last bite of my steak.

"Just thinking," she said with a difficult-to-read smile.

"About what?" I returned the look and her smile.

"Um...anticipation."

"Anticipation?"

"Relationships are sometimes like games, ya know. You need to take time to feel out your opponent, so to speak."

"Is that what you're doin'?"

"I suppose. I guess I really don't know." Allura sighed heavily.

"Sweetheart, I think you're wrestling with the 'us' issue a bit too hard," I said, noticing that she appeared a bit anxious.

"Really?" Sarcasm was all over her face.

"Really. I'll tell you what. How about you and I take a stroll to walk off some of this dinner, and we can discuss the future of you and I."

"You're serious?"

"Sure, I enjoy talking with you. I feel, I don't know...at ease talking to you."

"I'm glad to hear that, Lorenzo."

CYPRUS

Another busy Friday reared its head and plans for the four of us were the same as they'd always been. We would see each other at Dali's in the early evening. Still, some of us, had other appointments that needed to be handled beforehand. Though only a few weeks had passed since Fat Chicago Tone's "business" was taken care of, he wanted me to relax and "take it easy" for a while.

Chicago had a thing about keeping a low profile. He hated unnecessary attention and he loved anonymity. His line of work made being invisible of paramount importance. Chicago expected the same kind of behavior from his men. If anyone was ever caught by the police for something as ridiculous as hanging around a "hot" street corner with friends after killing or stealing for Chicago, they would catch hell upon release. Chicago's intentions for me were no different. He knew I was a well-known name in the city. Though it was that favorable reputation which caught Chicago's attention in the first place, he still felt that a little anonymity wouldn't hurt. My take on anonymity? Fuck that shit.

I was sitting on the hood of my car outside of my apartment waiting for him to pick me up so we could discuss this low-profile shit. I had an eerie feeling about the whole thing. I knew that Chicago would want something that I might not be prepared to give. I knew that while hooking up with him served as a great advantage, I kind of missed being a freelancer. Before I could piss myself off further, Chicago arrived.

We talked about nothing for a minute or two before Chicago got down to business.

"I don't know, man. It just ain't me," I confessed as we sat in Chicago's Humvee.

"Look, man, I know you like the streets and all, but it ain't like I'm askin' you to move out of the city," Chicago replied. "I mean, shit. I've already heard that you got some cop in your shit."

"Ah shit, don't even worry about that."

"Got to, cuz. That's how I keep my people outta trouble, makin' sure ain't no cops in the picture unless they on the payroll. That shit you took care of for me was no walk in the park. The average nigga would have fucked the whole thing up and got hemmed up in the process. You pulled that shit off with no problems at all. I'm talkin' quick and clean. That's the kind of shit that I need workin' for me. So this is the way I want it right now. I have to protect my investments..."

"At the expense of me sittin' on my hands?"

"Don't look at it like that. All I want you to do is stay off the block for a while and let me hand-pick your jobs."

"And what about money?"

"There's twenty grand in the trunk for the job from the other night. Hell, you earned it. I'll keep you busy with other shit in the meantime."

"Okay, stay off the block for a while. How long is 'a while'?"

"Damn, Cyprus, that's what I like about you—relentless, fuckin' relentless." Chicago checked his side and rearview mirrors. "It'll just be for a couple weeks."

I sat there looking outside the dark tinted windows of the Humvee. Chicago's offer seemed a fair one, but I wasn't too big on bein' off the streets. Shit, what would I do? How would I spend my time? To me, low profile sounded a lot like hiding and I never hid from no one. I mean it ain't the same when the streets is hot. In situations like that, everybody gotta take it easy 'cause everybody at risk. Still, there's a lot of ways to enjoy twenty grand. Images of hotel suites with bottles of Moet, bags of weed, room service, and the two young ladies from Chicago's club ran through my mind. Maybe a week or two wouldn't kill me. I remembered the time I took a week off to go to Los Angeles. I like L.A.

"So what's up, man, can you work with me on this?" Chicago asked.

"Yeah, man, fuck it—ain't shit."

"Cool, let's roll."

As we headed for one of Chicago's nightspots, I started to feel quite comfortable. This type of arrangement was what I'd been looking for. I lit a cigarette as Chicago made a right turn on to a busy intersection. The traffic light appeared to be yellow. Neither of one of us took notice, but a patrol car behind us did.

"Shit," I said, looking in the rearview mirror at the flashing red and blue lights.

"Relax, man," Chicago insisted.

"What...you got this?"

Fat Chicago Tone shot me a cocky glance as he sat there as calm and at ease as a fisherman on a foggy Sunday morning.

A white, plain-clothes police officer stepped out of the patrol car and slowly made his way to Chicago's Humvee. Chicago turned up his radio a bit. "I love this fuckin' song."

"Hey, Chicago, how ya doin'?" the officer asked, leaning down and looking into the vehicle.

"I'm aiight, man, what's the word these days?" Chicago calmly lit a half-smoked cigar that was sitting in the car's ashtray.

"Word is you're a busy man, my friend."

"Tell me somethin' I don't know."

"Well," said the cop, peeking his head up above the car, looking around carefully.

"You're a bit too busy, accordin' to some of the other families in the city. They think you're gettin' a bit greedy with all the shit you're bringin' in. They think you're gonna end up bringin' Fed' heat along with all that shit. They want a bigger piece of whatever you're givin' 'em now."

Chicago turned down the music. He was upset to say the least. Chicago was one of the few brothers who truly understood how the Italian Mafia worked, and in his opinion they were the ones who were greedy. He was no fool, however. He knew that saying "fuck it" to the whole thing would bring him more harm than good. He had neither the time nor patience to deal with those kinds of inconveniences. Chicago was more concerned with money.

"How much is a bigger piece?" Chicago asked irritably.

"Look, uh, they want twice what they're gettin' now, but I think they'd settle for fifteen. You know, just somethin' to show good faith."

Chicago paused for a second, then reached into his pocket, and pulled out an envelope. He handed it to the officer. "That ain't go'n happen, but set it up, anyway," he returned.

"Not a problem," said the officer, putting the envelope in his pocket.

As the patrol car drove off, I asked, "What was with the sirens and lights and shit?"

"I didn't think you'd catch that," Chicago answered. "Some of the cops on my payroll been catchin' some flack for bein' seen wit' me and all, so they sometimes go through the whole rah-rah of pullin' me over. You know, to look legit."

"Makes sense...So what's wit' the Italians?"

"You sure as hell ask a lot of questions."

"Got to," I said, wondering if I had offended him, but not really caring either way.

"Yeah, true, I guess. They put me on a long time ago when I was a kid, just a bit younger than you. I can't really cut 'em off 'cause they know more about me than the cops do. Plus, I don't need no extra drama right now, but more money is gonna be a problem," Chicago said, pulling off into the bustling traffic.

After talking over future jobs with Chicago at one his clubs, I picked up my twenty grand. I decided to have a couple of drinks at the bar before I left for Dali's. I engaged in a bit of small talk with the bartender and a young woman who was waiting for her husband. She seemed quite chatty, to be married. Still, I wasn't that surprised. It wouldn't have been the first time that I'd holla'd at a married woman. I always tell Blue that I got no plans on getting married.

"Can't trust no woman, man—'specially not a young one," I'd always tell him. I'd simply shake my head and release a heavy sigh when he told me of his problems with Avida. "Can't trust no woman." I was about to pay my bill when I happened to glance over the married woman's shoulder and saw Avida with two of her girlfriends. The three of them joined a table of three gentlemen. Like I said, can't trust no woman.

BLUE

Games made it over to Dali's first. While they drank, Dali spoke of how things were going for him and Allura. It was kind of funny. He sounded like a kid—gigglin' and talking all loud. He was happy. Perhaps happier than he had been for some time. Allura seemed to pull that out of him. He said she was funny. She made him laugh, and he always wanted a woman with a sense of humor. Someone to match his own I guess.

Nonetheless, he was beginning to become frustrated with Games' concentration on Cyprus. Dali's tolerance level for their tug-of-war had dwindled over time. He felt the whole thing was childish and boring. He would constantly remind both Cyprus and Games that even as adults they were still acting like young boys. Though the adult relationship between Games and Cyprus was now a lot more complicated, it was really starting to get on Dali's nerves.

"Games, I ain't tryin' to hear this tonight," Dali said, making himself another drink.

"Oh, so you on some ol' hear no evil, see no evil type shit now, right?" said Games.

"Here *you* go. Look, man, what you want me to do? I swear, man, twenty some odd years and nothing has changed with you two."

Games took some time to listen to Dali speak of the "good old days" and what had really been the good "new" days for us. Dali pointed out to Games that we, as a group, survived off the concept of trust.

Games may not have fully agreed with everything that Dali said, but it didn't matter. Dali accomplished his short-term goal of making Games back off of his present preoccupation with Cyprus. He was most proud of helping Games relax a bit by reminiscing about past times; old girlfriends, bar fights, Friday nights, and so on. They laughed about Dali's parachute pants days. And laughing is how Cyprus and I caught them when we made it through around nine p.m.

Cyprus called me and I picked him up from he bar. He said that he had something to show me. When he got into my car, he glanced at me, smiled, and opened a small duffel bag. It was packed with bundles of twenty-dollar bills. Cyprus explained that it was supposed to be twenty grand from Chicago but was actually more like twenty-five. The extra cash was what you might call a signing bonus. Cyprus was a very happy man.

✠ ✠ ✠

We strolled into Dali's apartment and engaged in the typical male bonding hugs, and handshakes. It was nice to know that all bullshit was temporarily put aside. Games immediately tossed us some "remember whens" while Dali made us some drinks. As far as drinking goes, Cyprus and I had to catch up. Well, I did. Cyprus had gotten started back at Chicago's club. Everything was cool, and some company Dali invited made it even more interesting.

Allura and three of her girlfriends came by. We all got along pretty well. There were no fronts or facades of any sort. My mind was somewhere else, and I didn't understand why. Something felt strange or out of place to me for some reason. My soul seemed to be trying to tell me something. It wouldn't have been the first time that I was internally warned to prepare myself for something. Then again, maybe it was just the weed. I was soon snapped out of my unusual mood by Dali's loud vice. One of Allura's girlfriends made the mistake of boasting that she could drink any of us under the table. Not only was her challenge met, it was countered by Dali, Games, Cyprus, and myself. In retrospect, the entire situation was juvenile, but what can you do? Occasionally, acting a fool builds character.

Hours later the four of them passed out. Dali, Games, Cyprus, and I continued to maintain and reign as the city's alcohol kings. Nothing to really be proud of, but you have to have something to hold on to at times. We continued to laugh and make fun of each other, until Cyprus felt the need to pull me to the side.

"Hey, cuz, I ain't trying to fuck up your night or nothin'." Cyprus began to slur his words.

"Then don't."

"I'm serious, man."

"What, man, what's up?"

"Aiight, I'm at the club chillin' and shit, gettin' my drink on after I got my loot from Chicago, right. And I'm sittin' there kickin' it with the bartender, Ray, and this other honey who said she was married. She looked good, too. Little beige skirt, big, brown legs looking real nice and shit, ya know. I was like damn I wouldn't mind"

"Cyprus, get to the fuckin' point. I'll be sober by the time you finish," I said.

"Oh yeah, right. So anyway, I'm chillin', and guess who I see?"

"I have no idea."

"C'mon, man, guess."

"Cyprus."

"Aiight, aiight. I saw your lady roll in with two of her girlfriends."

"Ain't shit, she told me she was goin' out wit' 'em tonight."

It ain't so much that as it is who they sat down wit'." Cyprus kind of looked around clumsily to see if anyone else was listening. Then he made eye contact with me as if he were giving me the worst news of my life.

"What you mean?" I questioned.

"Cuz, they sat down at a table wit' three dudes. Well dressed, pretty mufuckas, too. All of 'em were sittin' next to one of them niggas, Avida included. Now, believe me, man I ain't trying to be the bearer of bad news or nothin', but I figured you should know. I mean, I know you got shit locked down on the home front and all. If I were you I wouldn't read much into it."

I simply nodded my head because I really didn't have much to say at that time. I didn't know what to say or what to think. Cyprus, like the rest of us, did have a pretty good amount to drink that night. Perhaps, his memory had deceived him in one way or another. It's not like it would've been the first time that happened. I had my suspicions about Avida. One night out on the town could be totally innocent. Hell, look at me, in Dali's apartment with four very attractive, single women and my aim was to get drunk with some friends. Perhaps Avida's motives were similar. So I chose to soothe my internal stress with another drink. I figured I would pay my baby girl a visit and possibly do a bit of inquiring.

I went to the bathroom after my talk with Cyprus and walked out to find him and Games playing video games. Two of Allura's girlfriends had come out of their doze and were ordering Chinese food for all of us. And, there were Dali and Allura in his kitchen—engaged from the neck up, that is. At this point, I was quite confident that it wouldn't be too long now before they'd be waking up together. Everything was cool. For the moment, the residual funk between Games and Cyprus was squashed. One of Allura's girlfriends was rather fond of Games. She said she didn't care too much for cops, but she made an exception in his case. So we all hung out for another hour or two, and eventually made our way home. Well, all of us except Allura.

❈❈❈

I ended up at Avida's place before she got there. It was two forty-seven a.m. on the dot. After knocking on her door for a minute or so with no answer, my curiosity convinced me to wait for her. So I sat in my car for what felt like hours. It was actually only minutes. A gray Ford Explorer pulled up two cars in front of my own around three. I could see a female passenger lean over to the driver for a couple of seconds. Avida then got out and walked over to the driver's side. She leaned her head into the window. I was a bit surprised that she didn't recognize my car.

I watched her as she slowly strolled to her apartment, opened the door, and walked in. It wasn't like her to stay out *this* late. *Damn, she got balls.* I thought to myself. I continued to sit and wait for a couple of seconds. I was assessing the situation. I got out of my car and straightened myself up as best I could. This was a damn sobering situation. I soon found myself at her door, knocking. My heart was beating uncontrollably fast for some reason. I know I couldn't have been nervous or anxious about anything. There was no need for me to be. I hadn't done anything wrong. Still, I felt a bit weird—like I shouldn't have been there in the first place. *The hell with it*, I told myself, and kept knocking.

"Who is it?" A hesitant whisper came from the other side of the door.

"It's just me, sweetheart."

Avida took a second or two to check the peephole. Then the door cracked open cautiously, just like I had taught her. "What are you doing here so late?"

"What are you doing up so late?"

"Come in." Avida unlatched her door. "I told you I was goin' out with my girls. You comin' from Dali's?"

"Yeah."

"I can tell. You smell like a liquor store." Avida had a snippy attitude. She always got that way when she felt I had too much to drink or smoke.

"I don't know why you frontin' like you ain't never seen the bottom of a bottle before."

"Blue, please, you're right. I do get my drink on when I want to. I just don't end up smellin' as bad as you do," she countered.

"Yes, you do. I just don't tell you."

"Oh, that's fucked up." She giggled. "You hungry? I got some leftover curry chicken from last night if you want it."

"No thanks, I ate at Dali's."

She had taken off her shoes and some of her clothes, giving the impression that she was already quite comfortable.

"So what time did you get in tonight?" I asked as casually as I possibly could.

"Around one, one-thirty," she answered, getting some water from the refrigerator.

"Really." I laughed.

"Yeah why, what's so funny?"

"Oh, nothin', nothin'. I'm just trippin' on the fact that *you* stayed out so late," I said.

"I had a lot of fun actually, surprised my damn self."

"Where'd you go?"

"Just dinner and drinks, after that we just hung out at Janine's."

"I'm shocked you didn't go to any clubs, the way her busybody ass is."

"Nah, we really didn't feel like it tonight."

And that's where I left it. I could have gone on and started a whole fight and all, but to be quite honest, I was a bit too tired and too drunk. Besides, I didn't want to risk the loss of a titanic lie like this on her part. I would simply save this golden opportunity for a more appropriate time.

I wasn't feeling all that "frisky." The feeling was mutual. I took a shower at her request, and we both just went to sleep.

DALI

Allura and I fell asleep late that night after everyone left. We spent a lot of the following morning in my bed.

"I can still smell your perfume," I told her as I softly traced my lips from the bottom of her left ear slowly down the side of her neck. I finally stopped between the partially covered breasts I had dreamt about so often over the past couple of weeks.

"Oh God, you must still be a bit tipsy." She was somewhat embarrassed about her appearance.

"No, I'm serious," I said, brushing my fingers through her thick, jet-black hair. "Besides, brothers like me don't get tipsy."

"Oh really?"

"That's right. That's a woman's term."

"A woman's term? So then what do you call it when you bump into the wall, drop beer bottles, and slur your speech?"

"Oh that. That's drunk."

"And that's what you were—drunk?" Allura asked, laughing.

"Like a freshman at a frat party."

Allura laughed even harder, holding her stomach and cuddling up next to me, wrapping her legs up with mine.

She was a woman who was very aware of her emotions. She was familiar with the ups and downs that the heart encounters over a lifetime. Her comfort with herself spiritually and emotionally enabled her to be open to whatever might happen with me. At the same time, that comfort would protect her from any true damage that me or any man might cause—intentional or not. Was she falling in love? Was I? It was too soon to say.

She flipped herself over and looked me in my eyes. "Kiss me."

I did. Slowly, carefully, and methodically. We spent the early morning hours virtually attached to each other, fighting that strong urge to act like teenagers and say to hell with waiting.

We decided to go to breakfast instead.

GAMES

I woke up that following morning to a hangover and a couple of guests. I heard the repeated knocks. I managed to get myself out of bed. I made my way to the door, which for a quick second seemed a good mile away. Looking through the peephole, I stared at two faces I hadn't seen for almost a year.

"Open up, man, I see ya' ass looking through the peephole!" shouted a voice from the other side of the door.

"Fuck that, I can smell his drunk ass from here." A second voice laughed.

"How 'bout both y'all muthafuckas kiss my ass." I opened the door for two of my old cronies from the police academy.

I had joined the Marines after high school, and I jumped at the opportunity to join the police academy when my tour was up. I became closely acquainted with the two men now sitting in my living room, Rick Dove of Montgomery, Alabama, and Kevin Supreme of New York.

"So what's up, Games? What you been up to?" Dove asked with his thick, redneck accent.

"Working as usual, you know. Tryin' my best to keep these fools out here on they toes," I said, stretching and cracking my neck a couple of times.

"I hear that. Same with me and Supreme. I see you still drink like a fuckin' fish."

"Is it that obvious?"

"Mufucka ain't changed a bit, has he?" Supreme asked Dove rhetorically, pointing at me. "I told you, partner...," he continued, speaking to me again, "you gotta hit the gym wit' us, sweat the stress away. Not to mention, gettin' ya shit tight. You know you need that, dealin' with these crazy young niggas out here today."

"Shit," I said matter-of-factly to Dove, "Premo still don't know, do he? It's a new day my friend and size don't mean shit. Only muscle I need is my Glock and twelve gauge." I nodded over to both of those weapons, which I kept on my coffee table.

"You sound like a gangsta, dog," Supreme said.

"Gotta be the man to catch the man," added Dove as he rubbed his hands through his reddish-blond hair.

"What brings you two over to my neck of the woods, anyway?" I made my way to the kitchen.

"Well, we doing some work with the feds. Watchin' Fat Chicago Tone and the Italians he used to fuck with," returned Supreme, getting up to follow me.

"Used to? Try still is," I said.

"We know, we know," said Dove. "Look, we got word your ol' friend Cyprus been doin' jobs for Chicago."

"I know that, too. I'm workin' on it."

"Ain't good enough," Supreme replied in a calm but firm manner.

"Hold up, what's going on?" I interrupted.

"Alright, man, listen. Feds been after Chicago for years and we know you know this. What you don't know is that they got a damn good chance of gettin' his ass 'cause he's had the Italians breathin' down his neck lately." Supreme spoke a lot with his hands and they were working overtime as he spoke to me.

"What's with all the heat from the Mafia?" I asked, unskillfully working on making some coffee.

"Can't say. Looks like they think the brother's a bit too upwardly mobile." Supreme continued, "Anyway, I hear your partner Cyprus been rollin' wit' Chicago lately. That shit ain't too good 'cause we think Chicago's whole shit is comin' down."

I sat back for a minute. It was a great deal to take in all at one time. The information proved what I believed to be true from the beginning. Still, the cop in me warned that not only did something feel strange about this "situation," but it would also be damn near impossible to sell the story to Cyprus. I knew I would need to do some investigating of my own and sort everything out.

I entertained my old buds for another half-hour, recalling times from way back when.

I was a lot like Cyprus when it came to the issue of trust. As far as Dove and Supreme were concerned, maybe they should be watched. I gave them the impression that I was on the case.

After my guests left, I got myself cleaned up and made a bite to eat. I pride myself on being a fairly decent chef. I finished my protein-filled meal of steak and eggs and proceeded to call Cyprus. I figured Cyprus had just as much information about federal/criminal activities as any cop if not more. More importantly, I knew that I could trust Cyprus. That's the one thing so many people never understood about our adversarial relationship—trust. We both knew that no matter what the other did, we *always* looked out for each other.

"Whassup, nigga?"

"Ain't shit, what's goin' on?"

"Shit, man, still recoverin' from last night," I said.

"I hear you on that shit. Too bad you can't get wit' me on one of these Swisher Sweets and this dub I'm 'bout to roll. That's how this nigga 'bout to recover."

"I wouldn't mind goin' that route round about now."

"Damn, dog, that don't sound like you. What's on ya mind?" Cyprus asked with concern.

"I gotta holla at you 'bout somethin'."

"'Sup?"

I reiterated to Cyprus in code what I heard from my old buddies and added some speculation of my own. I told Cyprus that I wanted to do some checking around and asked if he would do the same on his end. He agreed but again cautioned me that he would proceed with his current activities with Fat Chicago Tone. I could accept that for now, but warned him just in case Dove's and Supreme's information proved true.

"I can live wit' that if you can," said Cyprus.

"No problems on this end."

"Cool. How's your son?"

"Oh, real good—handlin' his business in school, too."

"Hol' up for a second, lemme grab the other line." Cyprus returned with good news for me: a phone call from Chicago. "Hey, looks like I'm on first, but I gotta tell ya I don't like this investigative reporter shit too much. That's all I need is for muthafuckas to start thinkin' *my* shit is suspect."

"C'mon now. Don't even trip on it. Ain't nobody askin' you to turn snitch. Just keep your eyes and ears open, that's all."

"Aiight, aiight."

"Holla at me when you get a minute."

"I'll give you a hit sometime tomorrow."

"Aiight, later."

"Later."

CYPRUS

I hung up the phone not feeling as comfortable as I was when I answered it. I didn't like this move too much, but I did trust Games' instinct. It got me out of a lot of trouble in the past. For a second or two, I allowed my mind to toss around various theories and possibilities of these...well, circumstances. I thought about my adversarial, yet close friendship to Games. I thought about Chicago. I thought until I caught myself thinking too much. Unlike Blue, I don't think of myself as complex and I don't like spending too much time in my head. Philosophies and speculation ain't my cup of tea. It's just not my nature. Instead, after my phone call, I chose to continue with what I was doing before Games called, rollin' my blunt. I sat back, popped the cap on a Guinness Stout, grabbed my favorite lighter, and proceeded to watch *Goodfellas*—again. I had a meeting with Fat Chicago Tone the following day to discuss business.

✠✠✠

The young man who spoke to Cyprus hung up the mobile phone and informed Chicago that Cyprus would be present. Chicago was in the kitchen of one of the small restaurants he owned making a childhood favorite, seafood gumbo. It was a well-known fact among his men that when Chicago cooked, he had something pretty important on his mind. They said it appeared to help him concentrate and, though he didn't always make the best meal around, he made some of his smartest decisions and strongest moves after a culinary stand.

His gumbo had him pondering his situation with the Italians and the cops. Contrary to what some might have thought, Chicago was very aware of all that was taking place around him. It was why he had called some of his people, Cyprus now included, together for this meeting. This wasn't the first time that Chicago was under fire, so he knew what had to be done. Chicago was the founder and head of the first and largest independent Black crime family. He didn't get to that point by allowing himself to be outsmarted or taken advantage of.

✠ ✠ ✠

Things were now becoming complicated for all of us in one way or another. For Cyprus, Games, Dali, and myself, situations always seemed to get all twisted up without us ever realizing it. Our lives were tied together in a strange kind of way. What lay ahead for all of us was unknown. I guess that's usually the case, anyway. Dali appeared to be the only one content with this uncertainty. He embraced it actually. He was the only one taking the chance of going with his heart rather than trying to reason and rationalize everything.

DALI

I dropped Allura off at her two-bedroom condo in the 'burbs after our eventful morning of intimacy and breakfast at my favorite diner. I drove back home feeling pretty damn good about life. We made plans for a night at home—Allura's place. She wanted to cook for me.

I ran a few errands around the city and dropped by to see Serenity downtown at a flashy hair salon she had recently acquired. One of those places the sisters who date big-money fellas go and pay hundreds of dollars to get their hair and nails done. I didn't care too much for the spot. I was greeted by some dude who introduced himself as Twan.

"Oooh, can I help you?" he asked.

I ignored the question with an irritable frown and slowly strolled by the various shampoos, conditionings, retouches, perms, and the like being done to black and white women and men. It was a unisex, multi-racial, no-problem with-sexual-preference kind of place. Serenity liked it that way, which was ironic because she sure as hell wasn't brought up that way. She came from an affluent and conservative Anglo-Saxon New York suburb. The type of place where brothers get stopped by the police for waiting at a stop sign too long. Ever since Serenity was a teen and started partying with black folk in Brooklyn, The Bronx, Queens, and who knows where else, she's had an "in" with "us." None of the brothers or sisters I knew minded too much. One reason was because she never tried to act or be black. I suppose it would be safe to say that her motives have always been sincere. Then again, in my case "always" may have been too strong a word.

She approached me as I was glancing at a piece of art at the bottom of a spiral staircase, which led to her office.

"Hey, Dali, what's up, hon?" Serenity watched me as I continued to look at the work.

"Not much, just checkin' out this piece." My eyes remained focused in the same direction.

"Like it?"

"It's not bad, an old friend of mine, Vic…he'd paint circles around whoever did this, though." I pivoted around on one foot.

"Have him see me. I can always use new pieces."

"Sure, I'll probably see…." I said, turning my attention to Serenity. She looked fantastic.

One of the things Serenity was known for was how well she dressed. Today was no different. She was in navy from head to toe. A Versace business suit. The skirt displayed almost all of her tanned, golden thighs, which were accented by the matching pumps. It was a pretty classy ensemble.

I took in her appearance quickly. Well, quickly enough so as not to stare.

"So whassup?" I asked, thinking of the irony of that question as I followed her legs as they made their way upstairs to her office.

"Have a seat, hon'. Make yourself comfortable." Serenity motioned for me to sit at the chair in front of her desk.

"Nice," I said, taking a second to look at her office before sitting down.

"It's alright. Good place to get work done. Enough about the office. Let's talk business." Instead of sitting behind her desk, Serenity sat on the edge of her desk, legs crossed, directly to the left of me. Okay, let's just say she sat right in front of me.

"What kind of business?" She was making it very difficult to stay focused.

"How about a new gig, just for one night? Something to ooohh…let's say give you a taste of what I could get you into."

"I don't know. I like my gigs. I like my spot, and my band likes my gigs and my spot."

"Dali, honey, I know you've found a comfort zone in your club and all, but I just want you to simply think about this new spot. I know you'll love it."

"Okay, talk to me, give me some specifics."

"First of all, since this is a one-time run, it's all your show. I guarantee you'll make more in that night than you do in a whole weekend at your old spot."

"That's a big guarantee."

"Honey, half the people there are going to be folks who've already heard you at your regular gigs," Serenity replied.

"Alright, seriously—how much?" I questioned, taking all of her information into consideration.

"I'd say five thousand for you and your band."

"You'd say??"

"Sweetheart, cut me a little slack. I'm working with the money from the door. Anything can happen. How 'bout this? Worst-case scenario, you guys'll each leave with a grand from me."

It was a profitable offer no matter how I looked at it. I sat back for a minute, looking around the tastefully decorated office. She had to know something about something to get herself to this level of financial comfort.

"I tell you what, I'm going to be taking some time off tonight to relax. Give me some time to think about it and talk to the band. I'll call you tomorrow."

"No problem, take your time."

"Oh, one last thing," I said, rising from my seat and preparing to leave. "I was just wondering, Serenity, why so much energy invested in me?"

"Because my dear, you're young, attractive, and you play better than anyone I've ever heard. I'd be a fool to let someone with your talent just float by me."

"Interesting answer."

"Call me when you're ready. We'll talk more."

"I'll do that."

On my way home, I contemplated her proposal. I had to admit it was an attractive one. Like Cyprus, I wasn't the type to spend a great deal of time brooding over an issue. I usually just followed my heart. The one exception to the rule was my music. I never went with what sounded like a sure thing because it usually wasn't. One of the main reasons my band stayed loyal to me was because of my decision-making abilities. I always made them money and I always looked out for their best interest.

They trusted my instincts.

So here I was. Our current spot continued to come up short with our earnings. There were so many angles to consider for one small gig. How did things get so tricky? I just wanted to play. I found myself spending too much time and energy on the whole issue at this point. I focused instead on Allura and the opportunities that were possibly waiting for me. I played with the notion of what she would be wearing, how she would do her hair, what perfume she would have on...what would happen. I began to smile at how beautiful she was with her gentle disposition, magical hazel eyes, smooth almond skin, and flawless frame.

She was what me and the fellas call the wifey type.

CYPRUS

Fat Chicago Tone called a short meeting of his underbosses and a few representatives from their crews that night to discuss what he felt were immediate issues. A potential "situation" with his Italian counterparts and problems with the Federal Bureau of Investigation appeared to be imminent. He wanted to address them immediately.

Chicago generally made all of his business decisions alone and called meetings only to consult with the rest of the family. Tonight would be no different. He'd pretty much planned out what needed to be taken care of and would spend this evening delegating responsibilities. One of which would specifically require my assistance.

Chicago was always aware that he could have informants in his organization. He was known for being paranoid about the whole thing. As a result he would often randomly perform clean-up duties in an effort to better the family's home maintenance. Those duties were generally the kind where someone wound up dead when the job was done. I was chosen to perform one of these tasks.

✠ ✠ ✠

"I want you to postpone that deal with what's his name," Chicago told one of the eight gentlemen sitting in his dimly lit and lavishly bedecked, executive top-floor office. They were in of one of Chicago's smaller, more exclusive nightclubs. Three of the eight men were Chicago's advisers. There was Onassis Smith, Vaughn Dixon, and a Spanish guy they called Patillo.

"Who Savata, the Colombian?" Onassis questioned, referring to a deal with a guy I remember Games mentioning to me once. Savata was a major crime figure down South. He and Chicago had been looking to hook up for some time, but had been running into difficulty as a result of the FBI and cops like Games.

"Yeah, the one outta Florida. Stall 'em if ya can. If he gets frustrated and wants to go somewhere else, don't worry about it."

"That's a pretty big one, Chicago. Sure you wanna just let it go like that?" asked Patillo.

"It's a small concern right now. I got bigger fish to fry. Besides, that Colombian shit is as easy to come by as weed nowadays. Them muthafuckas line up to get rid of that shit. Like I said, don't worry about it."

"So what we gon' do about the Italians?" Dixon asked.

"That's the tricky part. Them guinea muthafuckas are patient, so that's what we gotta be for now. Patient. They think I'm movin' up too fast or on too hard. Cool. Sooner or later, they'll want to talk. We'll wait for that. Ain't no need talkin' 'bout wars and all that shit until then."

"Another thing," Chicago continued, speaking to Maxwell Sholtz, one of the top attorneys in the city and Chicago's lead counsel. "What's the deal with that kid, Magic?"

"Looks like he'll get a year and a half at the most. Probably won't do any more than a couple of months," Sholtz replied.

"With all that shit his dumb ass got caught with? How'd he do that?" Chicago asked.

Sholtz shrugged. "We couldn't get the case. DA got a hold of 'em. Can't say what happened after that."

"Three more of mine got pinched is what happened. Look, get Reese and his guys to catch up with him, talk to him, and convince him that everything's cool. We'll look out for him."

"Why? What you got planned that can't wait 'til he get in, or get out a year and a half from now for that matter?" Patillo asked.

"Fuck that wait shit. I want Cyprus to take care of it."

"Cyprus?" Sholtz questioned.

"That last job he did for us was fuckin' perfect and that's what I need right now—something done in a precise and thorough fashion. I want that big-mouth muthafucka gone and I know Cyprus can handle it."

DALI

The forty-five-minute drive out to Allura's was a long one compared to the places I usually went, but I didn't mind a bit. I chose to take the scenic route. I put my car in cruise control and popped in a compilation CD of the band's performances to analyze any mistakes we may have made. However, I ended up spendin' more time just enjoyin' the ride. I was like a kid in the backseat of the mini-van on a family vacation. I frequently gazed out of my window admirin' everything from the occasional mansion to the miles of woods populated with deer and other wildlife. I found myself at times focusing on almost everything but the road. I was excited, anxious—even a bit nervous, which was you know, kinda new for me.

I arrived at her door, paused, then knocked. The door opened and I stood there in her doorway for a moment. She literally looked good enough to eat.

"You comin' in?"

"Definitely." The mood was intimate. Allura lit candles carefully throughout her house. She had one of those living rooms that you have to step down into. She placed four candles on each end of the room. I always wanted a living room like that. Incense complemented the candles on two white marble stands. They sat on both sides of a huge, white, marble bookshelf that took up the majority of space on one of her walls. Like Allura, her home was modern, classy, and sophisticated. The walls were painted a soft peach. The sofa was ivory with soft peach pillows. The incense filled her living room and dining room with the aroma of sweet scents. I looked at the various pieces of art that adorned the walls as Billie Holiday played softly from her stereo. *She got taste,* I thought.

"Sooo...what do you think?" Allura waved her hand expansively around the apartment.

"You look great."

"Thank you, but I was talking about my place." Allura laughed as she gave me a big hug.

"Oh, oh. It looks great, too, but you didn't have to do all this for me," I said. "I feel kind of bad now 'cause you know how my place looked when you and your girls got there the other night."

"Your place looked fine."

"Yeah, but nothin' like this."

"Well, I wanted to do a little something special for you."

"I'm impressed."

"Thanks." Allura flashed a big smile, trying not to blush. At the same time, she seemed to relish the fact that she had done well.

"Did you have any trouble getting here, with the traffic and all?" Allura inquired, waving me into the dining room area, as she made her way to the kitchen.

"No, not at all. I had a very nice drive over, actually. Long, but nice." I casually stepped out of the living room and followed her to the kitchen, watching her ass, as she reached into one of the cabinets to grab a couple of wine glasses.

"Dali, did you take the parkway? Honey, that's the long way." She blushed slightly at catching me in the act of watching her.

"Yeah, I know, but it was cool. It's been a while since I've been in the country and all."

"Dali, this is not the country."

"Well, it's country-ish."

"Oh, stop." She laughed.

We met in the doorway of her kitchen as she made her way to the dining room with the glasses and a bottle of Merlot. There was a perfect moment of silence as we stood in front of each other, not too close but close enough. We stood there for a few seconds gazing into each other's eyes. My heart began to flutter. Allura must have felt the same 'cause she was the first to break. She brushed her hand down my chest, sighed heavily, flashed a beautiful smile, and walked into the dining room. I took a deep breath, smiled, and followed her.

We continued to talk about a variety of meaningless things while she put the finishing touches on her elaborate dinner. There was an appetizer of Cajun barbecued jumbo shrimp, a main course of grilled salmon, potatoes, and steamed vegetables. Then cheesecake, topped with cherries for dessert. I found myself more at ease and content with her than I'd been with women in the past. I noticed that I wasn't plotting, planning, or scheming on ways to get her into the bedroom. Tonight, my slogan was, "All good things to those who wait." I was cool wit' simply enjoyin' Allura's company.

I guess that's the interesting and sometimes disturbing point about men. On so many occasions, we spend so much time processing ways to sleep with a woman that we end up overlooking the opportunity to relax, and appreciate the "moment" for what it's worth. Men would probably get further with women in a shorter amount of time if we took this part of a relationship more seriously.

As we sat and ate dinner, we looked at each other with a silly, childlike glow that adults and especially men, like me rarely get. Another few brief seconds of silence passed. She seemed to want to ask me something.

"What?" I lifted my eyebrow, wiped my mouth, and took a sip of wine.

"Well...ah, forget it. It's nothing," Allura lowered her eyes and fiddled with her napkin.

"No, no, no, you can ask me whatever you want."

"I've been thinking about this since I've first heard you on stage...and I guess..."

"Spit it out."

"Alright, well, I was wondering...why do you play?" she asked, sitting back after finishing her meal.

"What do you mean?" I was both caught off guard and enticed by her curiosity.

"I mean why do you play...what motivates you? What's behind your...passion?"

"Good question. I don't think anyone's ever asked me that before."

"I don't know why. If you were a painter, everyone would want to interpret and know your inspiration for what you do. I mean music *is* art, and well, art is art."

"Good point. That's something I'd have to think about for a second." I paused. "Lookin' back," I continued, "I started playing when I was a kid. Actually, my father used to play and my parents got me into it to keep me outta trouble. So I practiced and played and practiced and played. As I got into my teens, people started sweatin' me 'bout how good I was. I didn't think about it much, really. I was kinda insecure 'bout my so-called talent back then."

"You insecure? I find that hard to believe."

"Nah, it's true. It wasn't until I started doin' gigs and makin' money with the whole thing that I realized that there was something in life that I was really good at. I ended up practicin' day in and day out, hour after hour after hour."

"What about school? Was college ever an option for you?"

"Uh, uh. I know it may sound ignorant, but me and the fellas ain't never been built for school. We hustlers—not in the literal sense but in the way that we never been big on living life like everybody else do."

"Well, what about money? You know…like how did you support yourself? Am I getting too personal? If so, let me know." Allura was, as we say sometimes, all in my mouth. She really wanted to know about me. *Damn, ain't this somethin'?* To have someone truly interested in me and my background was new.

"Nah, it's cool. Blue, Games, and Cyprus always brought in money in one way or another. During the real hard times, the fellas hooked me up wit' money and food. I was doin' the strugglin' musician thing and all. As time went on, I did one gig after another. The paychecks kept gettin' bigger and bigger and well, here I am."

"Now, Dali," Allura interrupted, "I know you're not going to tell me that you play the way you do just for the money."

"Oh, no, no…well, it *was* like that at first 'cause I'd been broke for so long. I was so pressed to make sure that I could keep a roof over my head that I didn't realize the degree of control I had."

"Control over what?" Allura stood, motioning for the two of us to move to the couch.

"Control over people. I know it sounds strange, but that's what changed me or moved me in a different direction. One night, I was playing and I had my eyes closed. I do that because it helps me concentrate."

I sat down next to Allura pantomiming that particular moment in my career wit' my eyes closed. My hands were in front of my mouth as if I were playing my horn. "Well, that night, I opened my eyes to see everybody in the club looking at me. They were feelin' every note, every tempo change—everything. I felt a sense of control, I guess. I don't know, it's hard to describe."

We were now sitting close enough together to easily smell and name what fragrance the other was wearing. We were extremely relaxed by this time, excess garments removed, feeling the effects of the wine, the music, and the mutually appreciated company. I leaned back on the couch. Allura was positioned to my side, sitting sideways facing me. I, with little success, tried to remain composed as I sat there taking in Allura's soft mahogany legs and inner thighs. Her small, black, spaghetti strap dress now appeared to purposely rise up and stop.

We talked more 'bout me and music and then moved on to Allura's dreams and aspirations. We were driving each other crazy, prolonging the obvious. We stopped talkin' for a brief moment, and looked into each other's eyes. I thought 'bout kissin' her, then followed that thought with the move to kiss her. Out of nowhere, her phone rang.

Allura stood up to answer. I got bold, grabbed her, and pulled her to me. As she straddled my lap, we kissed frantically, passionately, furiously. We were addressing the issue of sexual tension in the best way possible.

I moved from her lips to her shoulders, pulling her top down exposing her chest. My kisses literally left nothing untouched. I ran my fingers through her long black hair, grabbing a handful to pull her head back. She moaned loudly, showing everything but resistance. She quickly unbuttoned my shirt and put her hand into my pants. She pulled *me* before I could even consider protesting about slowing down to get into foreplay. *To hell wit' that*, we both thought. *We can do that later*. With a confident grip, she stroked, rubbed, and caressed my dick as she yanked my jeans. She admired the package I'd brought with me, which was now *standing* in front of her waitin' for her attention.

"Wait." I whispered. I grabbed her thighs right before she began to sit down, sliding my hands up to her hips, then her ass, looking to remove something that was never there.

"I'm not wearing any, baby," she hissed back as she stood over me.

"You're not..."

Before I could finish my sentence Allura, slid back on top of me—all of me—that was followed by a millisecond of silence and then...electricity—flowing through both of us—filled and generated by anxiety, tension, attraction, lust, desire.

We began slowly. I pulled her dress over her head, gasping at the view of a body I can only describe as one you might sell your soul for. I moved my hands over every inch of her body, from her feet to her ankles, her legs to her thighs, her ass to her back, her back to her stomach and breasts...her face to running my fingers through her hair. 'Cause of that, Allura got into a nasty rhythm. My eyes rolled into the back of my head as if my mind was being methodically possessed by the sex gods themselves. The whole while, my hands were working harder than they ever did with any music instrument.

Allura was right with me as she arched her back and moved like a dancer on top of me. She was sweatin' and her thick, brown legs began to tremble when she picked up her pace. She was calling for God, Jesus, and the Holy Ghost, Peter, Paul, and Mary and I was right there wit' her.

The slow start then sped up. Her sophisticated, classy home became a hotel room where we were showcasing our talents. We switched positions, and switched positions again, finding a comfort zone with me behind her. The subtle, sweet moans transitioned into screams of passion. I couldn't make up my mind. I focused on every inch of her body. Damn, she was hot. She called my name along with a few profanities as loud as she could.

We continued for a good while with enthusiasm and finally came together. That, however, was just the tip of the iceberg. We spent the rest of the evening and the following morning exploring and indulging. From the couch to the bedroom to the bathroom and even the kitchen, to say that we had chemistry would be an understatement, and that's without the consideration of our mutual orgasms.

BLUE

The incredible difference in how things were going in Dali's personal life compared to my own was almost indescribable. I spent about half of that morning in my darkroom focusing on work. It helped me relax for a while. It was a hidden perk. Granted, darkroom work was a tedious and methodical process. That's probably why I liked it so much. It allowed my mind to wander while I worked. It was like a mother sending her children out to play while she prepared dinner. It was all about details, focus, and concentration.

First, I would prepare the chemicals for the water bath, paying close attention to the temperature. Twenty degrees Celsius was the standard. Then, I had to check other stuff like my stop bath, fixer, and wetting agent. I moved from that point to loading my film, one roll at a time, into the developing tank. This was a bit of a pain because it included getting the film from the cartridge; you know, the ones that you drop off at your local drugstore for one-hour development, onto what is called a spiral. This was the true definition of darkroom because any light, natural or artificial, could ruin a good roll of film. From there, I transitioned to the developing and drying process, which involved a lot of repetition and what photographers call agitation. Oddly enough, I think photography is the only field that uses that word in a positive sense. Sometimes I would go through roll of film after roll in total silence—appreciating the art of photography.

That morning I was working on some shots of a female model for both of our portfolios. The ability to capture reality is breathtaking. Ordinarily, the focus on my bread and butter would be enough to carry me through the day. Distractions, however, prevented me from being productive past noon.

I spent a number of hours thinking of Avida. I knew I couldn't let her fabrication about her whereabouts that night just slip away. If I did, I ran the chance of setting a foundation for the same kind of shit in the future. Still, I wasn't exactly sure that the other night was a first. Hell, that betrayal could be one of many. I wasn't sure.

As I looked carefully at a particular nude shot of the model, I began to actually take notice of her as a woman more so than just…work. She was quite attractive, I thought, not a blemish on her brown skin. Her curves were hard and athletic. The black and white shot allowed the shadows and lighting to do her great justice, but I'd seen her in the flesh and she really didn't need it. The funny part about it all as I admired both the woman and the picture was that I never once regarded her in a "physical" sense. The desire strangely enough was never there.

My passion had always been directed toward Avida. For a minute, I thought about the pictures of the model and those I'd taken of Avida. I shuddered momentarily as I glanced over my shoulder toward my bed. I was looking behind my bed at something that really couldn't be seen. I'd hidden a collage of a good ten to fifteen photos of Avida behind my headboard. Sometimes when I had trouble sleeping, I'd place the collage on my nightstand and stare at it for hours. I'm not sure why. The funny thing about it is that the photos weren't professional, just various snapshots that I'd taken of her: a shot of her in an evening gown from a banquet we went to a few months ago; one of her in her T-shirt and underwear in her kitchen attempting to make me breakfast; a candid shot of her drunk ass coming out of the bathroom one Saturday night after throwing up for fifteen minutes. Another of her sleeping, half covered by my favorite mink blanket. I figured that keeping something like that where I did probably wasn't what one would consider normal. But hey, who's normal these days? I chose to ignore that fact and keep it as my own little secret. If the fellas found out, it would definitely be my ass.

I shook off that haunting image and began to wonder why Avida would lie. Why would she go somewhere else, to someone else? Why would anyone stray when they have everything in someone that they could possibly imagine? I continued working, developing negatives and figuring out what I could. I gathered that generally people in relationships, even good ones, stray for what could be considered damn good reasons. Anything from a lack of attention, intimacy, communication, sex; hell, even money problems can play a part in infidelity. Nonetheless, what if your special someone was given all he or she needed and wanted more piled on top of that. I suppose too much of a good thing could lead to a bad thing. It was all relative. Something that would just have to be worked out.

So as a result of me being in that darkroom for so long, my plan was just that—work it out. In many circles, I would probably be looked at as quite foolish, but I'd been through too much with my precious Avida to let her simply float away over bullshit.

I took a long shower before I gave her a call. I made an effort to feel good about the day—you know, thinking positive and all. I tried to concentrate on our first days together and how we could possibly get back to that point. I laughed to myself. Perhaps it was more so the realist in me being amused by the naivete of my idealistic side. Who knows? What I did know was that I wanted this relationship to go a certain way. Unfortunately, at this point I had no clue what Avida wanted.

I figured I wouldn't worry about the drama. Casually address it maybe, but I'd try my best to keep a level head. Avida had the strangest way of taking control over those situations when I acted with emotion rather than reason. So today would be a one of reason. I hoped.

"Hey," I said to the soft voice answering the other end of the phone.

"Hey, what took you so long?" she asked.

"So long for what?"

"To call me."

"I was getting some work in."

"You still could have called me this morning. I was thinking about you." Avida's tone came very close to whining. I hated whining.

"Oh, really. Why didn't you call me?"

"'Cause I figured you were working."

"Cute."

"Comes naturally."

"Yeah, if you say so. Hey, you hungry?"

"Sure, where you wanna go?"

"Let's go to that spot on the waterfront. It's quiet and perfect for what I need to talk to you about."

"What do you want to talk about?" I could hear the apprehension in her voice. Reason was feeling damn good right about now.

"Ah, it's nothin', really. Just some things I got on my mind."

"Well…that's cool, I guess."

At that point, I was feeling pretty confident with myself so I figured, what the hell, why not play around a bit.

"You dressed yet?"

"No, why?" She sounded relieved the conversation had changed its course.

"Just curious."

"Why?" Becoming more relaxed, Avida sounded rather spirited. She liked to play, too.

"What do you have on?" I ignored her curiosity.

"Just a T-shirt, why?"

"You go to sleep with that on?"

"What?" Avida's tone became mischievously stern.

"Don't worry about it. We'll talk when we go to eat."

"What? I hate it when you do that 'we'll talk later' shit."

I loved it. It usually made one-sided or shall I say her-sided discussions even.

"Get dressed. I'll be over in an hour."

"Fine, fine, I'll be ready."

I picked her up exactly an hour after we talked. We spent time talking about her friends and mine on the way to lunch. Though it was pleasant conversation, I was more concerned with more important things. She rambled on about one of her girlfriends in particular. I focused some of my attention on the nice homes we passed on the way to the restaurant. I chose to drive through the 'burbs that day rather than the direct route via downtown. I figured the serene surroundings would help the mood, so to speak. And it did, because she soon stopped talking about her friend and took notice of the nice homes.

"I like that one," Avida said, taking notice of one home.

"Maybe we can get one like that," I replied, looking at her.

"Maybe." She smiled. Her eyes spoke as clearly as her words. She was more powerful than she knew.

CYPRUS

I got a call to meet up with one of Chicago's people that afternoon to talk over some things. That morning, I spent some time thinking 'bout my present situation. I dumped twenty dollars' worth of marijuana into the empty shell of a Philly blunt cigar and smoked half of it before preparing to get cleaned up for that afternoon…all in an effort to relax. After undressin' and wrappin' a bath towel around me before heading to the bathroom, I looked at myself in my bedroom mirror. I thought about an Italian associate of mine from days long passed who had ties to the Chicago mob. I'll never forget his name. Mr. Manotti. Manotti owned a small corner store in our old neighborhood and took me in like a nephew when I was a kid. He let me work with him and his sons running numbers along with a few other things.

I headed to the bathroom, and looked in my mirror above the sink as I started to shave my head. The weed had now found a comfortable spot in my system and I continued to think about Manotti, specifically regarding my current situation and the phone call from Chicago Tone's errand boy.

"Sometimes you get called for, kid," Manotti told me one cold Monday morning.

"Well…what they want, Mr. Manotti…what's wrong?" I recalled asking. I remembered Manotti's oldest son, a good five years my senior, was standing next to him with an unexplained look of concern.

"Boys, look, it's really not important. In our line of work…" Manotti smiled at his son and me rather than explaining the situation. He gave both of us a hug and left. I never saw him again.

I smiled from my memory while shaving. It fucked wit' me a lil' bit remembering what happened to Mr. Manotti. It was referred to as being "called for."

Your presence was requested by the powers that be for regular business. In actuality, *you're* the business. You leave home. You don't return. I pondered over that idea, wondering to myself if the prior work I did for Chicago was a small part of a bigger game. I wondered was I being used.

"Fuck that shit," I whispered to myself. I returned to my bedroom after takin' a shower to light a cigarette. It really didn't matter what someone else was plottin'…they don't wanna fuck with me. Not only that, but I realized Chicago had no need to, and even if he did, he would have tried it by now. I also knew that no matter what the circumstances, I was more of an asset to Fat Chicago Tone than a liability.

I also couldn't forget about Games. Then I stopped wit' all the madness. Like I said before, I ain't that type a nigga, and whenever there was a chance I felt I was becoming a bit too emotionally involved wit' my thought processes, I stopped right where I was to get a grip on the situation. I committed myself to relaxing, watching my flat–screen, fifty-two-inch television that morning. I waited until it was time to leave.

Three hours later, I got the call. Nightfall was on its way and, as the sun set, the evening seemed to get a bit cooler. Clear skies made for an atmosphere unfitting of the night's upcoming event. I stood on the sidewalk next to my car and lit a cigarette. I took notice of a cool breeze blowing. It was a good day for work. The job this evening would be the elimination of Chicago's "Magic" problem.

The streets where me and my crew were camped out were unusually quiet, as if the street's natives were expecting the unexpected. I surveyed the surrounding blocks. They were uncommonly void of police, absent of kids playing, hustlers working, with the exception of a few. There was also a lack of liquor store traffic.

We were parked about a half-block away from the job. I'd been waiting for a while before Chicago's men, headed by Bobby Boca, finally arrived.

"What's happenin', Cyprus? You ready?" Boca asked.

"Not yet." I didn't bother to look at him.

"Cool. Chicago said it's your show. Let me know what you wanna do."

"You bring what I need?" I kept my eyes still focused in front of me.

"Yeah, got it up front. Bishop and Ray in the back."

"Give it to whoever sittin' behind the driver."

I briefly glanced at the dudes in Boca's Mercedes and began explaining to Chicago's guys how I wanted everything to go. "Aiight. Like I told the fellas here, this is going to be quick and simple, no cowboy, desperado shit. Your boy is parked on the right side of the block about six cars down. At least he was when we left him. He's in one of those old Ford station wagons."

"Who's wit' 'em?" Boca displayed a newness to the situation as he looked down the street. The whole time he was brushing his hands down his suit—making sure it was tight and clean.

"Don't matter." I finally looked at Boca, cutting my eyes at him in disgust.

"You sure?"

"Don't worry 'bout it. You ain't go'n be nowhere near it, anyway." Smoke from the last drag of my cigarette floated in Boca's face.

"What you talkin' 'bout?"

"You got another crew, don't you?" I pointed with my cigarette, then waved to an unidentified silver Cadillac parked across the street.

"Yeah."

"Well, have them drive by and check if it makes you more comfortable."

"Aiiight." The man sighed, as though realizing that this really *was* my show.

"Drive down and park one to two cars down from him if you can. Then wait for me. Make sure whoever's behind the driver has his window rolled down. The fellas here is my taxi home. They'll be at the end of the block lookin' for me. When I walk, they roll. You can stick around for the shot or bail. It's up to you. If it don't seem clear, don't worry 'bout it. *It will*."

"Oh, and Bobby…"

"Yeah, man."

"Anybody fucks this up…"

Bobby Boca looked at me as if he wanted to interrupt, but chose not to.

"They end up just like this muthafucka I'm taking care of tonight."

"Yeah, aiight, dog." Boca offered almost a challenging wink before he walked back to his car.

I watched Bobby Boca walk away, then looked back at Mo, Biz, and Sykes who remained in the car during the conversation. I walked over to the driver side window of the car where Sykes was behind the wheel.

"Remind me to handle that muthafucka when things quiet down." I looked at Sykes and then leaned against the car.

"You sure?" We watched the Mercedes and Cadillac pull off.

"Oh, most definitely," I said.

"What's wit' 'em, dog?" Biz questioned from the passenger seat.

"I don't know...somethin' 'bout his bitch ass I just don't like. Ya'll watch my ass on this one."

"You got it," said Sykes.

The streetlights replaced natural daylight as nightfall came into the picture, indicating that it was time for me to go to work. Bobby Boca's Mercedes slowly wove its way down the street a block parallel and to the left of where Magic was parked. The Mercedes then made two right turns, eventually positioning itself where it needed to be. I double-checked to make sure me and my crew were on the same page.

I walked a block over and made a left, so I was on the street parallel and to the right of where Magic was parked. I roamed down that block, observing any activity and saw that there wasn't much to look at, which worked for me. I made another left at the end of the corner, walked a few steps up that street and stopped. Out of the corner of my eye, I watched a police patrol car as it slowly passed behind me. I purposely fumbled about my pockets looking for cigarettes and a lighter. I began to walk up the steps of the row house. I tried to look as if I were heading home. The patrol car continued on.

I eyed the area again. I could see both Bobby Boca's Mercedes with good position on the right side of the block and just a piece of Magic's car on the left. At that point, I was where I needed to be.

I lit another cigarette, rubbed my head, and stretched a bit. I silently moved up the left side of the street. I crossed somewhere in the middle of the block and noticed my crew parked at the other end of the block, facing me.

Traffic on the block was practically non-existent. There weren't too many cars parked aside from the regulars. Most importantly, there were no children.

I walked to the Mercedes and leaned against the back end of the car, driver's side. The rear window was opened. I took a second to glance up the street at the old station wagon.

"He still there?" I asked.

"Yeah, behind the wheel smokin', I think," said Ahmad, sitting in the Mercedes behind the driver. "So what now?"

I tossed the rest of my cigarette on the street and simply winked at him as I calmly grabbed the shotgun from the car. "Watch and learn, dog."

I checked the streets again, then the gun to make sure it was loaded. I felt good, like everything was happening in slow motion.

I got into character as I slowly strolled up the block. This is what I do. I held the shotgun down behind my right leg as I walked. Sykes gradually maneuvered down the street toward me.

Just as I said to Chicago's men, this would be quick and easy, in and out. I approached the station wagon and immediately caught Magic's attention. Marijuana smoke floated out of the window as Magic tried to recognize this man in front of him. It was too dark and he was probably too high.

"Whassup, nigga, what you need?" Magic asked.

My tone was casual. "I'm good, playa. Got som'n for you, though."

The shots were quick and loud. I popped the first one in Magic's chest, then raised the gun a couple of inches to put another in his head. I turned around and Sykes was waiting with the door open. I got into the backseat and was gone as quickly and easily as I had come.

Almost seven hours later, in the early a.m., hardcore hip-hop bumped from the surround-sound speakers of the VIP section of Top Shelf, a popular bar and lounge for high rollers and hustlers on the outskirts of the city. I sat with Sykes, Biz, and Mo enjoying women, weed and liquor. I sat in silence and cautiously respected his marijuana-induced haze as I reflected on my work earlier that night. I hated taking the time to think about "putting in work," but I knew it was a necessary requirement of my job. The wild thing about it was that remorse and guilt were the furthest things from my mind. Killin' folk for me was just that…killin'. I didn't think much about it past the action itself 'cause I ain't never killed nobody that ain't had it comin'. My focus was on efficiency. And I was a bit irked with myself regarding that issue. Someone was sittin' in the passenger's seat of Magic's station wagon. For that reason alone I knew any kind of retaliation was highly unlikely. If I was wrong, it didn't matter. I'd take care of it if and when the time came. I wasn't perfect. Damn.

GAMES

When it came to Dali, Cyprus, Blue and me, coincidences and fate weren't a rarity. We've always been connected in one way or another. That's why it was really no surprise for me to be one of the investigating officers trying to figure out who was responsible for what was left of Magic. I pulled up about a few hours after everything was over.

"Jesus, somebody really fucked him up," I said, poking my head into the car., I took a sip from the strawberry milkshake that I'd picked up from a McDonald's a block away from the crime scene.

"You mind telling me what you find so amusing, Games," snapped a cold voice from over my shoulder.

"I take it you don't know who this kid is...was." I turned to face my lieutenant, Stan McAllister.

"Well, it seems a bit difficult since he's missing his fuckin' face. Hell, ya can't even tell if it's a man or woman. Whatever's left of the chest is layin' in the fuckin' backseat."

"Don't need a face, Lieu. For guys like this, name recognition is a wonderful thing—stupid, but a wonderful thing."

"What the fuck are you talking about?" Lieutenant McAllister curled his lip up in irritation.

"Look." I sighed. I put my milkshake on top of the station wagon, grabbed a pair of those plastic gloves, and reached into the car. I then grabbed the left arm of the corpse, pulled it out of the car, and laid it on the car door. I pointed to the huge, outdated and tacky four-finger ring, which read "Magic." Pushing up the sleeve on the arm I directed the lieutenant's attention to a tattoo on the arm, which read in Gothic lettering: "The Magic Man."

"He used to be a runner for Fat Chicago Tone. His name is Hakeem Pitts, a.k.a. Dariq Prince. Out here they call him Magic. I don't think David Copperfield could've got his ass outta this shit," I said, removing my milkshake from the top of the car.

"How'd he end up like this?" McAllister took his cap off and ran his fingers through his red hair, a bit baffled at my assessment.

"Looks like somebody shot his ass...twice." I sipped at the milkshake.

McAllister just stared at me. I think he was trippin' a bit at the fact that I could continue to peacefully enjoy McDonald's while standing in front of a body. What can I say? I love McDonald's strawberry milkshakes.

"Ol' Magic Man here was into a couple of things outside of what he was doing for Chicago. Hustlin', carjackin', armed robbery..."

"I don't need the kid's resume, Games."

"So what, it's over money?" McAllister and I were joined by a rookie detective by the name of Gonzalez from our precinct. Gonzalez was fighting to keep from throwing up at the sight of the body, so he chose to direct his attention toward me. By this time, in addition to Gonzalez, ten more cops had shown up. Some were forensics men looking for evidence. Others simply combed the area for witnesses and anything else that would be pertinent to the case.

"Naaah, I wouldn't say that." I leaned on Magic's car and searched my pockets for a cigarette.

"Why not?" McAllister questioned. "And get off of the fuckin' car."

"Well, 'cause Mr. Magic here got picked up in a stolen car some time ago. Third Precinct got him on theft and illegal gun possession in addition to the suitcase of heroin they found in the trunk."

"Shit." Gonzalez chuckled.

"Hey, go figure. The kid's no brain surgeon. Anyway, after a few hours of interrogation and the possibility of facing over twenty years upstate, he turned into a Wall Street businessman, cuttin' deals like the world was coming to an end. My guess is, as a result, some brothers got locked up who weren't exactly expecting to. Hakeem's out on the streets like nothin' ever happened. Yada, yada, yada, fucked wit' the wrong mufuckas, a big ass hole in his chest and no head, so on and so forth. Hey, shit happens."

McAllister stubbornly nodded in satisfaction with my summary of the events leading up to the murder. He directed the other officers to proceed with their search for any clues or witnesses.

I continued to look at the body. I again stuck my head in the station wagon.

"Fuck," I said, speaking to Gonzalez. "They won't find any witnesses for this shit."

"Why not?"

"Why not? Look at this mufucka, would you wanna end up like this?"

"Can't say that I would," Gonzalez replied cautiously, looking at the body again, this time with a handkerchief covering his nose and mouth.

"Whoever did this knew what they were doing. I bet it took no longer than a couple of seconds—quick and easy," I said, secretly impressed with the job, a job completed in a fashion that I'd seen before. I glanced around and noticed something. There was no one around. My guess was that there probably wasn't anyone around during the shooting, either, no one who would say anything, at least.

"Hey Games," Gonzalez asked as he shook his head and stepped away from Magic's car. "How you come across all that information 'bout Magic and Chicago and all?"

"I don't know—right place at the right time, keepin' my ears and eyes open, hell—luck." I took a glimpse up and down the block and again at the car. *Quick and easy*, I thought before throwing my milkshake away.

DALI

I searched my mind for the song that I wanted to run by the rest of the band.

"Forget it. It'll come to me later. I'll just write it down when it does. Anyway, we got an offer on the table, fellas."

I looked at the band as they tuned their instruments. My bass player, Barry or B-Heavy, fumbled around with two bass guitars trying to decide which one he was going to use. My piano player, Flip, finished up a cell phone call with what I understood to be a pretty demanding wife; and Bounce, my drummer, sifted through a bag of drumsticks looking for the pair he needed.

We sat in a plush, soundproof recording studio in the basement of a nightclub called Oasis in downtown Chicago. I had never actually hung out at the club, but I was good friends with the owner, who let us use the studio whenever we wanted to. It was impressive to say the least. The walls were all padded with the soft, white, pillowy-like material that looked like walls that would be in one of those mental wards to keep the nutcases from hurting themselves. One of the walls was covered with pictures of jazz greats like Miles Davis, John Coltrane, and Dizzy Gillespie. All kinds of musical instruments and audio and video recording equipment decorated another wall. We frequently used the equipment to record, then study the group's practice sessions.

I was looking for a buy in from the group regarding Serenity's business offer. Under her management, we would start playing at a different club. I had spent some time to think about the offer and even asked Allura's opinion. I usually discussed music matters with just the band members. I'd come to the conclusion that Serenity's proposal wasn't such a bad idea. I also thought about the fact that we never signed contracts of any sort, despite business rules. So I knew that we could play wherever and for whomever we wanted.

Waiting for a response, I watched the band as they looked at each other, shrugging shoulders, and toying with their instruments.

"Who's this again?" Bounce asked.

"Serenity," I returned.

"That rich white broad who comes to the spot sometimes?" Bounce questioned.

"Yeah." I nodded.

"The one wit' the ass like a sista?" B-Heavy chimed in with interest.

"Anyway, she wants us to hit at this spot in about a week or so. Seems we'll make twice, maybe three times, as much as we do hittin' at our regular, and that's after she gets her piece," I said.

"Why so short notice?" asked B-Heavy.

"That's my fault. I spent a week alone trying to decide if I wanted to do it. If you worried 'bout material, don't. We got more than enough."

"What makes you think we can trust ol' girl? This ain't the first time a mufucka done rolled up on us talkin' game and shit," Bounce asked.

"Hey, honey do got loot. I seen her up in the club, ours and others, hangin' wit' some pretty big players. Hell, she got like two, three rides," B-Heavy added.

"What we got to lose, anyway, Bounce?" Flip asked.

"I'm just sayin' I don't know. I hate wastin' my time on bullshit gigs. We did enough of that to get us to where we are now," Bounce replied.

"I understand where you comin' from, but I'm tellin' you Serenity's legit. She knows how to make money and she's been houndin' me for months to hook up wit' us. Look, we can try it once, if it don't work out we stay wit' what we got," I said, looking at the rest of the band members.

They eyed each other from different sides of the small practice room and nodded in agreement that they would give Serenity her opportunity to take us a step up from where we were at this juncture in our precious careers. Still, the vote wasn't exactly unanimous. Attention was now focused on Bounce who was playing with his sticks. He sat there twirling his drumsticks between his fingers, knowing everyone was staring at him.

"Aiiight, fuck it. One trial run wit' this bitch won't kill me. Besides, if things go right, I can get a DVD player installed in my truck," Bounce said.

"Cool, I'll let her know tonight. In the meantime…let's play. Oh, and Bounce—try to refrain from callin' her 'bitch.' It's bad for business."

"Whatever, man."

"Thank you, sir."

We practiced for about five hours that afternoon. Working primarily on two new songs they were now going to play at the new club. Rehearsal went well, and I felt good on the way home. Things were going my way. Not that they hadn't been before, but now I could actually *feel* them going my way. My naturally positive outlook on the world was strengthening itself with the idea of trying something different with Serenity and finding something once lost in spending time with Allura.

B L U E

Dali and I hadn't spoken to each other in a couple of days due to schedules, which wasn't particularly strange. Depending on the week, we would go several days without catching up. He called me when he got home with a request that surprised me. After a second or two, it actually sounded like a good idea.

"Hello," I answered.

"Hey, what's up, Blue?" Dali asked.

"Hey, whassup? Not too much on this end, just bullshittin' really. S'up wit' you?"

"Got in from rehearsal 'bout a minute ago."

"How'd it go?"

"Cool, same ol' same, really. Well, actually not really. We gonna try this new spot in a couple of weeks and see how that goes."

"Looks like Serenity finally got what she wanted, or either you just got sick of your current working conditions," I replied.

"Little bit of both I guess," he returned.

"Right. Brotha gotta do what he gotta do."

"True indeed. Hey, what you got up for tonight?"

"Shit, me and Avida up in here trying to figure out if we eatin' in or out."

"Well how 'bout this, dog? Allura's comin' through in about an hour. I got a couple pounds of shrimp, crabs, beer, and what not. Why don't you and Avida roll through? I got more than enough."

"That sounds like a plan. Hol' on for a second...Hey, you want to go to Dali's tonight?" I asked Avida.

"Why, what's going on over there?"

"Seafood and beer."

"Sounds a lot better than any of our other options," she replied.

"Yeah, we comin'. Give us 'bout an hour, hour and a half." I told Dali.

"That'll work. I need some time to straighten up, anyway."

"Aiight."

"Aiight, holla."

After hanging up the phone I glanced at Avida as she laid her head back at the other end of the couch.

"That mufucka's in a good mood," I mumbled, tracing my hand up from her ankle to the inside of her right thigh. She was quite cozy, stretched out on the couch. Her head lay on one end, her legs across my lap at the other. She was modeling a pair of my Calvin Klein boxer briefs.

"You think that color looks good?" Avida glanced at me from her end of the couch looking at the nail polish on her toes.

"I like it better than the red."

"Any color is better than red to you." She laughed.

"Red's alright, I guess..."

"You guess? You don't like red lingerie, red pantyhose, red high heels, red lipstick, red dresses, skirts, shorts, pants or tops. Shit, nigga, you don't even like red cars." She laughed even harder.

"True, true...I guess you gotta point there," I said as a shiver of disgust over the notion of that color shook me.

"I think they're dry now." She held her left foot out and wiggled her newly polished and now dried frosted Cappuccino-colored toenails. A satisfied smile tugged at the corners of her mouth. "Baby, I'm tellin' you, you missed your callin'."

"Here *you* go."

I had to admit however, that although I would never fancy myself the pedicurist, it was a job well done.

"Ready for the right foot?" I asked.

"Uh-huh."

She taught me how to do this some time ago. I remember the first time I tried it. I was apprehensive to say the least. Still, I never knew until that evening how much a woman gets out of having her nails done by her man. To a lot of women, it appears to be a rather stimulating experience. I know firsthand that it's led to damned memorable bedroom experiences. In my opinion, true and mutual affection comes in the form of manicures and pedicures, despite the closed views of any male ego. And so, I polished on.

I was proud of my selection of colors. I really had no clue what I was getting. I simply went with my gut. It seemed to pay off though. The Cappuccino didn't stand out on her toes and fingers the way I was afraid some of the other colors would. It actually blended perfectly with her blemish-free skin. Perfect. That's a word I rarely think about. Still, as I brushed the second coat, I stared intensely at her toes following her foot to the point where it became her ankle, then leg, on to her thighs, and finally a full view of—perfection. I continued to stare, knowing I would never tell her what I was thinking. Perfection would definitely go to her head.

"What's wrong?" She crooked her head to the side; a quizzical smile graced her face right before she wrapped her arms around me and looked me in my eyes.

"Nothin', just lookin'."

✠ ✠ ✠

Avida and I arrived at Dali's to find Allura already there. Neither Dali nor I formally introduced the two ladies to each other. My reason was simply because I knew Dali had the habit of appearing to have a steady woman one minute and not the next. I just wanted to wait him out and see what happened. This impromptu session was possibly his way of saying that Allura would be around for a while if things went his way. I didn't know what to expect, since Avida and Allura were night and day. Different backgrounds, tastes, personalities. It didn't seem to matter as they began to bond on their own, without any help from Dali or me. Differences in people, especially the extreme, can sometimes lay the best foundation for a friendship.

Dali had changed his apartment around a bit. The living and dining room looked different. He used to do this all black, kind of "keeper of the dead" décor with all black furniture, black drapes, solid black throw rugs, even these morbid pieces of art with themes of death and pain and all. He even had black vases, ashtrays, and candleholders. The fellas and I always felt that all of the ominous tones contrasted a bit with his creative artist's state of mind. I felt it was fair for me to assume that he'd been influenced by Allura. It worked. Though he did away with a lot of the black, he stayed true to the mood of his home, going with a lot of earth tones in his rugs, art work, and furniture. I took some time to observe his new set-up after calling for him.

"Where you at?!" I shouted, flipping through some of his CDs.

"Hey, hol' up. I'm tryin' to find a shirt...," he yelled back, his voice trailing off.

He came out of his bedroom to find my head in his refrigerator. He definitely had enough beer to please the masses, so I helped the ladies and myself to a few Coronas.

"Dog, please don't tell me you ain't started yet."

"I got tied up," he said, getting the kitchen ready to cook.

"Doin' what?" I asked.

He grinned and looked over to Allura who glanced embarrassingly at the both of us. She looked embarrassed.

"Jesus, never mind," I said, shaking my head and laughing to myself.

Dali and I stayed in the kitchen while Allura and Avida chatted in his living room. He told me about the new gig and what he and Allura had been doing over the past week or so, without disclosing too many details about the latter. He was excited, which wasn't much of a surprise since he was usually happier than the rest of us.

We eventually ate and continued to discuss issues ranging from music to Games and Cyprus. It was a tame version of how things were when just us guys were together, but it was fun nonetheless. It felt as though we could end up spending nights like these together quite often—kind of what I pictured married couples always doing. It was wishful thinking on my part. Avida and I rarely, if ever, hung out with other couples.

The four of us sat in Dali's living room drinking and talking, and everything seemed cool until Allura unintentionally threw a curve ball our way.

"So I hear you two have been together for a while. Do you have any plans on getting married?" She was sitting tucked up under Dali on his couch. Avida and I sat across from them. Avida sat in a big recliner and I was on the floor sitting between her legs.

Though I couldn't see Avida's face, I assumed her expression mirrored my own. Our response to her question was a blank stare accompanied by silence. The lack of an immediate verbal answer wasn't due to the fact that Allura asked something she shouldn't have. It was because Avida and I had never, and I mean never, discussed marriage or children for that matter.

"Damn, I'm sorry. That was out of line." Allura slightly twisted her mouth in embarrassment as a result of our reaction to her question.

"No, no, it's cool." I said before taking a much needed sip of my Jack and Coke.

"No girl, it's okay."

"I mean I guess we've been thinking about it but—" My feelings on the subject were cut short by Avida.

"Girl, we ain't at that point right now. We like a work in progress."

"What?" Both surprised and a bit irritated, I turned my head around to look at Avida.

"Blue, don't even think about making a discussion about this right now," she whispered bluntly in my ear.

My reply was a regulated smile, shoulder shrug, and nod. She hurt my feelings at that point, but under the circumstances, there was nothing I could do about it. Again, I'd been made a fool of thinking that my life and my woman were treating me as well as I had them. It was all right. Dali quickly changed the subject and I placed that moment in the back of my mind. Something just wasn't right when it should've been. There was something with Avida that I was either missing or simply didn't understand. In time, I would.

DALI

The following day I headed to Serenity's penthouse apartment to work out the details of our business arrangement. I wondered if the visit to Serenity's place, via her request, was a smart move for me. There was definitely a funky lil' hidden sexual tension between us, whether I wanted to address it or not. It seemed that I was puttin' myself in a rather compromisin' position, and I was never any good at resisting temptations of the flesh.

Serenity answered the door in a T-shirt and a pair of shorts so small that you probably wouldn't see them if she were to take them off right in front of you. It would be an understatement to say that standing in the doorway was a temptation of the flesh. She had a deceptive sensuality about her, similar to a drug that takes a while to set in. That straight hair of hers was the only "white" thing about her. She was as "full-bodied" and shapely as any ample black woman you could run into. Perhaps, this visit wasn't one of my brightest moves. I don't care what anybody said, she had the ability to seduce any man. It wasn't so much her looks, as it was her sophistication. She seemed to make everyone she interacted with feel important. I really needed to just leave her alone, but for some reason I couldn't.

"You'll have to excuse my appearance. I didn't think you were coming," she explained.

"Understandable, I guess, since I'm late." I tried not to pay much attention to her appearance by keeping my eyes focused on her face.

"No problem."

"Busy?" I asked.

"Nope, just watching TV. Taking some time to relax. It's been a busy week."

"I can understand that." I scanned her apartment. "Nice place, I've never seen it before."

"You'll see a lot more of it in the near future," asserted Serenity as she casually strolled to her kitchen.

"Meaning?"

"Meaning that if things go okay with you, me and your band, we'll have a great deal to discuss. I handle a lot of my business here in my apartment."

I nodded in affirmation.

"You seem tense. Can I get you something? I got juice, water, of course, uh...beer..."

"What kind?" I said as I plopped on her couch.

"Heineken."

"Heineken works." I became aware of a mysterious tension that never seemed to be apparent. It was like Serenity's presence alone was making my heart beat faster. I wasn't nervous but uncomfortably tense. In all honesty, I wanted to skip the pleasantries and get between her legs.

She brought two Heinekens and sat down Indian style on her couch beside me.

"So let me understand this, so I'm straight on everything. You guys are going to play once to see how things go. If they go well, you'll follow my lead for future gigs"

"If not...," I interrupted.

"I don't think in 'if nots,' hon'. I know you and the band will love the gig."

"And how can you be so confident?"

"Because I always get what I want," she exclaimed before sipping her Heineken.

"Really?"

"Really." At that moment, she gave a new meaning to the word nonchalant when she casually adjusted her right foot to let her arm rest on her knee and placed the other foot on the floor.

Ok, now that was uncalled for. I was screaming to myself as I looked at her. I tried my best to hold on. It was only a few seconds, but to me it seemed so much longer as I admired the tattoo of the number "69" on the inside of her right thigh. Now that just ain't fair.

She halted what could have been an extremely interesting situation by explaining motivations. It went back to her childhood, her father, so on and so forth. I'm not quite sure why she interrupted the "moment," but I was glad that she did. My feelings for Allura made for a mighty shield. Still, who knows long it would have held up.

Perhaps the whole thing was a tease on her part, which wouldn't have been anything new to me. I'd run into my fair share of flirtatious women and was always willing to participate in whatever festivities were necessary to get what I wanted. The shoe was startin' to slide to the other foot in regards to Serenity. Men who are used to playing the cat sometimes make easy prey as the mouse.

We went over details about the band's upcoming performance. I left about an hour after I'd arrived. Content that the visit remained professional, I headed straight for Allura's place when I was done and pushed the other aspects of this little meeting with Serenity to the farthest corners of my mind.

CYPRUS & THE HISTORY
OF FAT CHICAGO TONE

F at Chicago Tone was born Anthony Richard Brown in a hospital not too far from his neighborhood, the Cabrini Green projects, in Chicago. By his fifteenth birthday, he had become one of the smartest and most prosperous criminals in the area, which enabled him after some time to add the "Chicago" to his childhood nickname of Fat Tone.

He was a member of one of the city's gangs at twelve and quickly moved up the ranks with his ability to *use* his mind more than abuse it as he saw so many of his associates doing at the time. He also tended to stray away from the demented antics of friends and other gang members who, for some reason, seemed to be happier with jail and early graves than money.

At the age of eighteen, his talents for staying in the good graces of the almighty dollar and out of the grasp of law enforcement was recognized by one of the city's top Italian crime bosses, Alfonze Cicero. Generally, the mob didn't involve themselves with black folk too much when it came to business. But in the city of Chicago in the sixties money was tight for everyone, including organized crime. Cicero took the young Fat Chicago Tone, along with a number of his friends, under his wing.

Chicago continued to work smart rather than hard and eventually surpassed just running the gangs to being formidable competition for the Italians. Twenty-some odd years later, Fat Chicago Tone is still afraid of no one...and still respectful and cautious of Alfonze Cicero.

✠✠✠

"The old factory on the East side, five p.m., Saturday afternoon," said Chicago's associate and personal bodyguard, Big Loon, or Looney Tunes as he was sometimes called.

Chicago nodded, blowing smoke from a cigar.

"We'll be there," Loon replied to whoever was at the other end of the line in response to Chicago's nod.

Chicago rose from his custom-made office recliner to glance out of the fif-teen-story window of his downtown office. He remained quiet as his inner circle of colleagues stared at him, waiting for him to speak.

"Hey...uh...Chicago, you alright, man. Whassup?" asked Raymond, Chicago's childhood friend, who happened to be one of the most respected drug dealers in the state of Illinois.

"Just thinkin', cuz," Chicago replied.

"'Bout what, Tone? I mean you got us kinda spooked the way you been actin' lately wit' this Cicero thing and all."

Chicago turned around slowly as he continued to smoke his cigar. He casually eyed his large office, taking time to observe the expressions of the six or seven men in the room. He smiled.

"You gentlemen worried about somethin'?" he asked.

"Naa, we tryin' to figure out what's goin' on wit' you," chimed in Bobby Romano, one of Chicago's attorneys.

"Lemme ask you fellas a question. Any of you know Alfonze Cicero?" Chicago inquired. No one answered, but a few shrugged and nodded. Chicago took a couple of seconds to bow his head and massage the bridge of his nose.

"Man, no disrespect, Chicago, but ol' man Cicero is just that—old. The Italians don't run shit out here like they used to anymore."

"Let me explain somethin' to you," Chicago said as he sat back down into his chair. "Muthafuckas like Cicero was over here getting paid more than you do now when your fuckin' moms was a kid. They started this shit. I hear you. Nowadays damn near this whole state is ours. Remember this, though. It did-n't get that way by underestimatin' mufuckas, old folk included. We clear."

"Yeah Chicago, man, ain't no thing. I'm just sayin'..."

Fat Chicago Tone was through with talking and thinking about the entire situation. He made that clear by suspending his man's course of action with an impassioned glare.

He spent the next ten to fifteen minutes explaining what he needed from everyone for the meeting. He expected no foul play from Cicero, but wanted to assure himself that every angle was considered. Like he said earlier, he didn't get to his present position from underestimating his adversaries or old friends for that matter.

"Hey, where's Cyprus?" Chicago asked.

"Not sure right now, he might be..."

"Find him," Chicago interrupted. "I want him there, too."

"No problem."

CYPRUS

That evening I was hangin' out with Charlotte and Milan, the two women that I'd met some time ago in Fat Chicago's club. I took 'em to lunch at an upscale Cajun restaurant that I could now see as I looked out at the city from the balcony of Milan's high-rise luxury apartment.

I didn't know much about 'em aside from what I gathered from our previous encounter at the club, occasional phone conversations, and short visits over the past few weeks. Something 'bout these two was different. It was their chemistry. I could tell they were good friends. They seemed more than friends when they started spoon-feedin' ice cream to each other at lunch.

I sipped my Guinness Stout and watched and listened to them on Milan's balcony. That lunch shit had me trippin' 'cause I had no idea where things were goin' from this point. After puttin' out my cigar, I left the balcony and walked into Milan's living room. It was the kind with imported marble floors, Persian mink area rugs, Italian sculptures, and those fireplaces that you can turn on by clicking a button on the wall. I'd never seen anything like it in my life. This was a caliber of woman that I was not used to dealing with, but I didn't mind the challenge. I was talking to Milan when the phone rang.

"It's for you." Charlotte winked at me as she passed me the phone.

"Whassup?" I asked. "Where?...Cool, no problem, I'll be there. That's not a problem, either. How many?...They'll be there too...Aiight, later."

I hung up the phone and was handed another beer.

"So who was that?" Charlotte and Milan jointly asked.

I looked at the two of them and paused for a second.

"Friend of mine, why?"

"Just curious." Milan began to unbutton her shirt.

"A random friend of yours with Milan's home number?" Charlotte approached me, staring in my eyes as she stood in front of me. "And we still don't know what you do for a living." She purred as she caressed my head.

"Mmm, what do I do for a living?" I returned Charlotte's stare, then glanced over at Milan. "Well..." I slowly but strongly grabbed Charlotte by her hips and pulled her close to me. "I guess I do a little of this...some of that," I said, looking at her.

"You're being vague," Charlotte said as she looked in his eyes.

"Very," Milan added.

"I like that."

"So do I."

"You two are funny. You probably already know what I do. Shit, ain't too many folks who don't," I said before kissing Charlotte on her neck.

"True, we've heard some things."

"A lot of things."

We fucked around each other wit' that kinda shit for a good minute. They wanted it that way. I was in way over my head so I chilled and followed their lead. They continued wit' their strangely sensual way of speaking and inter-acting with each other. I loved that shit. For a second, I wondered if they were even human, not that it made a difference to me either way.

By late evening, it was obvious that I wasn't going home anytime soon. We went out for a light dinner and more drinks and were back at the condo around eleven. I figured, or rather hoped, things would get physical, but I had no idea how I would be able to hook 'em if the chance presented itself. They had worked themselves into a quiet frenzy. I needed an equalizer. Now was a good time to introduce the ladies to the high quality weed they'd asked me for previously. I never figured 'em to be the type to smoke, but they asked and I had no problem providing. I was wrong. They can smoke wit' the best of 'em. Fuck that, I brought that ugly shit. It wouldn't take long. All I would have to do is wait.

Candles dimly lit the living room and Milan put in a Miles Davis CD. I wasn't quite feelin' the jazz shit and all, until they got started.

"I'm hungry," Milan whispered.

"I'm hot," Charlotte added.

Here they go, I told myself.

Charlotte stood up, got undressed, and headed for the kitchen. She returned a minute later with a plate. It was filled with fruit: strawberries, pineapples, grapes, kiwi and mangoes.

She placed the plate on the floor next to Milan and politely requested that I sit on the couch in front of them. She then stood in front of Milan who was now also naked and sitting on the floor against the couch with the plate now situated between her legs.

Milan sat in front of Charlotte, wearing only a beautiful smile and a comfortably positioned six-foot, chocolate frame constrained only by a plate of fresh fruit. She casually caressed herself as Charlotte gradually ate some of the fruit and all of what was between Milan's legs. I sat watching, almost paralyzed, not quite sure if it was due to the weed or this crazy shit I was seeing.

"I'm still hot," Charlotte said, looking down at Milan who was at this point curled over on the floor.

"I'm still hungry," Milan gasped.

"Why don't you finish the fruit?" said Charlotte.

"Why don't you finish cooling off?"

Charlotte slid her hand from between her legs up to her stomach, then around to her back to her ass.

"Ah, ah, ah you know better," Milan replied. "Lay yo' ass down."

As I continued to watch, I was gettin' a lil' warmed up myself. I mean damn, dog. I ain't never seen anything like this. At least not in person. For the next thirty minutes or so, even though its hard to think about the time at moments like these, I just watched as these two women, now both completely ass naked, proceeded to eat every single piece of fruit from that plate from each other's thighs, stomachs, breasts, and pretty much everything else. They were just getting started.

Charlotte lay on her back while Milan kissed her feet, ankles, knees, thighs, and finally ended up with her tongue between her legs.

Giggling, as a result of an incredible orgasm, Charlotte asked, "Think we need a little something more?" as she looked at me.

"I don't know. Think he's ready?" Milan replied.

"The bulge in his pants implies he is."

Hell, I wasn't. Still though, nothing beats a failure but a try.

All sweaty and covered in fruit juice, they figured a quick shower was in order. And lucky me,...was asked to join. From the shower, we worked our way to a king-size bed, giving us the space we needed to pick up where they left off. I found myself in position after position—woman after woman—back and forth—underneath and on top for hours.

BLUE

While Cyprus was basking in the aftermath of his ménage à trois, I spent the following morning cleaning my apartment. My two-bedroom row house was my palace, my source of strength and solitude, and my kingdom. When the going got rough, I stayed at home. I took much pride in keeping it meticulously clean. Games and Cyprus used to joke about how my place and Dali's were definitely those of artists. My walls were filled with black and white stills of models, locations, and various people and places. It wasn't unusual for visitors to spend a few minutes simply looking around. I kept my décor pretty simple with a small couch and loveseat, accompanied by a few throw pillows here and there. I didn't have any kind of color scheme. Like Dali, I stuck with the earth tones. My favorite piece in my living room was a black and silver marble chess table and chair set with matching pieces that was given to me as a birthday present from a European client of mine last year. It truly gave my home an elitist look.

Games really liked it because he and I frequently played chess. He dropped through later that morning to join me for a game.

"You heard about that shootin' the other night?" Games asked, looking at me over the chess table.

"Uh, uh, what happened?"

"Nigga named Magic got fucked up." He kind of glanced off to his left, thinking about it while toying with one of my pawns that he captured.

"For real?"

"Yep. Hell, some mufucka hit 'em up twice wit' a sawed-off—one in the chest, one in the head. I'm sayin', man, half a dude was in the driver's seat, the other half was in the back," he said as he cautiously moved one of his pawns.

"That's fucked up...but, not as fucked up as this—check, cuz."

"Shit," said Games, looking at the board.

"Wanna go another round?"

"Fuck that." He sighed. "I don't know why I even fuck wit' you on this shit anymore."

"Me neither, really." I chuckled.

"Yeah, yeah, yeah...hey, you goin' to hear Dali this weekend?"

"Yeah, I'll be there. Probably take Avida."

"For real, how she, anyway?"

"Aiight, I guess. Unpredictable as usual."

"What you mean?"

"I don't know. It's like sometimes she just be off on her own shit, you know. It's impossible to tell what she's thinkin' or how she's feelin'."

"I hear that," Games said, stretching and taking a seat on the couch. "I think women are naturally more complicated than dudes are. But as they mature and start fuckin' around wit' niggas, they just get that much more difficult to comprehend. Hell, for the most part I like to think of women as always havin' like this emotional string that connects they heart to they pussy, you know. A nigga can't fuck wit' one without eventually fuckin' wit' the other."

"Well, Avida must of cut her shit...disconnected that mufucka. Either that or she got some kind of on/off switch I don't know about," I remarked.

"I feel you. Can't win for losin'."

"No doubt. Wanna drink?" I asked on my way to the kitchen to get myself one.

"Yeah. So what you think 'bout D's girl, Allura?" Games asked.

"Well, she's looks damn good, for one." I handed Games a beer.

"Besides that."

"I mean, hey, she's cool. Different ya know. She seems to be good for his ass. Every since he hooked up wit' her, the mufucka's been on cloud nine. Me and Avida was over there a little while ago. It was cool. We kicked it, talked a little shit, drank and all. You'd think they been together for years."

"Shit, if this new gig works right for him, I'll start thinkin' she brings that nigga good luck, too," Games said, taking out a pack of cigarettes.

"Well, either her or Serenity."

"Who, the white girl?" Games had an amused smirk on his face.

"Yeah, she set the whole thing up. If it hits and he likes it, she'll be around for a while."

"Damn, I don't even know if he should fuck wit' her ass. White women that fuckin' tight can't be healthy for a nigga," Games said, shaking his head.

"She be in his shit, too," I added.

"No bullshit?"

"No bullshit."

"That's got the makin's of a nasty situation."

"Nasty indeed," I said, sipping my beer. "But you know, Dali...that fool thrives on that type of shit."

Games hung out over my place for about another half-hour before his evening shift. He stopped by a lot before his shifts to talk or gossip. He got me into chess a little over five years ago. He's slacked off a great deal, and to his chagrin, I've sharpened my skills to the point where he hasn't beaten me in over a year. Hurts his ego more than anything. Such is life. He probably doesn't think about it at all after he leaves.

He was probably thinking about Dali's new gig. Actually, Cyprus and myself were without question thinking about it also. It was hard not to from all of the hype Dali placed around it. He had convinced himself that this was going to be both a good and big thing. I suppose that's a rather smart thing to do in situations like these. It was pretty much mandatory that we all showed up, preferably with someone. In reality, there was no need for him to worry about us. Games, Cyprus, and myself could all pretty much count on one hand the number of Dali's performances we'd missed.

DALI

I brought what was probably five days' worth of clothes over to Allura's to stay over, one might think. That wasn't the case, however. I guess I—and this wasn't exactly unusual for me—was having some trouble figuring out what I was going to wear for tonight's performance. So I went with the old adage, when in doubt, ask a woman.

I stood in front of her in a pair of black slacks, black Kenneth Cole dress boots, and a white tank top undershirt. That's where I got stuck. Allura and I went back and forth over dress shirts, ties, and sports jackets. Whatever I liked, she didn't and vice-versa. After almost an hour, we both looked at her clothes-covered bed, mentally exhausted by the whole ordeal.

Allura thought for a second and walked over to her closet. She looked, poked through, pulled out, and put back a variety of different dresses, skirts, and outfits until she found exactly what she was looking for. Something to complement and hopefully give assistance to what I would wear.

She chose to keep it simple. She held up an exquisite Liz Claiborne sleeveless, silver-to-black fade, pure silk dress with a draped neckline and V-neck back. It fell inches above her knees. As she tried it on for me, I considered cancelling the whole gig and spending the evening alone with her.

"Well?" she asked.

"Huh?" I mumbled, slowly coming back to my senses. "Oh, uh...that's gotta be the tightest thing I've ever seen on a woman in my life, and I don't mean the tight part literally."

"So you like it?"

"More than you could ever imagine," I said, continuing to stare.

"Wait 'til you see the heels I got to go with it," she said, removing the dress and placing it on the bed.

"Where'd you find it?"

"The dress? Actually, I've had it for a while. I just never had a reason to wear it."

"I just thought of a reason and it ain't got nothin' to do with my show tonight."

"Stay focused, sweetheart. Wait a minute. I just thought of what you can wear," she said, picking through his clothes. "Look, this and this right here would go nice with what I'm going to have on tonight."

I came back to reality and what I was actually supposed to be doin' when I looked at what she was speaking of. She was right. With my black slacks, I, too, would keep it simple wearing a matching black vest and sports coat with a vanilla button-down dress shirt. An hour later, we were ready.

BLUE

Tonight, we were all headed to Serenity's hand-picked club, State of the Arts, a relatively new venue where upwardly mobile young black folk took time off from their busy corporate schedules to relax, drink, and socialize with others like themselves. Though it wasn't our type of crowd, it did have the makings of a place we could get used to. Classy was the operative word as this place had Serenity written all over it.

It was what she called an artist's lounge. There were paintings from local artists on the walls, but it was wild because certain parts of the walls were extended as hands to hold the paintings. It had a bit of a Victorian feel to it, but everyone seemed to love it. There were also excerpts from local writers and poets enclosed in glass settings placed methodically along the walls, and pictures of dancers and musicians on random pedestals on both sides of the club's four bars. All of the staff wore Armani suits, many sported diamond earrings, watches and rings as if they were patrons rather than employees. They kept the lighting dark with only candles to create the mood for the evening's performance.

We all showed with company, per Dali's request. He figured the ladies would enjoy the club since Serenity raved so much about how exclusive it was. I had to admit it was definitely a five-star spot.

I arrived to find Dali already there with the band orchestrating how he wanted everything set up on stage. Avida, standing by my side, was already impressed with the club. She had a thing with environments that fed into the fact that the four of us were all well off.

Anyway, I talked with Dali for a quick minute before Avida and I made our way to a large booth he had reserved for all of us. We joined Allura who was ordering herself a drink.

She and Avida talked about whatever women talk about as I sipped on my double Remy Martin. The two of them were by far the most attractive women there that night. Cyprus arrived with his *two* new lady friends roughly ten minutes later to add to the mix. I'd always heard of situations where someone would walk into a room and everyone there appeared to stop whatever they were saying or doing just to look. I'd never seen it until Cyprus walked in with two women on his arms. The brother definitely earned kudos with his entrance.

There he stood with Charlotte and Milan, both women about six feet tall. They looked like black Barbie dolls. Long, black hair, chocolate skin, toned, and perfectly shaped bodies. They were eye candy and Cyprus knew it. He also knew that his newfound luck with upper-class women was due in part to his association with Fat Chicago Tone. It didn't bother the brother one bit. He joined the three of us after chatting a bit with Dali.

"Whassup, dog? How you doing Avida, Allura?"

"Hey, Cyprus," Avida and Allura said in unison.

Cyprus introduced his lady friends to all of us. The four women managed small talk although there was an undercurrent of "who's the sexiest" tension flowing amongst them. Cyprus and I ordered another round for the table and as the waitress left we heard our missing link.

"Damn, it's enough of ya'll up in here, ain't it?" Games' voice thundered from in front of the large table. Dali was with him now and he was with Allura's girlfriend from the other night when we were drinking at Dali's.

The eight of us sat at the biggest booth in the club, probably giving some the impression we owned the place. Everyone there seemed curious about who we all were. Dali loved it. If his performance went well, and I was confident it would, this place could definitely be a new home for him and the band. The band members were also enjoying all of the attention since their pictures were posted throughout the club.

Dali hung out with us for a couple of minutes until it was time for him to take center stage. He kissed Allura and looked at the rest of us with a confidence in himself that many could only dream of having. There was no doubt in our minds that they would give one of the best shows that club had ever seen.

He and the band took their time making their way on stage. Dali appeared overwhelmed by all of the familiar faces from his past performances who had come to show their support.

"I told you there'd be a big turnout," whispered a voice from over his shoulder.

"I was wondering where you were. Haven't seen you since I got here," he said, turning his head slightly over his shoulder with his response.

Serenity gave every sister there, whether they wanted to admit it or not, some damn stiff competition. Tonight, as the club's mistress of ceremonies, she pulled out all the stops. I suppose she felt she had just as much riding on this as Dali did.

"I look okay?" she asked as he quickly turned toward her in an effort to get it over with.

"You look" —he cut what was about to be a quite descriptive reply into—"fine."

"Thanks. Ready to shake 'em up again?" Serenity flashed a smile.

He released a cocky smile in response as he stepped onstage.

It had always been interesting to me that Cyprus, Games, and myself were never big jazz fans. Cyprus actually hated jazz. Still, when we were all kids, Dali practiced. We continued to listen in appreciation for this talent he had. We were impressed by his gift. To this day not much has changed. We're still impressed.

Dali's jazz didn't sound like the contemporary jazz you hear so many artist playing these days, with all of the songs sounding the same to the outside listener. He made music he knew everyone could enjoy and understand because it was real. Not to take anything away from any other artist, but Dali wrote what he knew and played what he knew. He strayed away from the more conventional sound when he began to come into his own. Dali knew pain, loss, confusion, anger, frustration, and unlike many, unrestrained fun. Like the rest of us, he knew the ghetto with all of its ups and downs. He could feel the streets and, in my opinion, he played them better than anyone. It was all in his style of performance and in the fashion his band played. They were all thugs with talent and you could see it when they played.

Everyone reacted to it. Dali literally played to the crowd. He could blow his horn so loud and so hard that he would step away from the microphone and walk into the crowd. Bounce, the drummer, would get so involved on some of the sets that he would play standing up. The same with B-Heavy and Flip as they would play off of each other and virtually invite anyone to come up onstage and sit with them. Dali and his band played so well and so hard that the rumor is that only one musician had sat in on a set with him and that was Branford Marsalis.

Tonight he would introduce the hard-knock life we knew to the State of the Art. Everyone was there to hear the city's jazz phenomenon. Dali was once described by a writer of *The Chicago Tribune* as being the urban streets' second coming of Miles Davis. His performances represented his lifestyle and attitude. He was what jazz musicians and fans considered a monster, or a truly superior player. That respect was apparent when he took center stage that evening. With a glass of cognac in one hand and his horn in the other, he walked through the crowd speaking to everyone. Then he stepped onto the small, intimate stage that practically reached out into the first row of seats. Dali placed his drink on the stool next to him, looked back at his band, nodded to each of them, and twirled his horn in his hand before addressing the crowd. He stepped to the microphone and prepared to speak. Instead he put his horn to his mouth and played.

They never knew what hit them. Dali's A Section, or the first part of his set, usually was with the rest of the band. This evening he soloed for the first six to eight bars, with precise riffs and runs that couldn't be taught in a class-room. Though it may have sounded like improv to many, it wasn't. Bounce, B-Heavy, and Flip jumped right in and never left the pocket. Their play halted various conversations in mid sentence as even the bartenders took a break to listen. The sound was smooth and elusive, delicate enough to relax yet inviting enough to hold everyone's attention. That was Dali's unique sound, ghetto jazz...filled with B-Heavy's slow, country gal thick, collard green, looping bass lines; Flip's committed, simple yet catchy keystrokes; and Bounce's dirty, gritty, hip-hop bounce on drums. I glanced over the room noticing couples holding hands, bopping, whispering in ears and others simply listening intently.

I would have to say it took Dali and the band around five minutes to entrance the State of the Arts' crowd. They made it seem easy when by their last set they had everyone dancing to a groove damned reminiscent of Parliament Funkadelic's prime. Dali lived up to the comparison of Miles Davis—one mostly based on Dali's talent for innovation and improvisation. In jazz, improvisation sets the professionals apart. Dali has always been a fan and student of Miles Davis, a lot due in part to improvisation. As a professional, many believe Dali embodied how Miles worked improvisation...in a modern sense. It was said that Miles would go into the studio with sketches or outlines of what he wanted to do. Dali was the same way. All of the practice that he went through with his band was more so for them. It was on nights like this where he would give them a lead and he himself would make the rest up as he went. I was proud of him. We all were.

The smoky throwback feel of the city's old jazz clubs was impressive and the culturally diverse crowd of designer and tailor-made suits, eight hundred-dollar dresses and six-figure salaries just added a new millennium style that was unparalleled regarding non-nightclub venues. I couldn't help but feel good for Dali. At the same time, I thought about myself. Though it was selfish for me to do so, I couldn't seem to help it. It seemed as if I should be a content and relaxed person, this evening, but I wasn't. Something was wrong with me and I just couldn't shake, it no matter what the distraction. I glanced over at Games, Cyprus, and his lady friends, then Avida. They all appeared to be enjoying the evening as I should've been, but that wasn't the case. God, if Dali wasn't playing I probably would've left by now and I couldn't understand why. I ordered another drink, managed a smile for Avida, and made myself listen to Dali.

Dali and the band finished the night with an irreproachable remake of James Brown's "Big Payback," vocals and all. The finale earned the band an unexpected standing ovation, which caught me off guard since I'm used to those being reserved for players with CDs out. Of course, I would poke fun at Dali about that later.

The band hung out with Games, Cyprus, me and the ladies down by the stage, while Dali took a couple of minutes to work out finances with Serenity. We decided that when Dali finished, all of us would grab a bite to eat afterward for celebration's sake—minus the band since they had made their own individual plans.

Dali's visit with Serenity would prove to be an interesting one. I would find out from him later that his business arrangement with her would be trickier than he expected. It ended up being a meeting that he couldn't wait to tell me about.

DALI

I stood in the club's management office talkin' wit' the club owner, a wealthy Nigerian they called Tookoo. Serenity walked in shortly after.

"Baby you were perfect," she said, placing a small attache case on the desk in front of me. She sat down at Tookoo's desk and gave him a nod. Tookoo took the hint, gave me a hug and handshake, and headed out.

"You think?" I picked up the case with a grin.

"I know," she said, looking at me intensely. "You know too, and since you know, let's talk."

"Alright." I sat on the table across from her. "Let's talk."

"Okay. This spot every Saturday night at a grand more than what I'll give you tonight," Serenity explained, her sex appeal placed on the back burner for the moment. She was all business as she sat behind Tookoo's desk, arms folded, legs crossed. The look on her face resembled a prosecuting attorney with the death penalty on the brain.

"Keep talkin.'"

"Good news travels fast, dear, and in this business, good news is profit. Do you like profit, Dali?"

"How much profit?"

"Mmmm, not so fast, Lorenzo."

"I hear you. You don't play around much, do you?" I stood up.

"Of course I do, just not when it comes to money."

"No doubt. I tell you what. You got me and the band every Saturday, this spot here and others if they're as...appreciative as this crowd."

"Deal?" she asked.

"Not yet," I said, looking again at the attache case.

Without pause, she got up and handed the case to me.

"What's your cut?"

"I already have my cut," Serenity asserted as she stood up and walked over to me. "That's yours. You all earned it, don't you think?"

"Depends..." I glanced into the case.

"On what?" Serenity whispered, standing inches in front of me, her professional body language turned personal as she seductively smiled at me and playfully brushed my face with her hand before directing my attention to the case.

I opened the case. "On...Jesus...how much is this?"

"About two grand over what we agreed on," she said confidently. "It won't be in cash next time. I wanted to show you how things can be if we work together. Well...deal?"

I hesitated for a second, then stared at the case again. "Deal." I extended my hand to shake hers. She offered me one better as she grabbed the lapels of my suit jacket and unexpectedly pulled me to her and kissed me. Now ain't that some shit. By the time I built up the strength to push her away, she calmly stepped away and straightened my jacket as if to say that I hadn't seen nothin' yet.

"I figure that holds more weight than a handshake," she said, gazing into my eyes.

"I don't know if I can disagree. We'll talk more later."

"No problem, call me sometime this week," she said, sitting back on the desk.

"I'll do that," I said over my shoulder on my way out of the office.

I came down and joined everybody at the booth where they were still drinkin' and talkin'. I let the band see what we brought in and from that point, it was on.

"Looks like things went well for you tonight, player," Blue said.

"Better than you know, dog," I said with a big grin. "Oh, I need to holla at you about something later."

"That's cool."

"Dali, let me get five hundred dollars from you real quick," Games joked.

"Hell no."

"Why not? Ain't like you ain't got it."

"I tell you what. Why don't you grab an instrument, hop up on stage and let's see how badly you need five hundred dollars."

"Fuck that. I'm better off leaning on Cyprus for it."

"Better call backup for that shit," Cyprus said as we laughed and pointed at Games.

"Seriously, though I just want to thank the band here for a job well done. We put a hurting on 'em tonight and this is just the beginning."

"So this is the spot now?" asked Flip.

"Looks that way. You okay with that?"

"I know I am if the money's lookin' like this on the regular," B-Heavy added, fingering through the evening's pay.

"I second that. The white girl's cool in my book." Bounce, too, was counting his money.

"Serenity dog, Serenity," I said, shaking my head.

"Whatever."

"Flip, you cool?" I asked.

"Yeah, dog, I roll where you roll…and the pay does work for a brother."

"Aiight, I'll call ya'll tomorrow to set up the week's rehearsal.

CYPRUS

I t was around two-thirty p.m. a day or two later as Fat Chicago Tone leaned against his gray Range Rover and smoked a cigar. He, along with five of his men, waited for the rest of his entourage for the meeting with Alfonze Cicero. I arrived with my small crew around three. We parked behind his truck, got out, and greeted Chicago and his men.

"What up?" I asked.

"Waitin' on Takoma Joe and his peoples," Chicago replied.

"Everybody who roll wit' you got names like yours?"

"Almost," Chicago laughed. "Let's see, uh, there's Takoma, uh, Mike Dakota, Vegas Black, you met Ohio Joe Maxey and Texas Pete. There's a couple others I can't think of right now."

We continued to wait. Takoma arrived ten minutes later with more men. Chicago called everyone together for a quick debriefing. He informed the group that he would be the only one talking, and he wanted them to give Cicero's men the same attention they would watching their children play at the park.

There were three cars: Chicago's truck leading with Takoma Joe behind him and me in the rear. They reached their destination to find Alfonze Cicero along with four cars of his own already waiting.

The setting was a tense one to say the least. The factory had been abandoned for sometime and much of the equipment had been either sold or scrapped. There were only empty buildings forming a circle of sorts around well, a lot of space.

The seven cars of the two families faced each other. Alfonze Cicero, and another gentleman, who was apparently an unfamiliar face to Chicago, stood in front of four black limousines, all of which had four Italians each standing next to them. Fat Chicago Tone, with his highest-ranking soldier, stood a couple of feet in front of his truck.

There was a minute or two of silence as both sides cautiously and yet patiently eyed each other and the surrounding area. Cicero extended his right arm gesturing for Fat Chicago Tone to join him alone. They walked a couple of feet before talking.

"Looks like ya still takin' care of yourself, kid," Cicero said, his voice experienced, old and raspy. He had a Brooklyn accent.

"You ain't changed much, either, old man. I see you still travel with more weight than the president. Who's your new face?"

"Him? He's from old family back in Sicily by way of New York. He's helpin' me out with some...problems."

"Uh huh," Chicago said, glancing at the gentleman.

"So, how's business, kid?" Cicero inquired.

"It's good. Hell, you should know, same business."

"Not like it used to be."

"Not much is," Chicago added.

"Times change, new players in the picture, more money, more unwanted attention, ya know what I mean."

"Everything's in control on my end," Chicago said.

"Is it?"

"What's the problem, Cicero? You got me out here. What's on your mind?"

"Look, Chicago, you've always been smart. Hell kid, I think you're a fuckin' genius. That's why I tried to look out for ya, 'cause I knew ya respected the streets, but shit, after a while ya grew beyond my control. Look at ya, a regular fuckin' black US Steel over here. I gotta give it to ya, kid, you're on top. I helped ya get there and I'm proud of ya. But I think I'm alone in my praises," Cicero said.

"Gettin' some pressure from the other families, I take it."

"You know the rules, Anthony. Ya movin' up way too fast and rollin' wit' too much weight for someone not to notice."

"So what they want from me?"

"More money, kid."

"No disrespect, Cicero, but fuck that. I can't do it."

"Anthony, listen, ya puttin' me in a bit of an imbroglio here, kid. Some unneeded shit, if ya know what I mean. Ya know what's gonna happen 'cause you would do the same. You say no, the families are gonna try and pressure ya. I figure I visit ya now instead of my friend over there visitin' yours later," Alfonze explained.

"Mr. Cicero," Chicago sighed as he puffed on his cigar, remembering for a second that he hadn't used "Mr." with Alfonze Cicero in a long time. "Look, as you said, times change, but you know as well as I do the rules don't. The agreement on the percentages was set a long time ago. They can't just change that shit whenever they want to 'cause my family's doing a whole lot better than they expected. The deal was ten percent no less on my part and no more on theirs. I won't fuck with anything more or less. They put *me* in a compromising position when they try to take money out of my pocket."

"What can I tell ya, Anthony? The bosses set the parameters we live by. You know that. Hell, they can make adjustments whenever they want."

"Not this time, old man. Those are your parameters, not mine."

"I guess things are about to get a bit complicated."

"I guess so, my friend."

"Well, take care of yourself, kid," Cicero said, taking a deep breath. "I hope everything works out for all of us."

"You do the same, old man...and so do I."

BLUE

Avida and I spent the afternoon doing her shopping with numerous stops at Neiman-Marcus, Macy's, Victoria's Secret, and a few others that have luckily slipped my mind. I, quite honestly, was ready for a drink. A *few* drinks.

We stopped for an early dinner and drinks at a favorite Spanish restaurant of ours. The food was always hot and the Coronas were always cold. Our relationship appeared to be making a change for the better recently. Not that things in the past were all that bad, but they tended to get a bit more complicated than they needed to at times. Lately, however, spending "quality" time together became a priority of ours. I sometimes wondered about her motivations, but I reassured myself that our feelings for each other were mutual and left it at that. Sometimes it doesn't pay to overanalyze things.

After dinner we took a walk, talked and held hands, which is something she'd always wanted from me. A deed I tended to shy away from. Tonight, I would make an exception since there are occasions where the ideals around old-fashioned romance have their benefits. I figured it wouldn't be such a bad notion to continue along my present course with a trick I learned from Dali sometime ago. When he showed me, I thought he'd seen too many of those old movies. I couldn't believe the reaction I got from Avida when I pulled a perfectly intact, long-stemmed red rose out of nowhere and gave it to her. I must tell you, old-fashioned romance is definitely underrated.

That was only the beginning. Though she planned the afternoon, the evening was all mine. We relaxed in my apartment a bit, drinking a red wine in front of my fireplace.

"You warm enough?" I asked.

"Sure," she purred, stretching out on the carpet.

"Good. I have something special for you."

"What?" she whispered.

"You'll see. Give me ten minutes."

"Okay."

"Oh, and uh, take off your jeans."

She was in the process of that while I made my way to the bathroom. It was a location where I appeared to continually excite Avida. As I have so often said in the past, tonight would be no different.

I set candles on the floor, sink, and left and right corners of the tub. Cinnamon incense burned as the bath water and bubbles filled the tub. The last added touches were for me. Once the water reached the right level and temperature, I added two gallons of milk, then rose petals. I figure most would understand the rose petal part, but the milk probably throws some off. My only response to that is a man knows nothing of sensuality until he views a beautiful woman submerged in a milk bath. It accentuates every curve, ridge, crevice, corner, valley, mountain, and any other "terrain" your woman may have.

I returned exactly ten minutes later to find Avida one step ahead of me, lying naked and smoking a cigarette right where I had left her. I escorted her to the bathroom where I received a response greater than the one for my little trick with the rose. I sat on the edge of the bathtub as she enjoyed her bath. I eventually joined her in the tub, well...she pulled me in actually. I didn't mind much since making love in a warm milk bath with this woman wasn't something that I'd actually complain about.

Some hours later as I lay there on my bed while Avida slept, I wrestled with the fact that Avida and I had a very, very strong sexual relationship. It was just an obvious point that I had tried to ignore at times with little luck. I assumed many would give their soul to have what we had in that capacity. I occasionally struggled with the fact that our relationship lacked depth. We relaxed with sex, relieved each other's stress with sex, celebrated with sex, even ended arguments and fights with sex—great, mind-blowing, body-exhausting, life-altering sex—yes. Hell, we rarely told each other "I love you" with the exception of when we made love. I guess I was somewhat worried that over time

Avida would also notice that something was lacking from our relationship and since she had the tendency to be rather unpredictable, I wasn't sure what that could lead to.

After glancing over at the clock I realized that I'd gone through two cigarettes and used up almost twenty minutes thinking this over. I regained some of my senses on my way to sleep. Romantic evenings similar to the one we just spent together would give me the piece of mind I needed to believe that everything would work out.

GAMES

"So what happened?" I asked, dribbling the basketball as Cyprus guarded me in our game of one-on-one.

"Not much, really. He met up wit' Cicero. They talked in private a bit about him bringing in all the cash he does without cutting the Italians in for more than what they're already gettin'," Cyprus replied.

"Anything to worry about?" I quickly stepped back to shoot a short jumper that hit nothing but net.

"Nice shot. Not really, if you don't count Nikki Movatto."

"Who's that?"

"*Who's that?* And them mufuckas say you do yo' homework? Man, Nikki Movatto is the hitman's hitman. Guinea mufucka got like fifty, sixty hits under his belt. He's from somewhere outta Italy or Sicily or some shit. Straight-up killa...uh oh, watch out, old man," Cyprus took the ball to the hoop for a lay-up, coming up short but getting the rebound.

"Why would Cicero bring him in?" I checked him and his ball movement even closer.

"Anybody's guess, really. I'm not sure. What I do know is that if we got to go toe to toe with that muthafucka, we got our work cut out for us."

"No shit?"

"No shit indeed. Speaking of shit, old man, taste a bit of this..." Cyprus faded to his left and spun quickly to his right before taking a two-step leap to slam and bring their game to an even ten points.

We always play hard. It was our way of releasing that tension between each other. Better on the court than in the streets. We also used the time to trade secrets that could probably land us both in serious predicaments, if anyone found out. That's why we always play one on one, without an audience.

The game was even as we neared the end of the tie-breaker. Both of us were winded. I guess we could cut down on the smoking, but I doubt that's going to happen.

"So where do you go from here?" I took a second to catch my breath before checking the ball for what I hoped would be the last shot of the game.

"See how it plays out, I guess. Put a couple of fellas on Movatto, to keep their eyes on him."

"This guy is really that much of a concern?"

"Hold up a minute," Cyprus said, raising his hand slightly to bring a brief halt to the game. "I don't trip off anybody in the game who on top or consider themselves 'that mufucka'. Italians, Colombians, Jamaicans, and whoever else—fuck 'em—ain't shit to me. But Nick Movatto...has been at this shit since he could walk. Mufucka got no family, no nothin'. You got to take special precautions with a man like that. I remember hearing 'bout his ass when I first started out. He's been known to do hits for free, just 'cause he likes to do the shit. And he don't just shoot muthafuckas. He get into that torture shit and the whole nine. I could tell you all kind of stories about Movatto. All I'm saying is that if Chicago puts Cicero in a situation where he's gotta put Movatto on 'em, Chicago got problems. His peoples ain't ready for a cleaner like that."

"On that note, let's call game—even," I said, soaking up everything I'd just heard.

"Game it is."

BLUE

For Games, Cyprus, Dali and me, the world was beginning to get unpredictable. We were now finding ourselves in new territory. For some of us that was good news—for the rest, not so good.

Dali fell into the not-so-good category. Although he was spending more time with Allura than he ever had in the past, he found himself thinking of Serenity.

He told me he was struggling with the fact that he knew he would have to deal with her for business on a regular basis. Those primal male instincts were fighting him. He needed to do what was right, which was to leave her ass alone.

That's the "thing" with men. We just can't leave ass alone. It's not in our nature. Hell, those who can perform this damn near impossible feat have been taught to by women or God. Women either leave us because we're ass greedy or they use their own ass to show us the light.. No matter how you look at it, men, are managed by ass. It may sound crass, rude, or for some, difficult to understand, but it's true and very real.

One of the hardest concepts for women to understand is why men act like men. To a lot of women, men are complex, confusing, and impossible to figure out. In my opinion, women simply try too hard to find answers that are quite simple.

Men are pretty basic, with the exception of those who have taken the time to look within and realize all that life has to offer. Aside from those few guys, the rest of us have basic wants and needs. If women are curious as to what makes men difficult, consider this: love, romance, and giving a woman the attention she wants are what the majority of men want nothing to do with despite what they tell women. What men tell women is what they want to hear—not necessarily what they really feel. There are exceptions, but not many. Smart women know this. They also know that a great deal of their control over men's concerns are physical.

Serenity is a smart woman and she didn't get that way by feeling that men are just too perplexing to figure out. We're not. Dali's a perfect example.

Dali and Allura as watched a rented copy of *The Sixth Sense*, Dali knew he wanted to have his cake and eat it, too. While a good woman won't allow that, not even her zero tolerance can stop a man from testing her resolve. It's simply the rules of the game. He contemplated being temporarily involved with Serenity, while at the same time being permanently attached to Allura. It was wrong and he knew this. If Allura wanted to do the same with him and another gentleman, he would have nothing to do with her. Taking all of this into account, he found himself still in deliberation over what he was going to do. He knew that his previous kiss with Serenity gave her an advantage that he wasn't too happy about. He just hoped she wasn't aware of it.

After the movie, they sat up and talked for a couple of hours about the story, Dali's last gigs, and several other subjects that came up. I've always felt that communication is the cornerstone of a strong relationship. And it was communication that distracted Dali from his dilemma. It would be this same communication in their relationship that would prevent him from making any hasty decisions.

Their evening ended quite similar to that of mine with Avida. Passionately. Dali forgot all about Serenity. Actually, with what Allura did that evening, it would've been damned difficult for any man to think of anyone or anything else. Dali tactfully told me the following day, he wished the entire event was on video for his lonely nights.

CYPRUS

It was business as usual for Fat Chicago Tone as he stood on his extended office balcony. It overlooked the dance floor of one of his downtown clubs. It was after his meeting with Alfonze Cicero. Chicago was amazed, yet not too happy with the fact that none of his close crew members had a clue who the gentleman accompanying Cicero was. He was happy with the job I was doing, especially when I clued in everyone on Nicholas Movatto's background.

Chicago, after a couple of drinks and cell phone conversations, called another gathering of four men. I was there, too. I would serve as a consultant of sorts in regard to the situation with the Italians, particularly Nick Movatto. He explained and predicted what everyone should expect and what he expected from everyone. Chicago figured Cicero would reluctantly send Movatto to add the exclamation point to the Italian's request. It would be nothing dramatic, but simply enough to get the point across. The message would push Chicago to meet with a representative from one of the families to work out an arrangement, which would be in everyone's best interest. That arrangement, as far as Chicago was concerned, would never happen.

During this whole ordeal, I was curious as to why Chicago would make things so difficult for himself. I figured even with a little more money going out, Chicago's business wouldn't skip a beat. Chicago was moving a lot of merchandise: money, drugs, guns, faster and in larger quantities than anyone else around. Any extra change really didn't matter. The issue was pride. Sometimes it's the only thing men have to hold on to. I couldn't see how Chicago could get tangled up in such a concept. In the game, pride was rarely practical and generally bad for business. Nevertheless, Chicago was calling the shots. He didn't get this far by making bad decisions.

BLUE

Another Friday evening. The debate was swirling around about going out to a club or bar, or simply meeting up at one of our apartments.

Games was pushing for the club. I suppose the lack of some consistent female companionship was beginning to take its toll on the brother. Still, in my opinion the last thing that he would find at a club was consistency. I mean let's be honest here. The nightclub environment isn't exactly a conducive place for meeting your soul mate. Unless one wants a man or woman who is going to be out every other weekend rubbing up on someone else. Then again, there are exceptions to every rule of mine. I just didn't feel like getting dressed for a night out.

Everyone ended up at my place around seven and for the time being, our late-night plans were tentative. The boxing match on my television kept our attention until one of the fighters found himself on his back as a result of a clean overhand right. There was a minute and a half left in the fifth round. We continued drinking and channel-surfed a bit after that.

Dali seemed rather distracted for some reason. This was unlike him. I figured the situation with Serenity was still bouncing around in the back of his mind. Actually, everyone seemed kind of detached from this evening for some reason. I could see in their restlessness that I would soon be out voted as far as our evening agenda was concerned.

Sometime after eleven, we all piled up in Games' Pathfinder en route to a club called Anastasia's. Although we had been a time or two, Games was the only one who remembered the directions. Perhaps, because he'd been the only sober one in the group. Anyway, Anastasia's was a club for older folk.

Perhaps "old" is too strong a word. The club was geared toward a mature audience. It was not the kind of place where the brothers fight over who stepped on whose shoe. It was Games' kind of place. By the time we reached the bar, he'd already bumped into a woman he had been involved with in the past.

Dali, Cyprus, and I clowned around a bit, flirting with women five and ten years our senior. The majority of the women in that club, though forty and up were just as attractive as the twenty-something-year-old pain-in-the-asses we tended to spend our time with.

Games found his niche at a table of three women not too far from the bar. We let him do his thing while the three of us got a booth and continued getting drunk.

Around nine Tequila shots and a number of Coronas later, we were engrossed in a conversation about...well, the details have evaded me for some reason, but it's not important. I noticed myself occasionally fading out and thinking of Avida. I suddenly blurted, "You know, man, I think I wanna marry Avida."

"*What*?!" Dali and Cyprus asked loudly.

"Nigga, is you fuckin' high?" Cyprus asked.

"What? I'm serious. I mean things between us been fuckin' like smooth sailin' lately," I replied.

"Yeah lately, but you be twisted up over how hot and cold things get with you and ol' girl," said Dali.

"I'm sayin,' shit is different now. It's like we fillin' in a gap that wasn't there before you know, so the whole fuckin' thing's like complete," I said.

"I told you about her being at the club and all," Cyprus said.

"What about what you told me 'bout dude droppin' her off at the crib and her lyin' to you about it?" Dali added.

"I told you that?"

"Yep."

"Well...I did say I was just thinkin' about it."

"Well, think some more, mufucka," said Cyprus.

"When you're sober," Dali added.

I had to chuckle at their concern. Perhaps, they were right. Only in their suggestion to think more about it, that is. I could not deny what I felt at that time and had been feeling for a while despite the couple of unanswered questions concerning Avida. I could always chalk that up to my own insecurities and paranoia, or the inhibitions of being drunk.

Anyway, our night went well, especially for Games. His joy was evident as he sauntered over to our booth as if he'd just closed a five million-dollar business deal. He rambled on about the phone numbers he'd acquired and all of his plans for the women who'd be on the other end of the line. He hadn't enjoyed himself this much in a while.

DALI

I woke up the next morning and sluggishly made my way to the cof-
feemaker in the kitchen and after setting that up, I headed straight for the
shower. Coffee and a hot shower were two of man's strongest weapons in
the war against tough hangovers. After the shower, a couple cups of coffee
and a small breakfast, I looked over some music for that evening's gig at the
club. I had agreed to stop by Serenity's place before performing, to work out
some final financial business. I decided against that commitment about twenty
minutes after I got up that morning.

The first reason was because I just didn't feel like leaving the house. The second was somewhat more complicated. I knew that my best defense to counter
temptation was to simply avoid it. Unfortunately, that method doesn't work
too often and even when it does, it's time sensitive. Meaning it won't last very
long. I casually limited my contact with Serenity to phone calls. I talked with
her for about fifteen minutes early that afternoon and she appeared to respect
my covert boundaries. Still, I believe she relished my attempts to push away
from her. I suppose she felt it made it all worth while, adding a degree of interest to the game.

Though usually an avid player, I was handicapped in this "game" with her.
I was taken and I knew it. I guess that's what makes it fun for people who are
not. Nevertheless, I had to play tonight and I'd trained myself to ignore any
external distractions when I played. I didn't change that for anyone.

That Saturday evening, the band and I played better than last time and the
club appeared to be twice as full. Everyone made it on our end with the
exception of Cyprus. Something pulled him away at the last minute. Games

showed with a woman that I'm guessing he met at Anastasia's. He seemed just as confident as I did that evening which was truly a feat since I was playing like there was no point in listening to anything else. If I was bothered by resisting temptation, no one would be able to tell from my performance. I prided myself on his ability to step up whatever I was doing in the face of adversity.

As the evening slowed and we all prepared to leave, I made my way up to the management office to meet Serenity for the night's returns. This time I brought Bounce with me.

"Hello, gentlemen," Serenity said, showing no sign of surprise that I was not standing in the doorway alone.

"Hey whassup, Serenity?" Bounce asked.

"So whad' ya think?" I asked as I took a seat.

"Better than the first and that was outstanding," she replied.

She had sorted our earnings into individual envelopes. Each one was filled with the amount she and I agreed upon.

"Dali, could I speak with you for a moment?" she asked.

Before I could reply with a roundabout "no," Bounce interrupted.

"Hey dog, I'll be outside."

"Aiight." I chuckled.

"What's so funny?" Serenity asked.

"Ah, nothin,'"

"Don't worry, dear, I won't keep you too long since you have someone waiting."

"You don't make things easy."

"Not much in life is."

"True."

"Since things are going so well with the club, I figured we should consider celebrating sometime," Serenity said this with poise, prepared for any answer I could think of.

"What, like all of us?"

"No."

"Oh."

"All of us is not how this came to be," she said.

"True. Well, I'll suppose we'll see, you know, how our schedules look and all."

"Clever answer."

"Safe answer," I replied.

"Okay, we'll see," Serenity agreed.

"Okay."

I wasn't sure what had just happened, but I'd come to the conclusion at that moment that I just might be dealing with the devil herself. There was a slight chance that my player/pimp powers at this juncture might prove to be... mortal.

CYPRUS

arrived at an old, rundown convenience store to find three gentlemen already there waiting for me. Everything inside was trashed, shot up, and burned. I stepped up to the doorway after lighting a cigarette.

"Whaddup, Cyprus?" asked one of the men.

"Ain't shit, what happened?" I asked, looking inside.

"Chicago says it's a message."

"What? Here? Chicago got places a lot tighter than this to fuck up?"

"This ain't Chicago's spot."

"Then why we here?" I was both confused and slightly agitated.

"It's his pop's store," replied one of the other gentlemen.

"You bullshittin'?"

"Nope. Couple kids down the street said they saw this tall white dude with a couple other mufuckas fuck the place up...said they was up in here tearin' up shit and blastin' for a while. Then they set the mufucka on fire."

"Where's his pops?" I walked through the remains of what used to look like a humble mom and pop corner store.

"At home. Chicago said he ain't been feelin' too hot lately so he been closin' up early. Hey, Cyprus you think dude did this?"

"Movatto? Maybe. Chicago pissed?"

"Off the principle of it, really...I mean he got the joint insured and all, you know. He can hook his pops up with another spot with no problem but shit, fuckin' with a nigga family..."

"I hear that." I glanced through one of the shotgun holes in the wall. "Damn, they fucked it up pretty good. Let's ride...see what Chicago got to say."

I followed the gentlemen to Chicago's home. One would expect a man who brings in millions a year to have a home which reflected that. Fat Chicago Tone, however, chose to let his home reflect his needs. He had a quaint, two-story house with its own customized circular driveway with motion-sensitive, alarmed airport runway lights to both accommodate and alert. Approximately half of Chicago's home were additions including security monitors, anti-bug devices, a hidden basement, and an anti-intruder system so high-tech one would think he worked for the CIA. Apart from that, it looked like something a lawyer from Maine would own.

We were greeted at the door by one of Chicago's bodyguards. He took us to the back of the house where Chicago was watering vegetables in his garden. Chicago said nothing for a while as we stood there...waiting. Seconds seemed like extended minutes of silence as he continued to water his garden.

"Hey, Chicago, you want us to..."

Chicago interrupted with only the movement of placing his index finger on his lips as if signaling to a child to be quiet.

I smiled to myself knowing that waiting patiently in a situation like this was the smartest thing to do. Chicago's men were as slow as I'd previously assumed. As I figured, it's probably not a great idea to irritate a man who is watering vegetables at night.

"Cyprus, you like tomatoes?" Chicago asked.

"Only if it's in a spaghetti sauce."

"I hate 'em myself. I still don't know why I grow these muthafuckas. Pops used to have this garden out in the country when I was a kid. Helped him relax, he told me. He got that store ya'll just came from when I was about twelve. I remember that bitch didn't have shit in it but fresh vegetables and beer. That was his spot, though," Chicago said as he put the hose down and motioned for us to have a seat at a table on his deck.

"So who did it?" he asked.

"We think it's probably the big Italian who was wit' Cicero," one of the men replied.

"Mr. Movatto. Well, that does make the game a little more interesting."

"That store ain't his thing. He'll be here for a while until he earns what he gettin' paid for," I added.

"How you figure? Better yet, how you know him so well?" Chicago asked.

"Bumped into him a couple of times."

"Looks like you fared alright," said Chicago.

"I said bumped into him, never met him."

Chicago chuckled. "Alright, looks like these mufuckas tryin' to turn business into somethin' personal wit' this shit. Street wars is just like any other wars—costly. If I say fuck it and give 'em they fifteen percent, it'll be twenty-five next year, so that ain't an option, either. I'll talk with Cicero alone in a day or two and let him know that the Italian families' current course of action will eventually lead to serious consequences. In the meantime, Cyprus, watch that guinea muthafucka, Movatto. The rest of ya'll, put the word out that all wops is cut off. No deals wit' 'em at all. No drugs, no guns, no hoes, no loans, no nothin'. We'll watch it from here and I'll take care of the shit wit' my pops. Cool?"

Everyone agreed.

BLUE

vida and I met up with Games on Sunday afternoon to take his son shopping for clothes, shoes, and toys. Games' ex-wife had told him not to buy any toys. Divorces are funny that way. We tagged along for a number of reasons. We loved seeing Games' son but we were also shopping for Avida. Relationships are funny that way.

We strolled around a local mall from one kids' store to another, one women's store to the next. My tolerance level dropped faster than everyone else's. I would be the only one leaving empty-handed. Such is life. At one point Avida and I separated from Games and his son to browse around Victoria's Secret.

As I watched them walked away en route to a video arcade, I felt a strange and unfamiliar sense of envy. I had always held Games in high regard because of his relationship with his son. Looking at them, I found myself feeling the need for the same kind of relationship in my life. So, for a second, and it was odd due to the fact that I had never thought of it before, I pondered the idea of Avida and myself having a family. Perhaps, I was still kind of riding off of the marriage thing and all. Avida as both my wife and mother of my child was beginning to feel better to me by the minute.

Browsing through Victoria's Secret gave me the opportunity to talk a little with Avida about the whole thing. We walked from bras to bathrobes, panties to pajamas, as she held up items, enlisting my opinion.

"No red," I declared, looking at the silk one-piece teddy she held in front of her.

"Forget about the color for a second. What do you think of this style as opposed to the one with the spaghetti straps?"

"I thought they were the same."

"You're ready to go, aren't you?" she asked.

"Naa, I'm cool."

"Good. 'Cause I wanna know how you like this over here."

"Hey, uh, you ever thought about us, you know, as a family wit' kids and shit?" I inquired as she looked at some pajamas. Actually, she stopped looking when I asked.

"Kids and shit?" she returned with a smirk.

"You know what I mean."

"Where's this comin' from?"

"I'm not sure really. Just curious, I guess."

"Well, I don't know. I've never really thought of myself as a mom. I spend too much time thinkin' about myself."

"At least you're not afraid to admit it."

"What, me as a mom or thinkin' about myself?"

"Both," I said as she grabbed a couple of things she wanted.

"Yeah, well, I can't say that the thought has never crossed my mind, but I figured since you never mentioned it, why should I? You know how cold you can get about things sometimes. I didn't want to look stupid, you know, bringing the subject up and all."

"So you want to have kids?" I asked.

"Yeah. Someday. But I don't wanna rush into it. I mean, from what I can tell, it takes a lot of work despite how easy Games makes it look. So where's all this comin' from?"

"Like I said, just curious."

As we left the store, we continued to play around with the subject. It was interesting since I never knew she actually entertained the idea as much as I did. We met up with Games and his son after we grabbed a quick bite to eat. They approached us laughing and carrying what I gathered to be prizes they'd won from their arcade visit. Though I knew Games was a good father to his son, I rarely got a chance to really see him be himself without the concerns of his job and the streets. He was relaxed. He had let down a guard I never knew existed.

I guess it was understandable, to a degree. A lot of men won't admit that they sometimes have to cover who they are inside. With children, you can be yourself. You can laugh, cry, play, or like in Games' case, just act a fool. It's okay. They won't take advantage of you.

I could appreciate that. Again, I found myself envious. I suppose our previous conversation made Avida think about settling down. I noticed her paying more attention to Games and his son than she usually did. Maybe Dali and Cyprus were wrong and I wasn't out of my mind to consider this woman as the one I would spend the rest of my life with.

So with that, everything seemed to be going quite well, if not exceptional for everyone within our little clique. We had all found a safe haven of sorts. Dali basked in his fruitful relationship with Allura and was using it to ward off Serenity's "evil" sexual spirit. Cyprus was now tucked comfortably in bed with one of the most profitable crime families in the city. Games remained centered in his bond with his son and his commitment to catching the bad guys, while trying to protect Cyprus. And I was simply happy with my woman.

✠ ✠ ✠

I've always felt that life was about searching for and fulfilling ourselves with that which makes us happy—relationships, money, safety, comfort, love, etc. We seem to exist from one day to the next working only to bring a smile to our faces. We spend time with friends, family, and lovers because we enjoy it. We both make and spend money, time and energy on the things we love in life. If you think about it, even our vices are in place for the sake of making us happy. We drink, smoke, and have freaky, unprotected sex with total strangers because it makes us feel good.

The four of us like everyone else in the world were in a continuous and unconscious search for that which brought us comfort and joy. Nevertheless, whether we realized it or not, we had all reached the proverbial mountain top in our quest for complacency. A point where Dali, Cyprus, Games and I said to ourselves at one time or another, "This is how life is supposed to be." Unfortunately, we aren't always in control of all the elements.

Life is dangerously unpredictable that way. Like a bad storm pulling, pushing, changing, and waiting. Life is relentless in its drive to make things difficult for the sole purpose of making sure no one takes it for granted. We constantly work at making our lives as stress free and easy as possible. We sometimes forget that if life was a human, he or she would say, "fuck you, try harder because the only way I get easier is with a little luck." And there's no such thing as luck.

The four of us were unable to predict the future, which made it impossible not to take advantage of the present. Our collective good fortune was on the verge of a collective change. As the common black colloquialism goes, "It's all good," but black folk ain't foolin' themselves. Life is never all good.

DALI

I had a busy day ahead of me and I knew it. I would be back and forth between the band members and Allura, not to mention running a variety of errands. My day started with Bounce, the drummer. I spent an hour or two with him discussing and practicing solos. I had a problem with how hard Bounce played. I would have to constantly remind him that we played funk-based jazz rather than hip-hop or R&B. Even though he didn't like it, Bounce complied with my wishes.

Though there were occasional creative differences between me and the band, I knew none of them would be bold enough to leave over something as petty as not being able to play a song exactly how they wanted to. Besides, I was the headliner and everyone understood that.

I then headed over to Allura's store to take her out to lunch. We decided to go to an Ethiopian restaurant. Allura decided actually. I would have never volunteered for Ethiopian food. Something about that no-silverware thing rubbed me the wrong way. We sat there eating funny-looking dishes out of this big bowl talking about what we'd be doing that evening. That's when the eating stopped.

"You told me that it wouldn't take you that long to do everything you had to do today," Allura said, her appetite disappeared after finding out that we might not spend the evening together.

"I know, baby. I don't know how long I'll be tied up. I'd rather just leave the night open than tell you I'll be over at whatever time and end up bein' late or not bein' able to show at all."

She was pissed. I've always been amazed at the kinds of things women get upset about. The same things that piss off women in a relationship wouldn't disturb a man in the least. I've never once heard a man say that he was upset with his woman because she didn't spend enough time with him, or she never bought him anything. We men have better things to get pissed about like not getting enough sex, or receiving credit card bills the size of dictionaries as a result of female sprees on clothes and shoes. I was gonna have to find some kind of happy medium to get myself out of a doghouse that appeared to drop out of the sky.

"Some things came up? What kinds of things?" she asked sternly.

"Business, Allura...I mean, c'mon now, you know that I don't just sit around all week, then go to the club on the weekend. I got daily work to do just like everyone else."

"Well, all I know is that this is the third time we've made plans, and you've put me in a situation where I gotta wait for you to do what you gotta do. I hate waiting."

"What do you want me to do, sweetheart?" I asked irritably.

"Right now, I just want you to get the check."

"I can't believe you're upset over this."

She simply cut her eyes at me and looked out the window. I was in for a long and lonely night even if I was able to see her that evening.

After dropping her off, I made some phone calls and arranged to meet the other band members and a potential female vocalist. They picked the worst time to try to sell her as a temporary addition to the group. I already had a major problem with female vocalists, who, for the most part, couldn't sing to save their lives. They kept their audiences with an abundance of cleavage and great legs. Don't get me wrong. Cleavage and great legs have their place in my life. I just don't allow the two to cloud my judgment when it comes to my music. My motto is if she can't sing, I want nothing to do with her. However, with the way I was feeling after my little tiff with Allura, the likes of Patti LaBelle, Aretha Franklin, and Billie Holiday all wrapped up in one would have to do a whole lot to impress me.

Well, to make a short meeting shorter, the young lady got to sing for about ten seconds before I tactfully stopped her and turned her down. On my way home, I called B Heavy, who arranged for me to meet her again and advised him against making arrangements like those a long-term habit.

I arrived at my apartment around ten that evening. Still boiling over my first disagreement with Allura, I decided to take the time alone to relax. I found comfort in one of man's ten commandments about women. If you truly fulfill their needs...don't worry, they'll always call back. Sometimes, still pissed, but they'll always call back. As chauvinistic as it may sound, those words are based in truth and overwhelming evidence.

I took a long, hot shower, poured myself a glass of red wine, threw on a CD, and began reading over some sheet music that Flip gave me.

The phone rang before I finished my second sip of wine.

"Hello?"

"It's me," said Allura, from the other end of the line.

"Hey."

"Hey, I wanted to know would you mind picking me up from work tomorrow. I have something thing for you."

"No problem. Is six okay?"

"Yeah, I'll see you then."

"Aiight,...hey, you okay?"

"Yeah baby, I'm fine...just a little tired."

"That's cool. Get some sleep and I'll talk to you tomorrow."

"Okay, bye."

"Bye."

I hung up feeling both relieved and a bit curious about what Allura had for me. I continued with my wine and sheet music.

I was interrupted again, this time by a knock on his door. It could've been anyone. I opened the door to find the last person I expected to see.

"Are you going to invite me in or what?" she asked.

"Oh yeah, I'm sorry c'mon in,"

Serenity strolled in dressed in a short black leather coat, which accented her flawlessly tanned and well-toned legs. Her six-inch-plus clear pumps only made things worse.

"Can I get you anything?"

"Whatever you're having would be nice," she replied.

I poured her a glass of wine and questioned her surprise visit.

"Well, we haven't had the opportunity to celebrate our little joint venture. So, I figured I'd drop by to either celebrate or find out why we can't," she gracefully explained as she sipped her wine.

"I see. Well, I'll be honest with you. I'm a bit intimidated by how complicated you could make things."

"Oh, Dali, sweetheart, the last thing I am is complicated. I'm kind of like a man in that respect. You know, simple needs, simple wants."

"Really?"

"It's true. This is a nice piece," she said, admiring the painting above my sofa.

"Thanks. My man Vic hooked it up for me. Took 'em a while, but it was worth the wait. I personally think it's priceless."

"Some say the same about me."

"What, that you're worth the wait or priceless?"

"Both."

At that moment, she slowly unbuttoned her coat to reveal...nothing. She now stood in front of me dressed in only that coat and those pumps. No dress, no skirt, no bra, no underwear, no thank-you note, no nothing but a body that seemed to reject any notion of imperfection. I'd never seen anything like it. Temptation of the worst kind confronted me and like any other healthy, sane, red blooded, heterosexual male—I was in trouble.

The silence in the room at that moment was deafening.

"So what do you think?" she asked.

"I'm not sure if I can *think* right now."

"Not to worry, it's not your brain I want right now, anyway," she asserted, walking toward me.

CYPRUS

Fat Chicago Tone and I arrived at the parking lot of an old Italian pizzeria around eleven that night. He parked back-end first to the left of a black Mercedes. It was the only other car in the lot. He kept his engine running while he waited. A second later, the driver's side window of the Mercedes rolled down. Chicago rolled down the passenger window on the right side of his car and looked in the Mercedes. Seeing that Cicero also only brought one passenger, both Chicago and Cicero turned off their engines and got out of their vehicles.

"You tryin' ta make a point, Anthony?" Cicero asked as he closed his car door.

"I figured the location would help you better appreciate the sincerity of this visit," answered Chicago.

"Jesus kid, I haven't been here in years."

"'Bout five to be exact. It's been closed up for a while," Chicago added.

"So what's wit' all the cloak and dagger shit, kid? What? Don't trust me anymore?

"I never did, old man."

"Yeah, I always told you that ya shouldn't anyway." Cicero chuckled.

"That's true," Chicago said, still glancing around the area for any unwanted surprises.

"There's no one else here, kid."

"Never hurts to double-check."

"What's on ya mind, Chicago?" Cicero asked as he lit a cigar.

"That shit wit' my old man's shop was outta line and you know it."

"I know, I know, but it wasn't my call."

"Yeah, but you were probably there when it was made."

"Ya right, I was there and I'll tell ya another thing. The calls are gonna get worse if ya don't give 'em what they want. Look, I don't want this, but there's not much I can do. I voted against the thing wit' ya old man. They made their own decision. Besides, Chicago, you cuttin' off supplies to everyone in the streets is just makin' things worse."

"I take it they're startin' to feel the squeeze a bit."

"Yeah, kid, they are. Hell, me, too, and none of us like it too much."

"It was simply a business move, nothin' personal."

"I hear ya, Chicago, but ya refusal was like a slap in the face wit' all we've done for ya'."

"And you know I appreciate that, especially all that you've done."

"Then give 'em what they want. It's fuckin' pennies to ya, kid."

"Pennies now, but it'll be more in a couple of years."

Cicero paused for a moment and looked around the area himself. "I'll see what I can do, Anthony, but I ain't makin' no promises. Besides wit' Nick Movatto in town and your whole stand on everything, it's probably too late anyway."

"I don't doubt that, but nothin' beats a failure but a try. A war over somethin' as simple as this is petty, but not unreasonable. I'm ready for any and everything. I'm just tryin' to put it out there that it doesn't have to be like this. What the families are getting from me now is more than what they're gettin' from anyone else and almost as much as what they make on their own."

It was ballsy talk from Chicago. Under the circumstances Cicero would have to take it for what it was worth and tell the other Italian families.

It was a delicate situation all the way around. Fat Chicago Tone was the city's only freelance gangster. He was previously tied up with the gangs and though he continued to operate in the same manner, he was now highly respected as the only Gangster Disciple alumni who didn't land himself in jail, dead, or even worse, in a typical nine-to-five job. He go to that point with permission from the higher-ups in the disciples and some help from a couple of the Italian mob families in the city who made some financial investments in Chicago. Investments, which Chicago felt had been more than paid off for some time now.

BLUE

I sometimes wondered why the word "perfect" is even a part of the English language. Nothing is or can be perfect. Especially life. If you believe in the concept of perfection, then you automatically set yourself up for disappointment when you realize that it's unattainable. Perhaps I'm looking a little too deep into the concept myself.

Avida and I sat on her couch, watching a movie she picked up from Blockbuster. I don't know what it is with some women and video stores but reason, rationale, and good taste in their choice of videos is definitely non-existent. I would be a millionaire if I got ten dollars for every time Avida picked an awful movie. She always made her selection from the romantic comedy category. So, here we are watching some movie about some guy and some girl and hell, I've tried my best to forget the rest of it. Now that I remember, Avida didn't even like it. She only picked it out because the title sounded "cute." After making it through that, we carried on with our sitting, and talking about nothing at all. I mentioned that I wanted to use her for another photo shoot sometime next week in an effort to work on my lighting.

"Nude?" she questioned.

"That's up to you."

"I don't mind, just as long as you're not showin' them to anyone."

"Sweetheart, I love to show you off, but I ain't tryin' to put it out there like that."

"Good."

"So, you think any more about what we were talking about the other day?" I asked.

"You're gonna have to be a bit more specific than that."

"You know?"

"No, I don't." She giggled.

"You know, about kids and all," I said almost embarrassed to bring the subject up.

She rolled her eyes.

"What?" I asked rather caught off guard by her reaction.

"You're really serious about this?"

"I mean, yeah, why not? What, you don't think it's a good idea?"

"Honey, it's a novel idea, but I don't..."

"Novel?"

"Now, Blue, please don't get upset and don't start cussin' at me, either. I'm just sayin' it sounds good, but I don't think it's realistic, at least not for me it's not."

"Why not?"

"Because, I mean, I just don't think I'm ready for somethin' like that right now. Think about it. We don't know where we're going to be five or ten years from now."

"Well, I was hoping we would at least be together."

"Don't take it there. Nothing's for certain and there are no guarantees in life."

"Where in the fuck is this comin' from?" I asked.

"Look, all I'm sayin' is that we're both young and I think it's kinda early for us to be talkin' like we ol' folks or somethin'."

"Okay, you're twenty-seven and I'm thirty. That ain't that fuckin' old but I see where you at."

"Whatever, forget it. I see that you're upset and there's no need talkin' to you when you get like this."

"That's cool. I think I've heard enough for one night anyway."

"So what, you're leavin' now?"

"Under the circumstances, I think it's a novel, yet good idea," I said as I got up.

"Fine," she snapped, sternly not bothering to look at me as I laced up my boots, threw on my jacket, and walked out the door.

I've always felt that love is much greater than just the acts of giving, sharing, and spending time. Love is where mind, heart, and spirit meet and agree to move in the same direction as one. Love is motivation to do things you wouldn't ordinarily do, feel things you wouldn't ordinarily feel, think things you wouldn't ordinarily think, and say things you wouldn't ordinarily say. Love is also vulnerability in its purest form. I found that out firsthand in my talk with Avida.

Like many times after leaving Avida's place, I drove around the city for what felt like hours. Confused and humiliated, I made my way to my second home and picked up a fifth of Jamaican rum from the liquor store. I tried my best not to overanalyze the situation or think back to how Dali and Cyprus believed I should look at it. Perhaps, she simply wasn't ready right now. I suppose it was understandable. I don't know of too many young folks who would jump at the idea of starting a family, since the general consensus is that they would have to sacrifice so much of themselves.

I decided to focus my attention on the rum.

An hour or two had passed and I was halfway into my rum and a Muhammad Ali documentary when the phone rang. *They always call back*, I thought.

"Hello."

"Whaddup, nigga?" Cyprus loudly popped from the other end. *Looks like I thought wrong.*

"Ain't shit. 'Sup on that end?" I answered.

"Me and Games up in his place chillin,' 'bout to get in some trouble. C'mon and ride widdus."

"Where ya'll headed?"

"Prob'ly over to G-Spot."

"Damn, G-Spot; we ain't been out that way in a while."

"I know, but Games say they got some new girls, topnotch. He was out there last week."

"For real."

"Is that nigga comin' or not?!" Games shouted from the back.

"Whassup, dog, you wanna roll?"

"Nah, I'm a chill tonight. I get wit' ch'all some other time on that one."

"That's cool. You got Avida over there?"

"Uh-uh, just got a little work to do."

"Aiight, dog, we'll get up wit' a mufucka next day. I'll let you know what you missed." Cyprus chuckled.

"Aiight, that'll work."

After speaking with Games for a quick second, I remembered how much fun we used to have at the G-Spot before the girls started to look like cheap whores. It was the strip club of all strip clubs before Atlanta jumped on the map. Three floors, twenty stages and, at one time, home of some of the most astonishing exotic dancers on the face of the earth. The place brought in all kinds of people. Men, women, black, white, you name it. Several of the girls even went on to become big-time porn stars and returned to draw crowds as big as their film audience. I guess the loss of some of the club's best dancers led to its drop in prestige. The word now was that Fat Chicago Tone bought the place a couple of months ago and was working diligently to return the club's class and splendor. I wondered if I should have just said the hell with it and went anyway.

CYPRUS

After an hour at G-Spot, me and Games were on the way to the second floor. I had a lil' trouble leaving the middle stage of the first floor because I'd found my future wife. At least she shoulda been since I'd just laced the woman's garter belt with damn near a hundred dollars. Still, Games was able to convince me to keep lookin' with a trip upstairs.

All three floors had themes. The first floor was fast paced and party-like, the second was slower and more seductive and sexy. The second floor was also where you'd find the rich folk who entertained more passive fantasies. The girls on this floor would come to your table. Me and Games arrived to find a large two-section room wit' mufuckas gettin' table and lap dances. The dancers were incredible. Every flavor, size, and taste imaginable walked around the room with only their bill-filled garters.

We liked the second floor as much as the first. The third floor was off limits to us tonight. Third-floor visits were by reservations only. We headed back downstairs after a couple rounds and another hundred dollars or so in tips for the "company." We took a seat at a table not too far from one of the stages where Games was focusing his attention. I ordered another drink.

"Make it two, on my tab," asserted a voice from over my shoulder.

"Hey," I said with a grin before taking a second closer look at who had just bought me a drink. "Hey!"

"You were expecting someone else?"

"No, no not at all. I guess I just didn't expect you," I said, smiling into the face of my future wife. *Oh my God*. She was dressed only in a top and bottom matching undergarment set, six-inch pumps, and White Diamonds perfume.

"I usually don't get as much attention or that much in tips from just one guy. I figured I'd come over here and personally thank you," she said.

"I appreciate that, but you don't have to thank me. I think you good at your job. Shit, the best I've seen actually."

"Thanks." She slid her chair closer to me. Games' timing was perfect. He got up and stood at the stage, not too far from the table.

"So what's your name?" I asked.

Before she could answer there was a loud blast at the first-floor entrance. It was followed by another, which was now clearly the sound of a shotgun. The blasts were followed by one of the bodyguards being tossed through the door before his body slammed into a wall. Confusion was replaced by chaos as six heavily armed Italian men entered the first floor and proceeded to fill the club with gunshots.

People ran about frantically for every exit. Strangely enough, the six men waited patiently for the floor to clear. Me and Games got out of sight behind one of the stages. Three or four of Chicago's men followed suit. Luckily, Chicago permitted his men to enter his clubs with weapons. Me and Games never went anywhere without ours. Before any of us could do anything, the Italians quickly spread out across the empty club floor. They shot up any and everything that looked like it could be worth something. That included the bar, bar stools, tables, chairs, stages, mirrors and even the DJ booth. Chicago's men attempted to return fire but instead made a run for the back exit. While they did, me and Games decided to return fire but found that we didn't hit a damn thing as they quickly escaped out the front entrance. We ran out after them but were only lucky enough to empty their clips into the back of a black van as it sped off.

"Tony Games, meet Nikki Movatto and company," I said, as we stood in the middle of the street.

"That was him?"

"Yep."

"Proficient muthafucka," said Games.

"Told you."

"He ain't hit nobody, though," said Games, glancing back at the club.

"I don't think he was tryin' to."

"His ass is mine," said Games.

"Get in line, nigga...aaah shit!"

"What?" Games replaced his clip.

"Man, I didn't even get ol' girl's name."

"Nigga, c'mon. We up in this muthafucka gettin' shot at and you trippin' off some stripper."

"She wasn't just some stripper. I was really gonna marry that woman."

"Whatever."

"I'm serious, turn her life around and everything."

BLUE

"Why are you being so quiet?" Avida asked, wearing only a black silk sheet and black high-heel pumps for my photo shoot with her.

"I'm working. You shouldn't be talking, either...it throws off the shot."

"You're still mad about us and the family thing aren't you?"

"Cover up your left; your nipple on that side showin'."

"I thought that's what's you wanted."

"I want art, not porn."

"Okay, so you have attitude."

"What makes you think that?"

"'Cause you didn't seem so high and mighty when we agreed to videotape us making love."

"I'm finished. Even though you're sittin' on my last nerve at this moment, I think these are gonna be good shots."

"So I'm gettin' on your nerves now?" She got up and wrapped herself in the sheet and walked toward me. "You're still pissed about the family thing?"

"Now, how could I be pissed about being in love wit' a woman who doesn't love me; a woman who doesn't know if we're going to be together five or ten years from now."

"Blue, wait..."

"No, you wait," I interrupted. "I want you to listen to me very carefully. I have never loved anyone in my entire life as much as I do you. I would kill for you. I would die for you and I live...for you. I have nothing and I am nothing without you. I don't know if I could..."

Before I could finish, a tear managed to slip from my left eye. I couldn't remember the last time I'd cried. It was an uncomfortable and unpleasant feeling, to say the least. She stood in front of me with a look of concern that I'd never seen before. My emotional state had me at a point where I was unable to tell if she shared my feelings at that moment, or just felt sorry for me.

I brushed what some men call a sign of weakness and women call sensitivity from my eye as if it were accidental and regained my composure as I took the film from my camera. Her corresponding actions took me by surprise even though they shouldn't have. She reacted in the same fashion she always did when it came to emotional tension between us. Sexually. I had no intentions of rejecting her advances. I don't think I would have had the strength to, anyway. She let the silk sheet drop to the floor before slithering her way to me. She whispered soft apologies in my ear as she unbuckled my belt and unzipped my jeans.

There are some women in the world who I consider sexually advanced. Avida is in that category. As a matter of fact, I think she sets the standard. Sexually advanced women stand above other women for the same reasons that great male lovers stand above other men. They respect and cater to others' needs above their own.

Avida has always known where, how, and when to focus on my needs. She continued to whisper words of love and desire in my ears along with soft kisses to my lips and neck as her grip inside my pants grew tighter and more passionate. She was like a machine. I guess she always had been in that respect. I began to wonder what the future would really hold for us as she proceeded with her assault. Before I finish the thought she dropped down to her knees and we enjoyed quite a long afternoon.

I woke up on my living room floor alone. It was a new feeling for me. I wasn't bothered by the fact that she left. It wasn't the first time. No, today I felt, for the first time, unfulfilled. Not by the sex, but by the relationship.

It was starting to happen all over again. Our emotional relationship was being dictated by our physical relationship. I showered wondering if she'd heard anything I said earlier. Did she realize that I was hurt? She treated my emotional wounds as if they were physical.

I honestly didn't know. I didn't know anything. Confusion was the operative

word for me. I couldn't seem to figure out how something as simple as settling down into a safe, secure, trusting, and healthy relationship could be so
difficult. Who was I kidding? If it was so easy, everybody would be in one.

I suppose I was trying to find that special answer to my problems with
Avida. Trying to find the answer to the why's and how's. If only relationships
were like businesses with policies, procedures and guidelines to work within.
They're not. Relationships are like storms, always in motion—changing,
growing, and diminishing without cause. I wanted to calm my storm. That was
my challenge, but Avida was like Mother Nature. Unpredictable.

GAMES

I returned without Cyprus to Chicago's strip club an hour after the shooting. I looked around as officers searched the first floor. I like to put things in perspective rather than work on instinct and hunches, which are luxuries I can't afford. I was puzzled, as I looked across the room. I'd heard about the situation with Movatto and Chicago's father's corner store. There was something about this evening's events that just didn't make sense to me. The two jobs seemed completely unrelated. As if they were done by two different people. The move on the store owned by Chicago's father had an obvious personal edge. The club, on the other, hand was strictly professional. There were two "places" destroyed with no substantial casualties. *Maybe it was nothing*, I thought. I knew however that in this line of work, that which appears to be nothing rarely is.

I continued browsing the leftovers of the club's first floor and came to the stark realization that whatever I was looking for wouldn't be found here. I was stopped by my Lieutenant.

"Games!"

"Shit," I whispered, noticing my boss stomping down the stairs from the second floor. "Yeah, Lieu."

"What in the hell is going on here?"

"Looks like there was a shooting, sir."

"Don't fuck with me, Games."

"No bullshit, Lieu. We got no real leads, but it does look like the shooters made a concentrated effort to fuck up the club."

"What?"

"Sir, no one was shot or even injured, well, except for the bodyguard but I really don't count him. Whoever did this, wanted to give the owner of this establishment a message."

"And what message would that be, Games?"

"Uh, shit, don't fuck wit' us. Hell, I couldn't say too much for motives here. We ain't got shit but a shot-up floor."

"Well, who owns this establishment?".

"Fat Chicago Tone, sir."

"Jesus, with everything else that's goin' on with that cocksucker, now I got this bullshit."

"Ain't life grand?"

"Shut up, Games, and find out who did this."

"Yes sir."

I had no problems about lying to my superiors. I didn't do it often, only when I felt it was necessary. I knew that too much information in the wrong ear would only make things worse. I needed to see the whole picture before I could explain what was going on to anyone else.

I needed an edge, so I went to outside channels as I usually did in situations like this. I called up my old pals Dove and Supreme on my cell phone as I drove around the city, hoping to get lucky.

"Dove, what's up partner? Supreme wit' you?"

"Yeah, 'G,' we both on speaker. What you need?" Dove answered.

"Hey, you here about G-Spot?"

"Oh yeah, somebody fucked that first floor up."

"Take me off the speaker phone and both of you grab two separate lines. I got somethin' for you."

"Aiight, hol' on....you got it, Premo? Aiight, he's on, what's up?"

"You fellas ever heard of the name Movatto?"

"Nicholas Movatto, outta New York?" Supreme asked.

"Yeah."

"Natural, born killer, dog," Supreme said. "Been in the game for decades and never seen the inside of a police station. Why?"

"He was the one who hit the club."

"Damn, that's two hits against Chicago wit' his pop's place gettin' fucked up and all," Dove added.

"That's what I'm callin' for, fellas. The two jobs are totally different and identical at the same time."

"Nick's unpredictable, man. The types of jobs he does are usually his call. That way nobody knows when he's comin' or where he's goin.' Wise guys don't give a fuck 'cause the mufucka never misses a mark," said Supreme.

"Shit."

"Hey, off the record, Games. It wouldn't be a bad idea to talk to Cyprus about some help on this one. 'Cause no bullshit, neither the cops nor the feds want shit to do wit' Nick Movatto. Besides, your boy 'C' thinks just like his ass," Dove said.

"Fuck that. The precinct finds out about that shit and that's my ass."

"I hear you, but you should consider it," said Dove.

I kept that piece of advice in mind as he neared home. Things were beginning to get a bit too sticky for my comfort. The game just had too many players and way too many angles.

When I got home, I checked in with my ex-wife to make sure everything with my son was okay. I made a couple of calls to the precinct and sat on the couch to figure things out. All I needed was a little time.

DALI

I sat on my bed for several minutes, overcome by a feeling that was as new to me as sex when I lost my virginity. What I felt, however, was a contradiction to the bliss generally felt after having great sex. Guilt had reared its ugly head in my heart.

Guilt to someone like me is kryptonite. I tried to shake the feeling as I showered and got myself ready for the day, but it stuck by my side like an old friend. Perhaps my days as a free agent in the dating market were numbered. I thought about Allura, her million-dollar smile, her touch, her voice and her essence; those thoughts haunted me. I went through my daily activities almost unaware that I was doing so. When the phone rang, I damn near jumped out of my skin. Knowing exactly who was on the other end, I stared at the phone as if it would answer itself. Granted, there was always voice mail, but I knew better. I needed to handle the situation as any true player in the game would, never hiding and staying focused and in control.

"Hello."

"Hey, hon," came Allura's voice from the other end.

"Hey, sweetheart, what's up?"

"Not too much, just waitin' for six o'clock to get here."

"For real, not too busy?"

"Please, this ain't Macy's. On any given day I can count on one hand how many people come in here and actually buy something," she joked.

I chuckled lightly in response.

"What's up with you? You alright? You sound kind of out of it or somethin.'"

"Nah, I'm cool, just got a lot on my mind."

"Nothing too serious, I hope."

"No, nothin' that deep. I'm probably just a little tired."

"I can understand that. You still picking me up?"

"Of course."

"Good. You should get some rest. I have an interesting evening planned for us."

"So, I take that to mean that you don't hate me anymore?"

"Sweetheart, I never hated you in the first place. Besides, I believe in letting the past stay in the past, don't you?"

"Definitely."

"So I'll see you at six?"

"I'll be there."

"Bye, baby."

"Bye."

I left the conversation, smiling to myself, yet a little voice made its first appearance. It was sucking its teeth, shaking its head, and drilling the words into my mind, *Boy, you ought to be shamed of yo' self.* I found it annoying. It was annoying enough to make me ask myself, *I know you're not going to be stupid enough to tell her what you did for the sake of honesty. God forbid.*

CYPRUS

"So what the fuck happened?" Fat Chicago Tone asked the six of us at the table as he looked at the wine list of the upscale restaurant in downtown Manhattan. I sat there, taking notice at how tense Chicago's men appeared and at the same time wondering if I'd be able to still catch the late flight home.

"Like I told you earlier. Mufuckas came in, swept the place and was out. Couldn't of been more than a couple minutes, and that's stretchin' it," I replied.

"You saw the whole thing?" Chicago asked me.

"Enough of it."

"Fuck you mean enough of it? You either saw the shit or you didn't? I can't have mufuckas on some ol' 'well I think it was this or oh, I thought I saw that,'" Chicago barked irritably.

"Tone, man, what the fuck. I was there. When I say the muthafuckas swept that bitch, that's what I mean. Anything I didn't see was probably 'cause a nigga was busy dodging bullets," I said sternly.

Chicago motioned for the waitress to take his order. He stared hard at me, then at the rest of his men. "Rest of ya'll muthafuckas ain't see or do shit, huh?"

His guys looked like all they wanted was to be somewhere else at that time. I sat there as cool as a spring evening.

"What ya drinkin', Cyprus?" Chicago smiled as he lit a cigar and glanced at the waitress waiting patiently.

"Tequila shot and a Corona."

"Cool."

Everyone else placed their orders and listened as "Chicago" explained what he was going to do in. His instructions were vague, but clear enough. We knew that he had things under control. Chicago knew that confidence was now his strongest tool. He realized that if he gave the slightest hint that he was losing his edge, his problems would multiply.

His trip to New York was simply to visit family and friends. Still, he was able to use the situation back home with the club to his advantage. Gangsters are gangsters are gangsters, and, as I said some time ago, they network like businessmen. Street businessmen. Chicago used his influence via a chat with a few reps from the New York families to figure out what would happen if a war started. What he found out was that the New York families were against him.

Two days later, he met with his higher-ups to discuss the details. I was surprised to find myself a member of that meeting.

BLUE

I was distracted from the turbulence in my life and mind by a generous payment from a long-time client of mine. It was for a photo layout, which he found near perfect. With a lot more in my bank account, I felt celebrating. With whom? Would it be the fellas or Avida...the fellas or Avida? I suppose the answer was quite obvious. I would enjoy time spent with Dali, Games, and Cyprus, but I had no desire to wake up next to them the following morning. Besides, I knew that Avida would appreciate my accomplishment, especially since she encouraged me along this road of full-time photography in the first place.

I called her twice over the course of an hour, only to talk to her voice mail. Nevertheless, I figured it wouldn't hurt to pick up a couple of things so I'd be set when I did reach her. I grabbed a bottle of red wine from a local corner store, along with some vegetables, pasta, and a few other things for dinner. There was always the option of going out for the evening, but on occasion I liked to cook.

On the way home, I thought of my business, my life, and Avida. My biggest weakness was process without action and the fellas never hesitated to bring that attention. There were so many things I wanted to do and be. I suppose a part of me envied my friends' unknown freedom to follow their souls. Though I cherished being able to work from home and earn a decent living doing so, I still felt that something was missing. A good woman was my guess, and although it isn't high on the list of priorities for some men, it was for me. I'd always had my difficulties being single.

As I approached my brownstone, there she was on her way down the steps and off to her car. Timing is truly everything.

"Hey! You wit' the black dress!" I shouted, disguising my voice. Her reply was simply a flicking of her hand in the air without even a thought of turning around to see who it was.

"Hey, you hear me talkin' to you!" I continued.

"Muthafucka, who you think you…" She turned around. "You know, you play too much," she replied, once she realized it was me.

"I'm sorry, sweetheart. I couldn't resist." I laughed.

Avida never had much of a sense of humor. Nevertheless, the jokes for the rest of the afternoon involved both of us as we played around with each other and spent time laughing. It was almost like it was a different her. She really only appeared to be comfortable and relaxed when I was pampering her in some way or when we were engaged in a sexual capacity. Today, felt like we were just as much friends as we were lovers. It was very enjoyable. I could definitely get used to it.

I had almost missed the fact that Avida was carrying a large overnight bag with her when I bumped into her outside. My best guess would've been that she'd brought clothes over to do laundry, which she's done on several occasions. I found an answer much to the contrary when I questioned her about it over the candle lit dinner I'd prepared.

"I meant to ask you, what's up with the bag?"

"Um, well," she said, somewhat nervously. "I was thinking about you and me and what we were talking about the other day. I guess it took some time for everything you were telling me to kinda sink in, ya know, and I was thinking that maybe I could hang out over here for a while. I don't know if that makes sense or not."

"How long were you thinking of staying?" I inquired.

"I don't know. Never mind, it's a bad idea."

"No, no, not at all. I think it's a great idea."

"You sure?"

My response was to simply hold her hand from across the table and look into her eyes. I wasn't quite sure what she really wanted or needed in her life or what she hoped to accomplish by staying with me. For that matter, I don't think she knew, either. Still, her move was one in the right direction. I had no plans to change it. My guard was still up in some way, instinct perhaps. Maybe it was just my paranoia kicking in, letting me know that it was best to proceed with caution. Avida had a lock on my heart and soul. She had the ability to literally turn my life upside-down. My love for her was more than she would ever understand. My only defense was reason and rationale. My mind would put me in check when necessary.

I didn't think another second about repercussions. We had a lovely dinner and a couple glasses of wine, then we ended up on the couch. We always made love with great conviction. Still, there was something special about Avida's performance this evening that I had not seen for a long time. Her emotions seemed to move with her ass as if this were the only place she ever wanted to be. My mind would be working overtime to protect my heart.

GAMES

The streets were quiet. Me and Big Tiny made our way on foot to meet with a local drug dealer. I hate fuckin' wit' hustlers. I'd have to put it on the back burner since I needed information that I couldn't get anywhere else. I made a deal with this kid to have some cops get rid of his rivals by way of a couple of raids and in return he'd tell me everything he knew about what was going on with Chicago and the Italians. I didn't have a lot of time and it was my safest bet.

"What's this kid's name?" I asked Tiny as we continued to walk.

"City Boy," he answered.

"City Boy?"

"City Boy."

"Fuckin' City Boy?"

"City Boy, Games."

"Jesus Christ, you gotta be kiddin' me."

Tiny simply shrugged in response.

"Why can't I ever get snitches with real jobs and real fuckin' names? Fuckin' City Boy, mufucka's probably from Montana."

"Wouldn't doubt it," said Tiny. "Speak of the devil, there he go."

"Scrawny lil' mufucka, too. Definitely no need to call his ass City Man."

"This name thing is really botherin' you tonight, ain't it?" asked Tiny.

City Boy wore a white T-shirt, black Tommy Hilfiger jeans, and black Timberland boots along with an assortment of tattoos, displaying gang insignias. His hair was in thin cornrows, which were not much bigger than his body. He was also younger than I had expected, no more than sixteen or seventeen. The three of us walked a couple of steps over to an alley between two buildings.

"You Games, right?" City Boy asked as he looked around cautiously. I nodded in return.

"You nervous?" Tiny asked City Boy.

"Wouldn't you be? Fuckin' police, man, I must be outta my mufuckin' mind."

"Who you wit'?" I asked.

"Why?"

"Who you wit'?" I continued.

"GD, why? What's wit' all the questions, cuz? I mean shit, a nigga ain't lookin' to be interviewed. Let's just handle this shit and..."

I glanced over at Tiny who in turn placed a gun in City Boy's neck before he could finish his sentence.

"Man, what the fuck? Ya'll niggas ain't no fuckin' cops," City Boy said, slightly choking from the pressure of the barrel.

"Hey, hey, hey, shut the fuck up!" I whispered. "I want you to listen very closely, understand?"

City Boy nodded.

"We *are* cops. Cops under a deadline. 'Dead' being the operative word here. Now, you gonna have to forgive the tenacity of my colleague and I, but we're very busy these days. We gotta lot a shit to do and, to be quite honest with you, I wanna hurry up. You see where I'm going with this?"

"Yeah, dog, cool."

"Thank you." I signaled for Tiny to lower his gun.

"Damn, your man on some ol' wild wild West, Doc Holiday shit. Nigga pulled that shit outta the fuckin' air. Goddam, David Copperfield ain't got shit on you, dog," City Boy said.

I took a long sigh and again looked at Tiny.

"Chill, nigga. What you wanna know?"

"What's going on with Fat 'Chicago' Tone and the Italians?"

"Same ol' really, ever since he started fuckin' wit' 'em, he's had problems."

"Ganster Disciples still back him?" Tiny questioned.

"Yeah, kinda."

"What else?" I asked.

"Fuck you mean what else? That's it, muufucka."

We stared at City Boy.

"Aiight, aiight wit' all the bullshit that's been goin' on lately they s'posed to have a meetin'."

"Who?"

"Everybody, cuz."

"What you mean everybody?"

"If you there, you'll see what I mean."

"When?" Tiny asked.

"Tomorrow night I think, probably at the..."

City Boy gave us the specifics of a supposed meeting between Fat Chicago Tone and the heads of three Italian families; including Alfonse Cicero. The meeting was expected to an effort to come to some kind of reconciliation.

"So you gonna hook me up, right?" City Boy asked humbly.

I sighed deeply. "Yeah, you straight, cuz."

DALI

I strolled around Allura's shop looking at things I would never buy for myself, or anyone else for that matter. Still, I admired Allura for being able to manage such a venture on her own. I don't think I'd have the patience to pull it off. I glanced at her and called myself stupid for what I'd done with Serenity.

I approached her as she finished up with her last customer for the day. As she closed up, we talked about how her day went and the plans for that evening. I thought we'd be dining out. She had other plans. On the way to my car she reminded me that she had a surprise for me.

A surprise from Allura at this point was good for me. One reason was simply because I like surprises. It also took my mind off of something not so good.

After dropping by my place, we took the long way to her home through the city. I always liked downtown with all its bright lights, aesthetic flashy colors, and non-stop pace.

Upon walking into Allura's apartment, I felt that level of comfort, which crept into his body when I first stepped over the threshold. Though I'd been there several times before, tonight seemed different. It was if her home had been waiting for me. I thought my mind was playing tricks on me. Allura passed me a glass of my favorite red wine before going to change into something more comfortable. The scent and taste of the wine blended perfectly with the scent of dinner coming from the kitchen. How in the hell could she have done all this while she was at work? Never before had a woman gone to such measures for me. That was my role.

"Close your eyes," Allura requested from around her hallway.

"Okay."

"You can open them now."

She stood in front of me dressed in a black silk teddy that left me speechless. She was holding her hands behind her back.

"Now, that's a surprise."

"Thanks, sweetheart, but this isn't the surprise. Here, it is."

She pulled an item from behind her back. It was practically impossible to acquire. I sat there, literally speechless as I carefully perused the cover of an old jazz record. It had to be at least fifty or sixty years old. I was now in possession of a collector's edition record that I'd been in search of for at least ten years. Allura was able to obtain this same item in a matter of weeks. I was impressed.

"How? Baby, how did you get this?"

"Well, I remembered you telling me a while ago about how there was only like a hundred copies printed or something. I know how long you'd been trying to find it. I just figured you might like it as a surprise. You surprised?"

"More than you can ever imagine. I mean surprised ain't the word. The only thing I can't understand is how were you able to find it when I had no luck for years. Plus, I knew where to look."

"Well, owning a shop like mine in a big city has its advantages. I do a lot of networking with people that specialize in old stuff, black stuff, and...old, black stuff. A colleague of mine from New York owns an old jazz/blues record store in Brooklyn. He would only sell a record like this one to someone who could appreciate it. I just told him you were that someone."

"Thank you, sweetheart. Thank you very, very much."

"You're welcome. You deserve it."

"You think?"

"I do. I also wanna apologize for the way I acted the other day. I know I can be kind of selfish sometimes, and I guess I just didn't think much about you and how you may have been feeling."

"Don't even worry about it, baby girl. Come here."

I chuckled to myself, briefly thinking, *She wants to apologize*. I didn't deserve a woman like this one.

CYPRUS

My follow-up meeting with Fat Chicago Tone was scheduled for the evening. I was up early that morning. I was in a place where I rarely wanted to find myself. In my head. I ain't big on introspection. It's for people who aren't sure of themselves. Me, I'm generally confident in ninety-nine percent of the decisions I make. That's what makes me a professional, choosing to know rather than think.

Still, I sat there on the couch cleaning three of my guns. I checked them before loading their clips. I unloaded them, checked them again, and cleaned them again. I went through this a few times as I thought about the situation with Fat Chicago Tone, the Italians, and Nikki Movatto. I thought about the fact that I had what I wanted, Chicago's respect and confidence. At that point, I stopped with all the internalizing. The overanalyzing was beginning to piss me off.

"Shit," I whispered to myself, laughing, "I'm up in my own spot trippin' like some pussy..."

Before I could kick my own ass anymore, I was snapped out of it by the phone.

"Yeah," I answered.

"Whassup, man, you up?" It was Blue.

"Yeah cuz, been up since nine, 'sup up on that end?" Cyprus replied.

"Ain't shit, me and...damn, nine, fuck you doin' up so early?"

"Had a couple of things to take care of."

"You aiight?"

"Yeah dog, I'm cool."

"Aiight...hey, me, Dali, and Games headin' out to Ugly Joe's spot around noon. You up to ride?"

"Ya'll shootin'?"

"Yeah."

"How we rollin'?"

"That's on you. One of us can pick you up or you can meet us there."

"I'll meet ya'll there."

"Don't front, mufucka."

"Bitch, please, I'll be there before ya'll."

"Aiight, see ya ass 'round noon."

"Cool."

I felt better already. I felt kinda stupid for the bullshit I'd just put myself through. I sat up on the couch and finished loading the clip of one of the automatics. I cocked the gun. It made a loud and sharp click. I aimed it and whispered to myself, "That's what I'm talkin' about, much better."

BLUE

Much to our surprise, Dali, Games, and myself spotted Cyprus leaning against his car, smoking a cigar as the three of us drove into the parking lot of Ugly Joe's Bar and Billiards Club. Joe's was a place where guys like us could hang out, drink, and shoot pool while listening to the music we liked to hear. Joe was what they'd called a stand-up guy. A Vietnam vet who put his disability money to good use. He unfortunately got his "ugly" name due to a bombing accident he suffered while on tour overseas that ripped his face up pretty bad. Nevertheless, he ran the tightest hang-out spot this side of the city.

"Took ya'll long enough," Cyprus commented, while puffing on his cigar.

"It's twelve oh-two. You probably just drove up ya damn self," Dali returned as we got out of the car.

"Whassup, balla?" Cyprus said, giving Dali a handshake and a hug.

We exchanged a few good-natured remarks in the parking lot before heading into the bar. We were greeted by the scent of cigarette, weed smoke, and the sounds of underground hip-hop thumping through surround-sound speakers that Ugly Joe had placed all over the bar. Young, black folk in their mid to late twenties and thirties milled about. Ugly Joe's clientele was a Who's Who of those considered "hip." Thugs, gangsters, wannabe thugs and gangsters, college students, college dropouts, rap artists both well known and local. There were also people like us, street guys, with a little free time on our hands. There were loads of women there who liked to be around those considered "hip."

We found ourselves a pool table after half an hour of sitting at the bar with a couple of pitchers of beer. We all must have needed the outing because we were opening up about damn near everything.

To no one's amazement, I spoke of how well things were going with me and Avida. Our current living arrangement was very satisfying to both of us. Avida's trial period idea was working out wonderfully. I now felt that I had hard data to support the notion of Avida and I as husband and wife. The fellas still felt they were looking out for my best interests by telling me that I should put more thought behind it.

"I'm just saying', dog, this ain't the kind of thing a man should rush into," Dali said, before taking his shot.

"Shit, I ain't say ya'll need to start gettin' fitted for tuxedos tomorrow. My point is that bein' with this woman on the long term is my plan," I said.

"What about what I told you?" Cyprus added, speaking of the information he'd given me of Avida's outing with her friends and their male company.

"It's been taken care of," I answered.

"What? You beat her ass?" Cyprus asked, laughing. Dali joined in.

"Here ya'll mufuckas go. That's why you missed," I commented, noting Dali's bank shot that fell short.

"Hey, cuz, don't trip off these fools, Blue. I think it's cool myself," Games said, as he prepared to take his shot.

"Right there, see, words of wisdom, age, and experience," I added.

"And he still missed," Dali interrupted.

"Well, I never said he was Minnesota Fats but he knows when a man is makin' a good decision. By the way, Games, you is on Dali's side next set," I replied. "You shoot pool 'bout as well as you been playin' chess lately."

"Aiight, Dali, what the fuck, man. I wanna know what's up wit' that tight-ass white broad. And don't fake wit' no basics, either," Cyprus said, before taking his shot.

"Serenity. The name alone brings drama," Games added.

"Dawg, I don't know what to say about that one aside from the fact that I just fucked up," said Dali.

"How's that?" I asked.

"I mean ol' girl came through the other night wearin' a coat..."

"What you mean a coat?" Cyprus questioned.

"I mean a coat, oh and a pair of porn-star pumps."

"What? Clear heels?" Games asked.

"Coat and clear heels, dog," Dali replied.

"Oh shit," I said.

"What you do?" Games inquired.

Dali simply looked at us in response.

"Oh Shit!!!!" Cyprus, Games, and I shouted in unison.

"I felt so bad afterward, I thought about throwin' caution to the wind and tellin' Allura," Dali said. At this point we had stopped playing and were just standing around the table.

"What???!!!" we now shouted in unison.

"Oh hell no," said Cyprus.

"I said I *thought* about it," Dali returned.

"So, I don't get it. How you figure you fucked up?" Games questioned.

As we continued speaking of Dali's sexual escapade, we were disturbed by two gentlemen inquiring about the table.

"Hey, cuz, ya'll go'n be long?" One questioned.

"Dog, we might be here a while. I think one of those other two over there might free up in a few minutes," Games answered.

"Nah, partner, I don't think you understand. We like to play here," the gentleman replied.

"We always play here," the other added.

"Oh, okay, I see your point. Now see mine. I don't give a shit. We'll be here for a while," Games said.

"What you say, muthafucka?" the first asked as he stepped up.

"Hey, cuz, I think you heard my boy wrong. What he was tryin' to say is *we* don't give a *fuck*," announced Cyprus.

At this point, Dali and I took a seat by our table and watched. We had gotten used to scenarios like this. We would involve ourselves on rare occasions, but it was evident that Games and Cyprus had things under control. One of the gentlemen motioned for another of their partners to help in the situation.

The guy they called over was huge, six-foot-four, six-foot-five and around two hundred-fifty pounds. Games and Cyprus looked at each other and grinned.

"Problem?" the big man asked, as he stepped up to Games.

"Nope." Games smirked, passing his pool cue to Cyprus.

"My man here thinks there is."

Just as the big man attempted to complete his statement, a large crack echoed throughout the bar. It was followed by a large thud as big man's large body hit the ground like a sack of bricks. Cyprus had cracked him over the head with Games' pool cue.

"The bigger they come," Games said.

The other two men who started the incident were now both angry and embarrassed. They tried to reach in their jackets for what were most probably guns. Before their hands could fully get a hold of anything, Ugly Joe had a shotgun aimed at both of them.

"I hope you two punk muthafuckas is reachin' for some money to pay ya fuckin' tab. And Cyprus, you and Games know better. This the third time this year," said Ugly Joe.

"Cyprus?" one of the guys questioned.

"You Cyprus?" the other asked.

We all just looked at the two of them.

"C'mon dog, pick 'em up, let's roll," the first told the second in reference to the fallen giant.

We continued where we left off with Games and Cyprus talking in code about what was going on with Fat Chicago Tone and the rest of that business. A part of me felt that there might have been a reason behind that. It was like having a stressful, dead-end job that you hated. The weekend was your time to unwind, relax and spend time with good company. Still knowing that Monday morning was soon to come, with even more stress. I had a feeling that this afternoon served as our weekend. We were all soon heading for more stress.

✠✠✠

Avida came in that evening around eight. I met her at the door with a hug and kiss as I had done every day since she'd been staying with me. I usually had dinner waiting even though she never ate much after seven. This living situation seemed to be going quite well for us. I noticed we hadn't been arguing as much. We talked as much as we made love. She frequently told me how she enjoyed us spending this much time together. Her constant verbal reminders of how much she loved me set the climate for what I felt would be the best move.

"How you feelin'? You look a bit tired." I took off her shoes and began to give her a foot massage. She sat on the couch and sipped a glass of white wine.

"I guess I am. Long day," she replied.

"Yeah, I hear life as a beautician can get quite rough with all the heavy lifting, you know with the weaves and all."

"Fuck you." She chuckled. "You're lucky this feels good."

I laughed and worked harder at my task of making her feel better.

"Listen, sweetheart, I was thinking," I said.

"About what?"

"About you and I, and how things have been going for us since you've been staying here."

"What? You want me to leave, don't you?" she asked, displaying insecurity for the first time.

"No, I was actually thinking just the opposite."

"What do you mean?"

"I want you to stay."

"Stay like what, another week?"

"No, stay like, move in."

"You're serious?"

"Yeah, I'm sayin' it ain't gotta be tonight. As a matter of fact, you ain't even gotta decide tonight. Just think about it. We can take it slow. Like we did this week. We can do another, then another, and go from there."

She smiled. I hoped she wouldn't make the decision tonight. It wasn't like I asked her to marry me, so I didn't feel there was any reason for her to rush. It was a big step for both of us. Ironically, though we had been together for some time, the idea of us living together never really crossed our minds. I suppose it was simply because we spent a lot of time at each other's places. We both had a thing about personal time and space. The latter was what probably kept us together for so long, anyway. For some time, I valued the fact that Avida never felt the need to always be up under me all the time. I wanted to move above and beyond that. I wanted her up under me.

"Well," she said slowly, still smiling, "I think it's a pretty good idea, especially the taking it slow part. I love being here and, more than that, I love knowing that I'll always have someone to come home to, but"

"Uh-oh," I interrupted.

"Wait a minute. I was just going to say that I want us to take our time with this and get everything right," she continued.

"I can live with that. So, how do you want to do this?"

"Let's work out the details some other time." She kissed me and slowly slid her hand down my shorts, keeping it there for a while, before replacing it with her mouth.

I hope being married to this woman is going to be this easy.

GAMES

The weekend seemed to arrive quicker than one for a death-row inmate's Saturday execution. I was working as if it were Monday morning. The "meeting" between Fat Chicago Tone and the Italians that City Boy previous spoke of had me running around like a chicken with its head cut off. I ran into some problems getting wiretaps, surveillance, and the like. The Lieutenant didn't trust my lead, which didn't surprise me. I wasn't really sure if I did. He still gave me the go-ahead to get what I could, but, for the most part, I was on my own.

That was fine with me. I called up Big Tiny. He was all the help I would need tonight.

CYPRUS

I called Dali to let him know that I wouldn't be able to make it through. Blue was already there. Dali told me that Games just called to cancel also. What a coincidence.

Fat Chicago Tone agreed to the meeting under the condition that he picked the spot. Oddly enough, he chose a small cafe owned by a Jewish guy who worked both with Chicago and the Italians. It was a strategic move on Chicago's part to show his "open mindedness" to whatever the Italians had to offer. The time was set for ten p.m., three hours after the cafe officially closed.

Everyone was there a few minutes before. It was a nice place. Chicago picked a good spot. The cafe was soft and light with pastel-like colors, small tables, and booths with matching tablecloths and chairs. A deli section spanned half the length of the cafe.

The block in front of the cafe was congested with Cadillacs, Jeeps, Benzes, BMWs, and even a couple of Hummers. Fat Chicago Tone waited for the Italians to go in first. It really didn't make much of a difference since it was understood that any foul action on either part was unacceptable.

By ten, the cafe looked like noon in the city's Central Business District on a busy, spring Friday afternoon. Alphonse Cicero sat with the heads of the two other families, Frank Delani and Tony Gatta. Chicago sat across from them. The entire room was split in half, the Italians with their backs to one wall and Chicago's people with their backs to the other. Me and two of my guys and three Italians waited outside.

"Chicago, I would ask you how business is going but if I didn't already know, I wouldn't be here in the first place," said Gatta.

"It's had its ups and downs," Chicago replied.

"Let's not get this started on the wrong, foot fellas. Chicago, thanks for takin' the time in helpin' us work this thing out," Cicero said.

Chicago nodded.

"Well, there's really only one thing on the table here, so...," said Cicero.

"Two things actually," Chicago interjected.

"What's number two?" inquired Delani.

"What's number one?" Chicago returned.

"This fuckin' kid." Delani huffed.

"Fuckin' balls," Gatta added.

"C'mon, Tone. Your bringin' in three—maybe four—times as much as you did from the initial agreement. We ain't blind, kid. You can't win makin' a go like this without cuttin' in the people who helped you get what you got," asserted Cicero.

"Can you believe this shit?" Chicago chuckled as he looked behind his shoulder to his closest associate. "You guys didn't help me get what I got. As a matter of fact, allow me to put this 'thing' into some kind of perspective. Several years ago you fellas saw me and my people as an investment. Business was startin' to change and you wanted a piece of what we were gettin' into. You put up sixty percent of what was needed and we paid back the sixty plus another forty to show good faith. Not to mention, the ten percent you all get regularly. There was never anything about profits doublin' or triplin' on my end and ya'll muthafuckas gettin' to up your take. That shit ain't right and you know it. You'd do the same thing if the shoe was on the other foot."

"Well, the fuckin' shoe ain't on the other fuckin' foot," Gatta replied harshly.

"See, I can tell already where this is goin'," Chicago returned.

"Hey, Tone, we didn't come here ta fuckin' argue," Delani said, lighting a cigar.

"Kid, we wanna make you an offer," said Cicero.

"What, one I can't refuse?"

"Funny fuckin' guy," Gatta replied.

"What is it?" Chicago asked.

"Look, the original agreement was for ten percent of what you make off the streets, right? You got about fifteen legitimate spots in the city. We all know that the real big money comes from the streets so let's say we'll forget about that ten for twenty percent off the top of the straight gigs you run," said Cicero.

"You gotta be fuckin' kiddin'," Chicago replied.

"Chicago, listen, your decision on this gets nobody nowhere," Cicero continued.

"Meanin' what?" asked Chicago.

"Meanin' we can't allow any fuck with balls and wild hair up his ass to just say no 'cause life ain't fuckin' fair. What, you think? You got a piece of all this 'cause we like you? No. We let you guys in 'cause we knew you could make money. Like you said, it was an investment. Just think of it like the interest rate got higher," Delani contended.

"Fuck that," replied Chicago.

"Fuck that?" Gatta asked irritably.

"Fuck that," Chicago maintained confidently.

"Chicago, you're puttin' our backs against the wall on this one. This kind of behavior gets around; other families begin to question how we're runnin' things here. Makes 'em think we can't keep our dogs on their leashes. Makes us think more persuasive actions need to be taken," said Delani.

Chicago laughed in response. "I guess that brings us to number two."

"What's number two?" Cicero asked.

"Conduct unbecoming," said Chicago.

The three bosses sat in silence, staring at Fat Chicago Tone. Chicago stared back with the same intensity. The meeting at this point had come to a deadlock. For a few seconds, the four gentlemen just sat there looking at each other coldly, waiting. Chicago's words were similar to a judge's gavel bringing order, silence, and from what it looked like, an end to the talks.

"Everybody kicks back, kid. What do you expect when you piss all over us?" Delani questioned.

"I expect to be treated with the same amount of respect that you give my money. I expect you to act toward my shit in the same fashion you act toward those young up and comin' Ciceros, Gattas, and Delanis over in your neck of the woods. They piss all over you a lot more often than I would ever consider. By conduct unbecoming, I mean that shit with my pops was out a line," Chicago returned.

"Fuck this gang-bangin' cocksucker! You got some fuckin' balls, Chicago. What makes you think you would ever get treated the same as any fuckin' wise guy?" Gatta asked, as he quickly rose from the table, starting a chain reaction. His men stepping promptly to his side caused both Cicero's and Delani's men to do the same, closing in on the small table, closing in on Chicago. Chicago's family returned the gesture.

There they all stood—and sat. The word tense at this juncture would be a grave understatement.

GAMES

This whole thing had me on edge. I'd been watching and listening to everything from across the street with a high-powered audio/video camera.

"Jesus Christ, can you believe this shit? Cyprus can't see it from the door. Shit!" I told Tiny as he continued to glance through his camera.

"None of 'em want it to go down like this. Way too risky. Give 'em a minute," said Tiny.

We waited. Tiny was right. It was just too many people in one room. Too much firepower on both sides for either side to chance a bold move. Fat Chicago Tone, Alfonse Cicero, Frank Delani, and Tony Gatta all knew that. It would have been stupid to act upon that at their emotions.

"Easy, relax," Chicago calmly informed his men.

Cicero, with a raised hand, relayed the same message to the soldiers of the three Italian families. Everyone backed off.

"Fuck," I said.

"Told you," said Tiny.

"Yeah, yeah, yeah." I turned the camera to Cyprus who had his eye on his Italian counterparts outside the door of the diner. I shook my head and sighed.

"Thanks for your time, gentlemen," Chicago said as he got up. The three nodded in acceptance.

"Take care, kid," replied Cicero, watching Chicago and his crew make their way out of the entrance.

Gatta took a deep breath, before glancing over at Delani and Cicero. It looked like they were going to plan B.

"Go get Movatto. Tell him it's time to earn what he's here for," Gatta said.

"Fuck," I said, removing the headphones from my ears.

BLUE

Avida slept in Saturday. Both my troubled soul and mixed-up mind had found solace in a committed relationship that I painfully questioned on frequent occasions. Half-awake, I glanced at her naked, full-bodied, five-foot-nine frame as she slept peacefully, chuckling quietly to myself. *Damn, this is a lot a woman,* I thought. I was impressed now as I was our first intimate night together. Her physique had not seen a blemish, stretch mark, scratch, bruise, nothing. I decided to wake her up.

"Are we still going to hear Dali play tonight?" she asked as she showered and I shaved.

"Yeah, I'll make some calls in a little while to get the times right," I replied.

"Get the times right? Ya'll been doin' this shit for years and you still callin' each other like you goin' out for the first time? I just think ya'll niggas like talkin' on the phone," she joked, as she stepped out of the tub.

"Look who's talkin'?" I said, hugging her, before she could towel off.

"You're gonna get all wet," she whispered as she kissed me.

"So are you."

We carried on in the bathroom like newlyweds for the next hour, basking in each other's presence. We eventually cleaned ourselves and the bathroom up and then headed out for a late lunch.

I noticed that I wasn't spending as much time worrying about our more than active sex life but rather appreciating it for what it was. I prayed that things wouldn't change once she moved in. Avida seemed different in a good way. Her high level of pettiness and insecurity seemed to dwindle over these past few days. I specifically couldn't say why and I really didn't have a desire to ask. I suppose the idea of us living together alleviated some of the stresses and strains on our relationship. Things were going quite well, so I thought, but the analytical side of me still pondered. Living in the here and now can be notably deceptive at times.

CYPRUS

It was around six on a busy Saturday night and we were all going to hear Dali play. But some loose ends had to be tied before we would have time to hear him work.

I sat at the biggest table of Fat Chicago Tone's favorite soul food restaurant. As I smoked a cigarette, I became aware that I was happy with myself. Of course, I made damn sure that no one sittin' at the table with me could tell. At the table were five other gentlemen. Three were Chicago's advisers, Onassis, Dixon, and Patillo. The other two in the chain of command were just a hint above me.

"Aiight, let's hurry up and go through this, so I can eat," said Chicago.

"Shit's 'bout to get hot," said Dixon.

"Real hot. Look, wise guys ain't too happy at this point. They're more pissed off now than before the fuckin' meetin'," Chicago said.

"What happened?" Patillo asked.

"They didn't get what they wanted and chances are pretty good they're gonna make a move real soon," said Chicago.

"What you wanna do?"

"Same thing we been doin'. Shut down the streets on them muthafuckas and I mean everything."

"Sounds like the makin' of a war to me, Chicago," said Onassis.

"Maybe, but nobody gets paid if muthafuckas start killin' each other."

"I think that's why they brought in Movatto," I added.

"What you mean?" asked Chicago. Everyone's attention was now focused on me.

"Nick Movatto is a professional. The moves on your father's spot and the club was like a warm-up. Almost like a smoke screen. Gets you thinkin' war, but that ain't what he's here for. He don't even get paid for shit like that."

"What? They bring this mufucka in from New York just for Chicago?" Dixon asked.

"Movatto gets paid to liquidate. I'm talkin' crisp and clean and he's gone. No mistakes. He was brought in to get rid of some kind of problem. I mean, Chicago's been back and forth in negotiations for a while right?" The gentlemen nodded in agreement as I continued. "Each meetin' seems to be gettin' farther away from what the Italians want. If the meetin' last night was as bad as you say it was, then it's only a matter of time before he starts workin' to earn his money."

"I think I asked you this before. How you know so much about him?" Chicago asked.

"To be honest, it's been some time since I last seen him, but don't be confused, this ain't the first time Movatto's worked here. I seen what he left of few fellas some time ago. He ain't the muthafucka to overlook."

Chicago sighed deeply. He trusted my instincts now more than ever. He respected me as a professional in the same manner that I respected Nick Movatto.

"Aiight, like I said, business as usual. Cut 'em off. They'll make one hard run, maybe two. After that, we wait," said Chicago.

"Wait?" asked Patillo.

"Wait. Like I always say, dog, timing is everything. We wait, then we hit Gatta," Chicago answered.

"Why Gatta?" Dixon asked.

"'Cause Gatta's hot-headed and he can cause a lot more problems than the other two. My guess is that it was his idea to bring in an outside gun. I don't doubt that Cicero picked who it would be. He's always been a 'top of the line' kind of guy. Besides, with him out the way the other two'll fall in line," Chicago replied.

He continued with specific instructions for everyone. While his strategy was not totally appreciated by some of his associates, I clearly understood what was going on.

GAMES

I spent the early part of the afternoon in an argument with the Lieutenant. It appeared that my surveillance work was effective. However, the Lieutenant didn't feel that threats were enough to warrant the kind of action I wanted. I knew he had a point, but I needed some damage control. After getting the details of Nicholas Movatto from the ball game with Cyprus, and hearing the call for work from the Italians, I wondered if Cyprus would be able to handle what he had gotten into.

I wouldn't be able to get the help I needed from the Lieutenant. I now felt that I would have to be on patrol with Cyprus as I had done for so long. I'd have to start tonight at the club.

As I got dressed for the evening, I talked with Dove and Supreme.

"Hey, partner, I don't think you wanna be no where near this shit when it goes down. Even the feds wanna wait and watch, you know. Clean up the garbage afterward," Supreme said.

"C'mon now, I know you two don't think I'm a hang back and fuckin' wait just so I can stand in line with ya'll, the DEA, and the feds. I'll be left with nothin' but dead bodies and a couple of bullshit leads to follow up on."

"I don't know why we bother talkin' to ya ass sometimes, Games. You got backup?" asked Dove.

"Not really."

"Now you do," said Dove.

"Cool."

With Dove, Supreme, and Tiny's help, I had just enough resources to throw a huge monkey wrench in any unlawful plans over the next couple of weeks.

DALI

suited up for this gig with an uneasy stomach. I found myself fighting to stay focused on what I'd be doing at the club. I contemplated being forthright with Allura. That notion disappeared quickly. I then moved on to thoughts of discontinuing my business relationship with Serenity, but the money convinced me otherwise. I contemplated a hiatus from playing to "get myself together," but I knew the band wouldn't be able to do much without me.

I took a page from Cyprus' book and trashed the introspection.

"You ready?" I asked as Allura came into the room wrapped in a towel.

"Ready? Honey, I just got out of the shower." She looked over at the clock. "We don't have to leave for another hour and a half."

"Hour and a…" I caught myself as I looked at the clock knowing that my mind was definitely somewhere else at this point.

"You okay, baby?"

"Oh, yeah, hon, I'm cool. Guess I just got a little bit too wrapped up in how me and the fellas were going to perform tonight."

"I never thought I would say this about a musician, but you work too hard." Allura's towel dropped, and she began to finger through some of her outfits.

"Maybe you're right. All work and no play can." I admired her backside before being cut short.

"Dali?" Allura pivoted around on one foot.

"Huh?"

"Are you looking at my ass?"

"Uh-huh."

"Isn't that how we ended up late last time?"

"Uh-huh."

"Do you want to be late tonight?"

"Uh-huh."

"Well, I don't."

"I kinda figured you were gonna say that." I walked over to her, grabbed her, and gave her a kiss.

"I guess we're going to be late again."

"Fashionably, honey, so don't worry," he returned.

"I won't."

BLUE

Avida and I prepared for Dali's gig like the world was ending tomorrow. She now had her essentials at my place; clothes, hair products, and an array of lotions, creams, perfumes, and other accessories. She never left the house "undone," but she seemed to put in extra effort when we went to hear Dali.

I constantly joked with her that I hoped she wasn't doing it for him, because he didn't like her due to the stress she caused me. A "fuck you" was generally her response.

Although running a bit late, Dali and Allura still managed to arrive a couple of minutes before the rest of us. He escorted Allura to the same booth where we all generally sat when we came to hear him play. He ordered a drink for her and sat for a quick minute to keep her company. Avida and I were right behind them. We made our way over to the booth and exchanged hellos before Dali headed for the stage.

Games and Cyprus arrived around the same time. I was not the least bit surprised when I noticed that the two of them came alone. They sat with Allura, Avida, and myself for a little while before taking a stroll over to the bar.

The club was no different on this night than it was any of the other times Dali and the band had played there. It was packed with folk who'd either heard him before or heard about him. Serenity worked every corner of the club in true diva fashion, welcoming and chatting with everyone.

"Goddamn, that is one tight-ass white woman," Bounce said, looking over Dali's shoulder at Serenity.

"You think?" Dali asked in a rather indifferent tone.

"What, you don't?" Bounce returned.

Dali shrugged coldly as he slowly turned around to look at her.

"What's wrong wit' you? You aiight?"

"Yeah, I'm cool. Ya'll ready?" Dali asked.

"Everybody's set," Bounce replied, literally bouncing up and down and twirling his drumsticks.

Dali stepped off the stage at the same time Serenity was walking toward it.

"You look good," she said.

"Yeah, well, we try to keep an image," Dali said.

"I said *you* look good."

"I think we may have to talk after the show."

"I agree," Serenity said before stepping up to touch her chest with his. Dali simply smiled, and stepped back with confidence and attitude. "I take that to mean you're ready to play."

"*We're* ready," Dali said, as he stepped back onstage.

Dali and the band were introduced with the usual "without further adieu" thing. They received their usual hearty welcome from the crowd. And, it was at that point, this gig for Dali became different from all the others. I noticed that Allura was observing Dali's interaction with Serenity. She was staring intently. I tried my best to divert her attention but to no avail.

Once I realized that my attempts weren't working I turned my attention to my own woman. Her eyes were taking interest in someone else. He was staring back.

"Do you two like what you see?" I whispered softly in her ear.

"What are you talking about?" I could feel that attitude of hers coming as she began to raise her voice.

"Listen, I want you to do three things for me, sweetheart. Relax, answer my question and don't even think of actin' an ass up in this bitch," I said. I placed my arm around her shoulders and kept my lips to her ear. "Do you two like what you see?"

"Baby, I do not know what you're talking about. You two who?"

"You and the Tyson Beckford look-a-like over at the table to our right."

"What? Honey, I don't have any control over what that nigga's eyes do and if you think I was looking at him, you're mistaken."

I simply sighed and chuckled softly as I removed my arm from her shoulders. I signaled the waitress for what was now a needed Tequila shot and Corona. Ordinarily, women can easily put a stop to a man's interrogation.

Avida had done so many times in the past, but her powers were beginning to wear thin and her body language was speaking louder than her words. Then again maybe it was that old paranoia of mine resurfacing. I don't believe the latter was the case.

I got up and joined Games and Cyprus at the bar. The two of them drinking and laughing as if they were co-workers from the same company.

"When that mufucka Gatta said, 'Fuck this gang-bangin' cocksucker,' I thought I was gonna shit. I was like, fuck, any second now and all I'm a hear is shots," said Games.

"Hell, it would've made your job easier," Cyprus said.

"Why you bullshittin'? I'd never get that lucky. So what you go'n do 'bout your boy?"

Cyprus asked, "Who? Chicago?"

"Uh-uh, Movatto."

"I ain't got no plans to do shit 'bout Movatto. I'm crazy, nigga, not stupid. I'm just go'n keep my ears and eyes open and look out for his ass. You?"

"Little bit of the same, I guess. Wait for him and anyone else for that matter. Try and move when they move, so watch yourself."

"Please. I'd see yo' ass comin' a mile away," said Cyprus.

"Good, then you shouldn't have a problem stayin' out the way," Games said arrogantly.

"True, but that can work just as much against me as it can for me."

"What the fuck you talkin' 'bout?"

"I ain't tryin' to be the only one who don't get caught if shit really gets rough wit' ya'll."

"What? I know you wouldn't take a pinch for these muthafuckas?" Games asked, truly astonished at Cyprus's response.

"Think about it. There ain't never been a situation where my peoples got busted wit' me around, without me gettin' busted along wit' 'em. The same goes on the other end. Now, whatever happens when niggas like Mo' and the rest of 'em get caught out there alone is between them and you. All I'm sayin' is keep doin' what you do and let shit fall where it's gotta. 'Cause if me and three other mufuckas get the same charge, I ain't tryin' to be the one gettin' out before everybody else. Might as well shoot my damn self."

"I hear that," Games replied, taking in all Cyprus had to say. "Aiight, cuz, I'm a stop beating around the bush wit' this. Besides, I'm on my way to gettin' drunk and I don't wanna miss anything important."

"What *you* talkin' 'bout?"

"I'm just tryin' to get a peg on what you know. A nigga ain't tryin' to see nothin' happen to either one of us."

"Man, I know you ain't go'n believe me, but I know what you know."

"No bullshit?" Games asked Cyprus, staring intently into his eyes.

"None at all," Cyprus, replied returning the intensity.

Games nodded in satisfaction, knowing that it was the truth.

"One thing's for sure," said Cyprus.

"What's that?"

"Shit's about to get ugly."

"No doubt." Games nodded again and laughed softly in response. The two of them continued to talk about everything but their jobs as they listened to Dali play. They were odd like that sometimes. Their relationship was a lot like a chess game with a concentration on the players as much as the game itself. Though they tended to work each other's nerves around what the other did for a living, they also seemed to leave the game as a game when they stepped away from the chess table.

Dali, too, seemed to be pretty comfortable though the manner in which he was playing was a bit different than I was used to hearing. The song he and the band were playing was fast-paced, filled with Dali's horn. The drums and bass served simply as background. Dali stood center stage blowing hard, leaning back, his eyes closed tight. He held his horn as if it were the only thing in life he ever owned. His frenzied blowing was burning his name in the hearts of the crowd. They loved it. I swear, it looked like no one in the club could look at anything but him. I was somewhat concerned. I knew Dali didn't play like this; angry, wild, and without control.

The band stayed with him for some time before they realized that something wasn't right. The last minute was nothing but Dali and Bounce, horn and drums. Their audience had never heard anything like it before. At this point, they were mesmerized. Mind you, this was only the first set.

Dali spent half of his break arguing with some of the members of his band and the rest with Cyprus, Games, and myself at the bar.

"'Sup wit' you?" I asked, looking to find out where his head was.

"I'm cool, whassup wit' ya'll? What's wrong?" he asked, staring at the three of us. I was a bit surprised to notice that Cyprus and Games picked up on the same nuances in Dali that I did.

"You tell us," Cyprus replied.

"What you talkin' 'bout?" Dali questioned. We'd known him too long. His mask was unconvincing.

"'Sup wit' how you playin', cuz?" Games asked.

"'Sup wit' how I'm playin'? How you sound? We hit that first set," Dali answered. The energy that motivated his performance was now becoming more apparent.

"It ain't about the set. The shit was tight. We just tryin' to figure out what's wit' you," I said.

"You ain't seem too much like yourself up there, cuz. Yeah, mufuckas was feelin' you and all. But that style ain't you," Games added.

"So what's up dog?" Cyprus asked.

"Nothin'. I'm cool. Damn, ya'll startin' to sound like therapists," Dali replied.

We followed his lead and ignored whatever was bothering him. It's probably why men have so many pent-up emotions. Women will talk anywhere about damn near anything with their close friends.

We weren't women, so we sat there for the few minutes of Dali's set break chatting about this, that and the other. We disregarded what we should have been discussing. I had a feeling that Allura and Avida were doing just the opposite. My guess is that they were taking this opportunity to get to know each other better and spend a little time commiserating.

I went back to the table sometime later to find the two of them engrossed in a conversation that probably revolved around men and our shortcomings. They looked at me as if they'd just found out I was sleeping with both of them. I didn't really give a shit. I was already pissed over Avida's previous behavior. Dali's little funk just seemed to add insult to injury. This was not how I had envisioned my evening.

The night finally came to an end with Dali returning to his old self during the last set. Games and Cyprus ended up leaving early. I wouldn't have minded following suit, given the opportunity. Avida and I hadn't said a word to each other since our argument earlier.

Allura waited for Dali as he went through his usual routine of meeting with Serenity to collect the evening's earnings. Ordinarily, Allura had no problem with waiting. She would spend the time talking with the servers and hostesses who knew her quite well. This twilight however would see Allura's ass on her back. She had more attitude than one of those guests on Jerry Springer's show. She was pissed off about Dali's interaction with Serenity.

DALI

Worldly women have an instinct for picking up on cues that men tend to ignore. Allura was definitely aware of the fact that something was wrong. I'd make my visit with Serenity a short one. I needed just a little time to nip a possible problem in the bud. It may have been too little too late.

"That was different," Serenity said as I stepped into the office.

"What was different?

"You just didn't seem much like yourself up there tonight, that's all."

"I didn't hear any complaints."

"Hey, I said it was different, not bad. Actually, all that energy you had up there was quite sexy. Reminded me of the other night." Serenity slowly began to approach me.

"Speaking of which, stop right there. I'd like to treat the other night as just that. One night and only one night. It's not good for business."

"Not good for business? Now that's new. From what I understand, sex is sex is sex as far as you're concerned. Business, pleasure. Who gives a shit, right?"

"Well, things change."

"Do they now? Let me guess. That little queen bee of yours that you bring here all the time must be getting to you. Amazing. Lorenzo Dali born again." She chuckled.

I had no response. I was being upstaged and flat out fronted on. Things like that never happen to me.

"Look, let's just settle up and leave it at that."

"It's on the table," Serenity sat down on her couch, smiling amiably at me as I grabbed the band's earnings. "I'll tell you what, hon. I'll keep it warm for you until this 'thing' of yours passes. We can just look at tonight's chat as water under the bridge."

I said nothing and simply left. As I walked out, Serenity chuckled again and shook her head before lighting a cigarette. The evening wouldn't get much better for me as things heated up before I could even get out of the club.

"You spend damn near as much time up in that office at the end of the night as you do on stage," Allura pronounced as I brought her coat to the booth.

"What's that supposed to mean?" I shot back angrily.

Allura's neck brought her head back far enough to where she looked like a mother who'd heard her child swear for the first time.

"Take me home, Lorenzo."

I could tell that the drive home would not be a pleasant one.

BLUE

I couldn't talk though. The evening wasn't a particularly spectacular one for Avida and myself. The drive home on our end just made things worse.

"So, who else are you fuckin'?" I asked nastily. I took the scenic route to my apartment.

"What? Fuck you!" Avida shouted.

"No, sweetheart, I already know about myself. I'm trying to figure out who *else* you're fuckin'?"

"I'm not sleeping with anyone else and I'm gettin' tired of this shit. I can't help it if somebody wants to look."

"I don't mind looks, but sometimes I get the strange feeling that you might be trying to fuck me over."

"Well, I'm not."

"That's cool. Just know though, tip out on me if you want to..."

"What you go'n do, Blue? Beat my ass." Her manner indicated that she knew I would never lay a hand on her.

"Of course not, baby. But I will kill you."

"Whatever, Blue."

We both chose to go to bed and get some sleep that evening. Still, the cool thing about long-term relationships though is that apologies go a long way.

The results of a sincere "I'm sorry" after an intense argument can be quite rewarding if your timing is right. So I offered the repentance the following morning.

Though there may have been merit to my argument, my approach lacked finesse. Men need tact more than women do in relationship-related arguments. I've heard women throw caution to the wind and lose it when it came to their men. I mean shouting, screaming, cursing. In public. She could be wrong as rain, but she's allowed that latitude. Then again, I guess depends on the man because some brothers won't hesitate to beat·the shit out of their woman. I'll leave trifling brothers out of the mix for 'arguments' sake. My point is, a man who loses his temper and flies off the deep end with his woman, usually ends up apologizing for losing his temper. Whatever he lost it over becomes secondary.

I say all of this to say that Avida more than likely was doing a little flirting with the Tyson Beckford look-a-like the previous evening. However, since I was insensitive in bringing my frustration around the matter to her attention, I'm the one bringing her breakfast in bed the next morning.

DALI

Allura didn't say a word to me during the drive to her condo. When we arrived, I attempted to speak but my words were met by a door slam as she got out of the car. I sat there for a couple of minutes after she went inside. Eventually, I chose to go home and speak with her the following day.

I wondered on my way home if Allura actually knew about Serenity or was she only hip to my going-ons due to women's intuition. Both were considerably dangerous, but I knew that I had a chance with the intuition thing.

I followed up on my decision to talk to Allura the following day. I don't know what in the world possessed me to call her at seven in the morning. I was definitely slippin'. I got her voicemail, so I had to settle for waiting until she woke up. I waited and waited and waited for what seemed like days before calling her again at nine.

"You up?" I asked.

"Yes, Lorenzo. What do you want?"

"Baby, what's up wit' you? Why you actin' like this?"

"Like what?"

"What's wit' the attitude?"

"Let me guess. You have no idea why I would be upset? You're totally clueless? My behavior just doesn't make sense to you, right?" Each question seemed more sarcastic than the last.

"Yeah, somethin' like that."

"You really must have dealt with some simple bitches in your past."

"What?" I was astonished by her language.

"Are you fuckin' that white girl?"

The inquiry was shot at me faster than I was prepared for.

"What?"

"You heard me, Lorenzo. The white woman. Serenity. Your manager or whatever you call her."

"Allura?" I called her name as if to again question why she was behaving in this manner. In all honesty, I didn't know how to reply. I'd passed the point of lying to Allura.

"You know, honey, I trusted you. More than that, I think I was falling in love with you." Her voice was now beginning to shake. "I know I can't prove shit. I don't have a videotape or pictures, but I'm not a fuckin' fool. I've had the misfortune of being around enough triflin'-ass niggas to know when something's going on."

"Allura, sweetheart, what are you talking about? Why you trippin'?"

"Trippin'? Lorenzo, I asked you a question earlier that you still haven't answered."

And I still couldn't. All I could do was sit there, silent. I didn't know what to do or say.

"I guess I should be glad that you didn't lie to me."

"Allura, listen," I said calmly before taking a huge breath. "How about I come pick you up and we can go out for a bite to eat. You know just you and I and maybe we could talk or..."

"I don't think so."

"Baby, wait a minute."

She hung up before I could finish.

CYPRUS

fuckin' spent half the week searching for Nick Movatto. Hoping to find him before he could get to Fat Chicago Tone. My patience was beginning to wear thin. I was at a point now where I remembered why I turned to a life of crime. Taking orders was not my cup of tea and all of the running around was starting to get on my nerves.

I like to let the drama come to me, rather than hunting it down. I can see everything coming that way. As I saw it, you go looking for trouble, nine times out of ten you'll find it. I supported Chicago's decisions in the past, but I felt that this one was hasty. Movatto was called for a job. That meant he was coming and there wasn't much you could do to stop it. To me, that's an even playing field. Sending guys out to find Nick Movatto was like being a quarterback and sending all your players out for the Hail Mary. There's a good chance someone might catch the pass. There's also a good chance you might get sacked before you can get the ball off.

As I drove around in circles through various neighborhoods in the city, I took a minute to look at my current situation. En route to Chicago's home, I thought about what I wanted out of my affiliation with Chicago. The answer was obvious. The same thing every up-and-coming gangster wants: power and respect. Money is a given. Now that I think about it, so are the other two. Even still, I knew that I'd never be able to obtain such entities as a henchman. Though I was known for just that, I also knew that survival and success took ninety percent brains and ten percent brawn.

I thought about how I got myself into a situation where as Chicago both trusted me and respected my input. I wanted and needed a promotion. I realized, as I neared Chicago's home, that I could only get one by being patient and playing my cards right. Basically that meant dealin' wit' Movatto in the way I wanted. Sometimes, personal agendas can be a great thing.

I arrived at Chicago's to find him surfing the net for information on the FBI and CIA. It's amazing how far gangsters have come since the days of Prohibition and Tommy guns. I stood and waited a couple of minutes before I was able to speak with Chicago.

"FYI, Cyprus, I don't care too much for unannounced visits," Chicago said as he logged off and led me to his study.

I glanced around the large room to find what looked like a public library. Books covered the four walls with only a black marble table and four matching chairs occupying the floor. It wasn't exactly what I would put in my place but I was still impressed.

"You read much, Cyprus?" he asked, motioning for me to have a seat.

"Probably not as much as I should."

"You should work on that. You can find information about damn near everything in books. Years from now, all this shit we do is gonna be in somebody's book. White kids be readin' 'bout us. Then again, nowadays technology is pretty much phasin' out all that library shit, anyway. I had to catch up and make that Internet move myself."

I nodded.

"What's on your mind, cuz? I know you didn't come up here to hear me talk about books."

"It's about the Movatto thing."

"What about it?"

"To be honest, we ain't go'n find 'em if we lookin' for 'em."

"Why not? If you need more people, that's no problem."

"Won't help."

Chicago again asked the question "Why not?"

"Look, Movatto's a ghost 'til show time. The same way you wanted me to lay low after that job I did for you. He ain't gonna be found and no bullshit, if somebody just happens to get lucky and stumbles across his ass"

"No good for them, either," Chicago interjected.

"None at all."

"I gotta tell you, Cyprus, I'm a bit surprised at your amazement with our friend, Nicholas. I knew you understood what kind of work he did, but I now see a definite respect for him on your part. I'm not quite sure how to take that."

"You can take it how you want." I shrugged my shoulders. "I wouldn't get too far in my line of work if I just brushed off every bad guy in the business. Movatto got more hits under his belt than anyone I know and I'm familiar with damn near everybody's work. He's not your ordinary bag man."

Chicago sat quietly back in his chair. I waited for a response.

"So what do you suggest?" he asked.

I suggested that Chicago keep me right by his side at all times for a while. I'd be the only one ready enough to deal with Movatto. The Italians brought him in for one thing. To kill Chicago and make it look good.

GAMES

knew that just waiting would leave me like a family showing up at a Fourth of July kick-off five minutes after the fireworks show—disappointed. I'd already heard that Cyprus was out combing the streets to find Movatto. I was unaware that Cyprus now had a new plan. I did the regular asking around, but it was to no avail. I considered shaking up a few of my snitches for information but I wasn't sure who to try. Besides, it would take up too much time. I thought about giving Cyprus a call, but decided against it. I'd been in this situation before and I hated it just as much now as I did then. So I continued to wait.

DALI

I was in pretty bad shape by the end of week. Allura wouldn't take any of my calls and wouldn't see me. I hoped she simply needed a little time. Calling her four to five times a day was probably only making things worse. I canceled practice sessions with the band and was seriously considering canceling next weekend's gig. Allura had pulled another first on me. My mind was now consumed by something other than music.

I spent the past couple of days cleaning my place. It was spotless by Wednesday. I suppose it was apparent that I wasn't sure what to do with myself. A part of me was lost without her. I was now reduced to a lovesick high school boy.

I was head over heels in love with a woman who had unknowingly stripped me of all of the garbage that make men troublesome for women. Now that my place was clean I had to find something else to do.

BLUE

Avida had come home late a couple of evenings. She told me she was hang-ing out with friends. On one occasion she said she stopped by Allura's to talk for a while. Those two getting together didn't sound good but I let it ride. I've always been one of those pick-your-battles kind of guys.

Avida chose this evening to come home at three forty-five a.m. Call me old-fashioned, but I've always had a problem with people who stay out to the wee hours without their romantic partner knowing exactly what they're doing. To me, that behavior is reserved for single folk. It's a sacrifice you make when you commit yourself to someone. I just think a phone call never hurts. I've slipped up myself a couple of times, but Avida is notorious for this. I never know where she is and she generally catches an attitude when I question her about it. Unluckily for her, she'd be going to bed with an attitude. She arrived to find me sitting on the couch playing my Sony PlayStation.

"Hey, baby, I didn't expect you to be awake," she said, coming in and locking the door behind her.

"I have trouble sleeping when my woman's out 'til damn near four in the morning and doesn't call."

"Don't start. Besides, why didn't you call me?"

"I did. Twice."

"Twice? You sure? I didn't..." She fumbled through her purse to find the pager that she never answered.

"Where were you?" I asked.

"I was out with Cheryl and Denise."

"Cheryl and Denise? What happened to Keisha and Diane?"

"Keisha and Diane? Oh...change of plans," she replied.

"Change of plans?"

"Yes, change of plans. What's with the third degree?"

"It's cool, hon. I was just worried about you, that's all. Come here for a minute."

"What?"

"Come here, please."

She walked over slowly and stood in front of my open legs, as I sat on the couch. I gave her a big hug around her thighs and behind, sliding my hands up her thighs under her skirt. I brought my hands back out and as I reached up to undo the button of her skirt, she stopped me.

"What's wrong?" I asked.

"Oh, nothing. We were over at Cheryl's, dancin' and playing around and shit. I just need a quick shower, that's all. Give me a minute, I'll be right back."

I loved her more than life itself. Loving someone that much can either give you a sixth sense or make you dumb. I knew Avida well and, she couldn't lie for shit. She'd been out hundreds of times dancing, working out, doing whatever women do that could possibly cause them to perspire. If there's one thing she should know about me it's that I could give a shit about her period, let alone a little sweat. Was my paranoia possibly kicking in again? I don't know. I was getting sick of using that as an excuse for having my head up my ass.

CYPRUS

The weekend crept up on all of us. It rained all day leaving the early evening wet and cold. Friday never seemed so dark. Perhaps, a stage was being set. The way I see it, you can't have shit hit the fan without the mood being right.

Chicago was now traveling with a small caravan of three cars, his own Lincoln Navigator truck with four of his men and another car. Me and my crew followed. We would spend the evening at one of Chicago's clubs where he would feel safe. A place where there was no such thing as the unexpected. Chicago was hungry, and, ironically, wanted to stop at his favorite Italian restaurant for an early dinner.

Me and my crew were waiting as Chicago got out of his truck and began to make his way to the restaurant. I saw that we'd been followed the whole time. Chicago's caravan had parked in a back lot behind the restaurant. A lot with only one entrance.

Chicago's people looked around casually under the impression that everything was okay. I walked to the entrance of the lot to find three vans parked directly in front of the restaurant door.

"Shit." I made a quick U-turn to the parking lot. Chicago and everyone else were heading toward me, en route to the entrance.

I signaled for them to turn around, but it was too late. Someone in one of the vans must have spotted me. I heard all the engines of the vans start up. In a matter of seconds, the three vans blocked the entrance of the parking lot. I walked briskly to Chicago and his entourage looking back over my shoulder every couple of seconds.

"What's up?" Chicago asked, as I got closer to them.

"Looks like it's time to go to work," I said, and with my reply came company. As Chicago and everyone made their way back to the cars, they saw what I was talkin' about. The parking lot quickly filled with men from the vans. More guys than I expected, but I was ready. It turned into a small war. Chicago's young soldiers were hungry and ready. They posted themselves behind any and everything they could find.

Within ten seconds the parking lot was full and the two sides opened fire. To see it would be to watch one of those big-budget action movies. It looked like no one was getting hit and, at they rate they were going, the Italians would back off. That wasn't going to be the case. The parking lot had only one entrance, but it was an entrance for cars. Movatto's shooters managed to find a backway opening to the lot.

Now only two vans were blocking the entrance. The third van was parked behind Chicago and his men. Chicago's soldiers tried to hold their post, but they were outnumbered. They began to drop like flies. They were able to cut down anything in front of them, but they weren't expecting the attack from behind. Me and Chicago returned fire from the back of his Navigator. It was only to be defensive. All they could do was shoot to keep from getting shot. It took everything in my power to keep Chicago from jumping out and assisting his young warriors.

"Fuck!" Chicago shouted.

"I told you this would happen. Just be cool, you'll get your time, trust me."

"Fuck that shit! I can't go out like this, fuckin' sittin' around..."

"Shit."

"What?" Chicago asked

"Grab that M-16 from the backseat," I instructed Chicago.

"Why?"

"Round two."

Seven of Chicago's men along with my crew lay dead in the lot, but it was only the beginning. Movatto had only lost half of his men. That left at least another dozen. Shots now opened up on Chicago's truck and the two vans blocking the entrance now moved into the lot. I spotted Movatto in the passenger seat of the second van.

"You may wanna think about openin' that bitch up 'cause we ain't got nowhere to go." I noticed that the vans continued to block the entrance of the lot.

"Don't worry about it. This muthafucka's bulletproof. Now where the fuck is Movatto?"

We hopped into the driver and passenger seats of Chicago's truck. I was behind the wheel. I spun the truck quickly to the left and right as Chicago sprayed bullets out of the passenger side window at anything he could see. The shots continued at the truck from everywhere. I knew that it was only a matter of time before someone got a piece of the engine.

"Fuck this muthafucka, Cyprus! Spin this bitch around so I'm facing his punk ass."

"Fuck that, Chicago," I wanted to let the combination of Chicago's bulletproof Navigator and the M-16 assault rifle work for us.

"Don't fuck with me on this," said Chicago.

"Shit." I spun the truck around where Chicago and Movatto were face-to-face. They opened up on each other with gunfire but it was Movatto who came out on top. Movatto and Chicago seemed to pull triggers at the same time but it was Chicago who dropped his gun. He was shot in his arm and shoulder. Movatto got out of the van and methodically walked toward the truck, continuing to shoot out the tires and grille. I turned the vehicle to face him. The lot was clear at this point. Movatto's remaining gunmen retreated to the vans, leaving only Movatto, me, and Chicago. I kept the engine running as I looked over at Chicago. Movatto stopped to reload while I waited. All I could think to do was hit the gas and head straight for Movatto.

Movatto was locked and loaded. The muthafucka smiled at me. I revved the motor hard as Movatto raised his gun, but before a shot could be fired and I could put the truck in drive, a large spotlight from a police helicopter hit the parking lot like a ray of sun. The helicopter came over the back end of the lot and was accompanied by patrol cars at the entrance. With that, Movatto quickly made his exit.

"Hey C, I want that muthafucka's ass alive, hear. Bring him to me," Chicago said, his voice tired.

"I got 'em. You aiight?"

"Yeah, shit went in an out. Go 'head and get his ass."

I got out of the truck and took off after Movatto on foot. The police got everyone left from the three vans.

I ran full steam down a nearby alley. I knew Movatto couldn't be far. I was blocked at the end of the alley by a blue sedan. It seemed to be waiting for me.

"Oh shit." I said Cyprus, stopping a few feet from the car.

"What the fuck you waitin' for, get in!!!" Games shouted.

I ran over to the passenger side of the sedan, got in and Games hit the gas.

"What the fuck are you doin' here?" I was confused but happy to see the detective.

"You can't be serious." Games replied smugly. He looked at me as if I was a complete fool. "It took me fuckin' forever to get all that backup and you talkin' 'bout 'what am I doin' here'? Shit, I'm workin.'"

"Hey, no bullshit, dog, I can't say that I ain't happy to see ya ass. You got timin' like a muthafucka. Wait. Wait a minute, hold up. Stop the car."

"What?"

"I can't believe it."

"What?"

"Right there."

"Oh shit." Games saw Movatto calmly walking down the street just five or six blocks from the restaurant that was previously a war zone.

"You see 'em?" I asked.

"Yeah, hold on."

Games slowly drove up the street, closing in on Movatto. The streets were empty.

This wasn't the first time me and Games had "worked" together. Ever since the first time we found ourselves after the same person, we had an understanding between us. No matter what happened, I had to leave the area. Games would get the official credit for it. We were fine with the arrangement.

Games pulled his car to the corner and parked. We got out and waited. Movatto halted calmly as he approached the corner. Tilting his head, he stared at the two men in front of him.

"Your call," Games informed Movatto.

Nick stood motionless for a second. It was my guess that he was preparing himself. He raised his hands and carefully pointed to the inside of his coat.

"Slowly," Games returned. His gun was aimed at Movatto. I stood behind Games' car with my gun out by my side.

"Fuck that," I added.

"If he's carryin', I wanna know," said Games.

"Shit, man, I don't know." Movatto cautiously unzipped his coat to reveal two 9mm's in holsters under his arms.

"Nice," Games stated. "You're gonna have to come up off of those."

Movatto took a deep breath, but said nothing.

"I think we 'bout to have a problem." I said.

"I think you're right,." Games replied. Something in Movatto's eyes indicated he had no intentions of submitting quietly.

We were right. Movatto reached for his 9's and opened fire. We returned fire at the same time. It seemed that at least thirty shots were fired in a matter of seconds. The result appeared to leave the three of us wounded, if not dead on that corner. Games with two shots to the chest and me with bulletholes in my side, arm, and shoulder. Movatto took more than we did. I was sure he took several hits to his chest, lower body, and head, for that matter. I was sure.

Games managed to prop himself up on the door of the sedan.

"Shit, that hurt." he said as he unbuttoned his shirt and removed his bullet-proof vest. "Cyprus?"

"Yeah."

"You alright?"

"Yeah, but I need to get patched up pretty quick. This bleeding shit ain't cool."

Games walked over to the other side of the car. I was sitting against the wheel of the car getting ready to light a cigarette.

"Can you drive?" Games asked.

"Yeah. I got somebody not too far from here should be able to tighten me up. Where's Movatto?"

"Muthafucka should be right over there where we left his ass, dead." Games helped me to my feet.

"I knew he was gonna reach for his shit 'cause—"

"What the fuck!!!" we exclaimed simultaneously.

We were reacting to what we were looking at. No blood. No body. No Movatto.

"Take the car," Games told me as he walked to the small piece of cement where he could have swore was...

DALI

I still didn't want to speak to anyone but Allura, so I spent the entire week at home. I canceled my first gig ever. Serenity went nuts, but the band was okay with it. They had no trouble making money on the side.

I sat on the couch that weekend, smoking weed and flipping through the channels. My phone and caller ID were close by. Stepping outside of my normal behavior, I chuckled frequently. I couldn't believe that I turned down a gig because of a woman. I hadn't practiced for days. I just didn't feel like it.

BLUE

Both Dali and I had reached a point where emotional stress, distractions, and love had both of us questioning everything. I started to feel as though we could start a support group for men in relationships that had grown beyond our control. Unlike Dali I realized that no one person can control a relationship. I knew that either my paranoia had gotten the best of me or my love for a woman had brought some clarity to a clouded mind. Avida had lied to me and we both knew it. More than that, she'd done so in the past and we both knew it. I also knew that to lose her would be to lose me.

I believe that is why people sometimes run from the truth, because it occasionally hurts beyond imagination and understanding. I would prefer to lose my own life than to lose Avida. Would I have to pay that price to uncover her possible betrayal?

I spent a long time wondering about my next step. Was it right? Was it morally and logically sound? I decided to go with my gut. So this weekend, she had plans. I had my own. I was going to follow her every step of the way.

DALI

It was Sunday afternoon when common sense found its way back into my thick skull. I would apologize my ass off to win back the woman I loved. Over the course of a week, Allura arrived at work each day to find an array of flowers, gifts, and cards of poetry waiting for her. More of the same awaited her when she came home. I went all out, using the city's oldest and finest florist to inundate Allura with the best. I made sure that every gift and bouquet of flowers was accompanied with a personal letter explaining my feelings for her. I also apologized for not being truthful with her.

Monday became Wednesday, and Wednesday eventually fell into Friday. My time, emotional torture, and sensitive efforts eventually paid off. She called.

"Hello," I answered, looking at the caller ID. My heart was beating a mile a minute.

"Are you trying to get my attention, Lorenzo?"

"Only if it's available?"

"Why do you keep sending me stuff and how much did all of this cost?" Allura asked.

"Like you said, I'm trying to get your attention. As far as cost is concerned, there's no price for repentance."

"Lorenzo, I don't know if I'm ready to talk to you. I mean I—"

"Baby, I know you have every reason to hang up the phone and close the books on me."

"What do you want from me, Lorenzo?"

"I just want you to know how I feel about you. Honey, I've spent two weeks doing absolutely nothing but praying that I would get an opportunity to talk to you again. Dig this, I could make two weeks a month, a year for that matter. I can't practice, I can't play, I can't concentrate on anything but you."

"What do you want me to do?"

"Dinner and that's all. All I want to do is see you and talk to you."

Allura waited for a couple of seconds before replying to my request. I didn't say a word. I awaited her answer in the manner a fighter would wait for a decision about a championship belt.

"I'll expect you at eight."

"I'll be there at five 'til."

BLUE

The following week would be one of waiting, watching, and worrying for me. As Dali was working toward repairing his bond with Allura, I was in the process of trying to figure out if my role was that of a stupid fool in love.

I briefly and separately spoke with Games and Cyprus that Monday. They told me the short version of their story. Though a part of me was certainly happy that Games and Cyprus were okay, ninety percent of my brain was fastened on Avida. I'd decided mid-week to rent a car and follow her after work. Was that legal?

The week floated by quickly. Either Avida was really slick or my fear was continuing to get the best of me. I followed her for three days. She went from work to one of her girlfriends. From work to the store and from work to a series of errands that ended up running me tired. Eventually, I said to hell with the whole thing. I was beginning to feel like even more of a fool, than I had when I came up with the idea.

I returned the rental and drove back home in my own car. If disloyalty was playing a part in my relationship, it would have to raise its head.

DALI

I arrived three minutes before I was supposed to. I'd been in the doghouse before, so I knew not to push my luck with anything. The mood was a light one between us. We made small talk about everything imaginable.

Our conversation over dinner was pretty much the same. One would wonder why we were waiting to get to the nitty-gritty. Finally, I simply couldn't take it anymore.

"Honey, I don't know if I should bring this up or not, timing being everything and all, but what are we gonna do?"

Allura took a deep breath before answering. "I don't know, Lorenzo. I have to say that I now know the true meaning of mixed emotions. I don't know if I'm ready to just let the past be the past and jump back into the way things were."

"I understand. I guess I just don't want things to end like this. I mean I'm not perfect, never have been really, and I know you don't expect me to be. What I'm tryin' to say is that there's something about you that's found a place in my heart. I just don't want you to leave me over this. I know I'm triflin' and I know you got no reason to believe anything I have to say. Hell, I know you probably heard this speech before. But I've come to realize recently, that there are some things in life more important than myself."

"I appreciate your honesty. I think there can be a way to make you and I, we again, but it's going to take time. I'm sick and tired of bullshit with men."

I nodded in agreement.

"I don't expect you to jump back in bed with me like this ordeal never happened. I don't want you to be a man with the tolerance of a two-year-old, moving on to something else because you're not getting your way," she declared.

I continued to nod. I never listened to someone that intently in my life. My mother would've been shocked. And, after she finished speaking, I suggested something amazing.

"I can settle for being friends. You know, kinda let the future be the future and take whatever it has to give as far as we're concerned." I said.

"I like your thinking, Lorenzo," Allura returned with a smile.

We treated that discussion as we did dinner, allowing it to sit on our system and slowly digest. We ordered dessert and picked up where we left off with the small talk. It was new territory for both of us. I hadn't been solely a friend to a woman since I was a kid. Allura was exploring unfamiliar aspects of herself in trusting a man even the slightest bit after he'd betrayed her. I suppose you can't always treat relationships and people as you would a job. The manuals, policies, procedures and rules don't always apply. True love is without limitations and could care less about how-to books on managing and maintaining your man or woman. *True love* is just that. *Love* and *truth*.

BLUE

The weekend arrived to find Avida and I at home in bed. Oddly enough, we weren't engaged in much outside of just talking. Living together seemed to give our relationship a new breath of life. She'd only been there for a couple of weeks and, though it wasn't a long period of time, I knew it was something that I could get used to. Everything was perfect for me. I had decided to ignore my suspicion about Avida. As I looked at her sometimes, I saw my mind clearing itself in the way clouds do when they make room for the sun, after a storm. My dementia, neurosis, and overall fear of losing her no longer felt like a great concern to me. Being in love with a woman no longer felt like a chokehold. It felt like the blessing that it really was. My feelings for her were liberating. Like Dali, I could identify with a child exploring something new, something good.

I smiled to myself as these thoughts ran through my head. What in the hell was wrong with me? Nothing. Nothing but entirely too much worrying and way too much thinking. And Avida. She made her home my home now and, as far as I was concerned, that was all that mattered. That was the only thing of importance and my heart knew that she felt the same.

"What are you smiling about?" she asked, leaning on her side, facing me.

"Oh, nothin', just thinkin'."

"Uh-oh," she said sarcastically.

"No, no not like that. It's good thinking."

"What about?"

"You and me, really, not much else."

"What about you and me?" she persisted.

"Well, I was just thinkin' about how literally crazy I've been over the years. You know, losin' my temper and all. I guess I just had a uh, what's it called, a uh...moment of clarity, you know. All that shit just seemed a little...stupid."

Her reply was simply a look of surprise. We continued to talk about various things before being interrupted by a phone call from Cyprus. He was feeling better from his ordeal and wanted to get together with everyone available. Just to do a little bullshittin' and drinkin' as we'd been doing before things started to get sticky. I was game. Avida said she would spend the evening pampering herself—bubble bath, manicure, pedicure, and the like.

I was en route to Cyprus about a half-hour after I got off the phone. I was feeling damn good. The four of us had been through some interesting shit over the past month. Everything seemed to have worked out for the best.

I was looking forward to spending time with the fellas. I informed Avida that I planned to be out all night and probably into the morning. I arrived at Cyprus' place to find that I was the only one able to make it. Games got tied up with work and Dali was working to re-establish a strict "business" relationship with Serenity. She wasn't too happy about that. Cyprus and myself would catch them the next time. It actually worked out quite well for me because there was more food, weed, and liquor for the two of us.

Cyprus and I spent a good part of the night drinking and smoking as he narrated, with boyish excitement, every detail of what happened with Fat Chicago Tone, Movatto, Games, and himself. He received the promotion he was looking for. It seems Chicago appreciated both his initiative and his ability to keep them both alive, even though he was unable to actually catch Movatto.

"So what happened to 'em?" I asked.

"Who?"

"Movatto?"

"Oh, shit, dog, I don't know. I mean we hit that muthafucka, a lot. A whole lot. I swear we wasn't but a few feet away from his ass," Cyprus replied, filling our glasses with the last bit of our second bottle of Hennessy.

"What? He just up and left?"

"Disappeared."

"Bullshit?"

"I'm serious, mufucka vanished. Ask Games."

"That's some weird shit." The alcohol and marijuana were now truly having its way with my motor skills. I fumbled around like a novice with a cigar, in my attempt to roll yet another blunt.

"Man, who you tellin'? I had to tell Chicago that me and Movatto both got hit and his ass managed to hobble away before I could finish him."

"I hope you left out the part about Games being there."

"Oh, hell yeah. Them niggas would have my head if—"

A phone call managed to cut Cyprus off before he could speak more on the repercussions of his friendship with Games. The evening was going well. We'd been eating buckets of spiced shrimp over the course of the night so the heavy alcohol and drug consumption had us only drunk as hell, rather than ready to pass out. I called Avida at one a.m. but she didn't answer. I figured she was in the shower and didn't think twice about it. As I continued to fill my lungs with smoke, I could tell from Cyprus' end of the telephone conversation that he was looking to make other late-night plans. Word gets around fast. And word of Cyprus' injury made its way to his two divas, who were of course, concerned.

"No, no, I'm alright. Just a little sore, that's all...ya'll wanna do what?!" he said almost choking on his drink. A devilish grin was slowly forming on his face. He didn't have to say much more. After hanging up the phone, he leaned back slowly on his couch and let out a laugh which sounded almost hysterical. "Dog, I got to tell ya. I've been shot three times and you would not fuckin' believe how much pussy you can get because of that shit. No bullshit, you gotta try it."

We both enjoyed a laugh at that. Cyprus may have been one of the dirtiest characters on the face of the earth, but he was always honest. I gave him his respect and made him promise to give me details as I departed.

Though our evening was cut short, and I was heading home two or three hours earlier than I expected, I left feeling better than I had when I arrived. I made my way home slowly. God forbid, I screw up my chances for sex by getting locked up for a DUI.

All that I had feared for the four of us was gone now. The past was present and the present was working to our benefit. There was a time when I considered myself a troubled soul. Even then, I wasn't exactly sure what it meant. Now, I didn't care. Things were going my way. I was finally happy.

I made it home safely but I found some old friends waiting for me. Old friends who I'd recently broken off my relationship with. Old friends who made me believe that no one would truly love me. Old friends who taught me pain, anguish, frustration, paranoia and mostly importantly, the remedy for a destroyed heart—psychotic abandonment.

My old friends were the demons I'd carried with me for so long that they'd become a permanent fixture in my life. Trying to lead me to what I refused to see. They made me look at the gray Ford Explorer parked directly in front of me. I swear to God Almighty above, I tried not to.

Looks familiar no? they asked. Like the car that dropped her off some time ago. The car you questioned her about. The car that you chose to forget about because you love her so much. And she, of course, loves you, right?

I ignored what I saw, though I could not deny my eyes. I tried to remind myself that I was drunk and whatever I'd smoked must have been playing tricks on me. I stood looking at the familiar back license plate numbers of that vehicle. The plates I promised myself to remember. They were the fucking same. Just a coincidence, I reassured myself, making my way to the door. Just a coincidence.

Unlocking the door silently and walking in, I thought of something I once heard. *If you think you're losing your mind, you most probably aren't.* BULLSHIT. Insanity is as clear and concise as reason. It is only the sane that don't realize it.

I crept into my apartment. She wasn't alone. I know I didn't just hear a man's voice coming from my bedroom. I had to be dreaming. What did I ever do to deserve this? I felt a calm overtake me. Was it to relax me? Was it to console me in preparation for the truth?

Cyprus got himself into some trouble a couple of years back and gave me something to hold. I thought nothing of it at the time. Under any other circumstances, I don't doubt that I would have forgotten its location. I looked at it now like a newborn child. In essence, that's exactly what it was. My baby. Given the fact that I didn't have a use for them, I'd never been big on guns. This one, however, provided me with comfort as if I'd bought it myself.

The stroll to the bedroom was longer than usual. She had the fuckin' nerve to have the door wide open.

"Hello, sweetheart," I said, pointing the pump shotgun at the nude gentleman lying on my side of the bed, actually cuddled up next to her.

"Oh, my God," Allura gasped, her hand to her mouth.

"It's a bit too late for that call now, hon'. You two look cozy. Is that my bottle of wine?" I aimed the pump shotgun toward a bottle of Merlot that I'd been looking forward to enjoying when the opportunity presented itself. It looked like they beat me to it.

"Hey look, cuz, relax. This ain't even how it—"

Some folks just don't know when to keep their mouths shut. Out of pure disgust, I let the shotgun finish his statement for him. He had fuckin' balls to even consider opening his mouth to speak in a situation like this.

The funny thing was that I had planned on letting him get dressed and leave. Instead, there was blood all over the place from the two shots I fired. All you could see was his head and legs, which was fine by me. Everything else in between was pretty much a wet, red mess. I understood at that point what Cyprus got out of this gun action. It was damn exhilarating.

"What's wrong, hon'?" I asked, now turning my attention and the shotgun toward Avida.

She jumped instantly when I shot Mr. "Let Me Explain." She was standing next to the bed crying hysterically, shouting, "Oh, my God."

"You're fuckin' crazy!" She cried, looking at the splattered blood on her chest.

"Maybe, but it's not like you're in a position to point fingers, if you know what I mean," I calmly replied.

"You didn't have to kill him," she said, continuing to cry as she looked over at him.

"See, there you fuckin' go again. Your priorities are all wrong, baby." She kind of pissed me off by being more concerned with the dead fuck lying in my bed.

"Blue, I'm sorry," she said, sobbing uncontrollably as I aimed the shotgun at her head.

"I know, sweetheart. I wish I had the time and patience to sit and listen to you explain your way out of this one. It's just too late for that now. Besides, I told you before not to fuck with me."

"Please, Alex, I'm sorry…" She began to walk toward me.

"If it's any consolation, Avida, I'll always love you and I'm sorry, too."

The burst from the shot sent her body across the room like a teddy bear being tossed in a corner by some child. I stood there for a second and then I walked over to the nightstand. I poured myself a glass of the wine. It was better than I thought it would be. By that time, I could hear sirens outside. I took one last look at my apartment, grabbed one of my duffel bags, filled it with photo albums, my portfolio, two bottles of Tequila and the shotgun. I chuckled to myself and a tear managed to bless my face.

I bumped into several police officers as I came off of the elevator and strolled through the lobby. I tapped one of them on the shoulder and said that the shots fired came from apartment 523. I wondered, as I got into my car, how long it would take them to figure out that it was my place.

I promised myself earlier that evening that I would try to lay off all the heavy thinking I used to do. I couldn't help it at this point, though. I found it interesting that I felt pretty good. Murder is actually quite liberating. Still, I knew my relaxed mood wouldn't last long. It was only a matter of time before reality made its way back into my life. I also wondered if I would be haunted by what I had just done. Again, as I drove around heading for an unknown destination, there was an emptiness forming inside me. I was beginning to become more content with that than afraid of it.

Life had dealt me an interesting hand and I had chosen an even more interesting way to play it. I'd lost my soul in my apartment that night. Either because I decided to, or because I had no choice at all. I suppose that's what living is all about. I believed after things were going well with Avida, I had thought everything through, figured out the questions, and come up with the right answer. I should have seen Avida's overactive social life a mile away. Actually, I probably did. Still, I wanted her.

The details of the shootings, oddly enough, were slowly starting to become distant memories. Today would mark a new beginning for me. I was one with an unclear past and unknown future. Things hadn't gone the way that I wanted them to, but I was now in another place. I was moving on with some regret, a little resentment, and no remorse.

GAMES

I was the investigating officer for the double homicide at apartment #523. I don't know how that happened, but I wasn't surprised. I didn't have much to say when I arrived at the apartment that I'd spent so many good times in. It seemed so familiar to me at one glance and simply like a crime scene in another. The cameras, fingerprint dust, and officers all over the place made me physically cold. I perused the area and gradually made my way to the bedroom.

"What do you think?" the coroner asked.

I walked over to Avida's body and knelt down then glanced over at the body on the other side of the bed. "I don't know."

"You don't know? C'mon, Games, look around. From what it looks like, he pops this fella over here twice, then shoots the girl. Witnesses said a little time passed before the last shot. Maybe two or three minutes."

"He was talking to her," I said.

"How do you know?" the coroner questioned.

"They were goods friends of mine."

"Well, we got an ID on these two. What's the shooter's name?"

I chose to leave rather than answer. Blue knew I'd be looking for him. It's my job. It was a raw deal. I wasn't sure if I'd ever find him. There were times when Blue would be seen only when he wanted to be.

EPILOGUE

Before moving on, I stopped by Dali's place to see my friends one last time, one last Friday. It was good to see that they were still getting together. I watched them from across the busy boulevard in front of Dali's. The three of them emerged from Cyrpus' car with what appeared to be bags from the liquor store. They looked different from the last time I saw them, not as many laughs and smiles. Cyprus headed inside and glanced back at Dali who was still standing next to his car.

"'Sup, dog? You comin'?" he asked Dali.

"In a minute," he replied.

Dali must have had one of those feelings you get when someone's staring at you. He looked around for a couple of minutes. Searching for nothing but allowing his eyes to be aware of everything. They moved slowly from his left to his right before they met what they never expected.

Dali and I looked at each other for only seconds but it was long enough to exchange a smile. The destruction and disappearance of a dear friend plus a busy boulevard can play tricks on one's eyes. For with a blink of his eyes, Dali was only watching the traffic and nothing more. Still, I had not gone far. I would always be with the three of them, in some form or fashion. And they all knew it. Especially Dali.

That was the world that we lived in. One where the bad guys don't always get caught. The guy doesn't always get the girl, and life itself is rarely, if ever, fair.

ABOUT THE AUTHOR

Kimani Kinyua has been a resident of the Washington, D.C. area for more than fifteen years. He graduated from Howard University in 1995 with a Bachelor's Degree in Journalism. He is currently an Information Technology professional in Washington, D.C. with a number of published technology-related articles in trade magazines. He is also a single parent and uses his experiences as a father in many of his literary projects. Visit www.kimanikinyua.com

IF YOU ENJOYED "THE BROTHERHOOD OF MAN,"
BE SURE TO LOOK FOR

A DANGEROUS RETURN

BY RIQUE JOHNSON

STREBOR BOOKS, SPRING 2007

PROLOGUE

Jason fulfilled his promise of taking his soul mate to dinner and later returned home for their chosen dessert selection, each other. Afterwards, Monique lay with her head on his chest comforted by the simple, but alluring embrace. She held her hand out in front of her, seemingly admiring a make-believe ring. Jason broke her comfort, sat up and gazed into her eyes, somewhat caught between a thought and a hard place. Monique glared back, identified his expression as one of concern.

"What is it, Jason?"

"I want you to have something, but first I need to know if you'd accept it."

"It…as in?"

"It's best if I show you."

Jason excused himself, walked to the closet, and returned with a medium-sized box. He rambled through its contents, then found and handed Monique a diamond solitaire, two-plus carats in size.

"What is this?" Monique asked, barely able to contain her excitement.

"It's yours if you'd accept it."

"Why wouldn't I?"

"It belonged to Sasha."

Monique looked into his eyes. She saw such emotion that she took time to reflect on the knowledge of his relationship with Sasha.

"Jason," Monique said carefully, "if my memory serves me correctly, you once told me that it was the memory of Sasha who helped you love me."

"Something like that. As strange as it sounds, Sasha spoke to me some way, somehow. I received whispers from a troubled heart, my troubled heart, and her spirit showed me all that I needed. She lifted the pain that I was feeling and released me to love you."

"With this in mind, I'd be honored to wear this symbol of your love. I don't want you to ever forget what she meant to you. I'm indebted to her, we both are."

At that moment, Jason realized that this and more amazing times were in store for him. He took the ring from her hand, placed it on her finger, and then politely kissed her on the lips. The simple act caused Monique to blush.

"Excuse me," she said in an excited state. "I could definitely get used to this."

For the next few moments, they coexisted in silence. Monique was curled comfortably in his embrace. They seemingly had blocked out the television that played in the background until the words "twenty-eight days for twenty-eight million" awakened their consciousness. They left their solitude and directed their attention to what the newscaster was saying. When the segment ended, they shook their heads in awe.

"I know that the person who bought that ticket is feeling sick," Monique said.

"Probably not, dear...it seems to me that if someone has twenty-eight days left to claim twenty-eight million dollars, then it stands to reason that this person either lost it or does not realize that he or she has the winning lottery ticket in their possession."

"That makes sense. I can see myself doing that. Sometimes I can't remember my words, much less remember to check a lotto ticket."

"Say that again."

"I'm saying that I often forget to check my ticket after a drawing."

"No, you said, remember my words."

"And?"

Jason didn't respond. He basically stared through her as he attempted to recall why those words were so familiar to him. Out of the blue, his subconscious mind blurted, "Sasha."

"What about her?" Monique asked.

"Who?" Jason responded after snapping back to reality.

"You called Sasha's name."

"Did I?" Jason asked rather dumbfounded. "It was Sasha who said those words to me that night I proposed to you."

"What are you talking about?"

"It's a long story. Remember my words," Jason recited again as he sat on the side of the bed. "Remember my words. She must have been referring to her journals."

It became clear to him, clearer than the brilliant VS-rated diamond Monique was wearing. His mind bounced to a bookmark located in one of her journals and he recalled thinking how strange that a lotto ticket would be used for such a purpose. Jason reached into the box of Sasha's possessions and blindly began removing the journals in search of what was calling him. He placed each gingerly on the bed as if they were delicate glass.

On the fourth try, it felt right. It *was* right, a small block of paper was extending from the journal's pages. Jason held the journal up to Monique's eyes. Without even looking, he said, "This is it."

"Jason, truly I'm lost," Monique confessed.

"That piece of paper," Jason announced as his eyes focused on it, "is worth twenty-eight million dollars."

"No way, things like that don't happen to ordinary people like us."

"Your statement is flawed. We are extraordinary people. Take it."

Monique found what Jason was saying well beyond belief, yet somehow his conviction to his statement, the sentiment it carried, made his words all too real. Her heart raced as she plucked the paper from the pages.

"The prize amount is?" Jason asked.

Monique flipped the ticket over, cut her eyes from Jason to it, back to Jason. Suddenly her mouth became dry. She swallowed before she spoke. "Twenty-eight million," she replied with a crackled voice.

Jason stood, smiled, and walked into his home office. In a few seconds he was browsing through Virginia's Lottery page. Monique was too nervous to walk. Even sitting down, her knees trembled as she anticipated the outcome.

"Angel," Jason called, "Come in here, please."

"Honey, I can't, just tell me."

Jason stood in the doorway. "Well, it appears that we have a new-found fortune."

Monique's mouth opened without a sound. She gazed at Jason in disbelief, seemingly discarding his words. Jason allowed Monique to gather her composure before he sat next to her. Immediately, her arms held him in a strong, silent embrace.

"This is," Jason spoke calmly, "quite a turn of events considering my poor upbringing."

"Remember, I knew you back then, things weren't that bad for you."

"You're looking at it from the outside because things weren't good at all. I remember one Christmas my mother wanted to get me something to wear and something to play with, but money was tight. So, she bought me a pair of pants and cut the pockets out."

Monique's face dove into confusion. She stared at him, followed the gaze with a smile and then a burst of laughter. "That was silly."

"Silly enough to make you laugh."

"Here I thought we were having a serious conversation; somehow, again you manage to add humor."

"We needed something to break the tension."

"It's strange, seems to me that we would be overjoyed with the money, but we're acting differently."

"Believe me...inside there is a fireworks display grander than the Fourth of July celebration at the Washington Monument. I guess everything surrounding how we became wealthy is mind-boggling."

"So..." She smiled. "What are you going to do with your free time?"

"I've always wanted to learn how to play golf."

ONE

Monique bathed in the hot sun topless. This piece of paradise was the last stop on their vacationing tour before returning to Virginia City. They had spent two weeks respectively in Aruba, Barbados, St. Thomas, and Bermuda, and concluded their extended vacation in Puerto Rico. She and Jason lay on beach towels tanning their bodies that had beads of sweat rolling down their oiled skin. They indulged themselves on the bow of a rented yacht that ironically was named "Monique's Pleasure," anchored in the Caribbean Sea. It was a one-hundred-ten-foot yacht that had every amenity imaginable. They had sailed to a secluded cove off of the main Puerto Rican island for their own private sanctuary on the water.

"Honey," Monique said, "does it get any better than this?" she asked with her eyes closed.

"Nothing can be better than quality time with the one you love," Jason responded.

Monique turned her eyes away from the sun, toward Jason and opened them slowly as if he were a Christmas present that she hardly believed she had received.

"I love you, too...even before the riches, but I can't complain about being spoiled beyond my wildest dreams."

"Yes, early retirement never felt so good. Are you ready to get back to the real world?"

"Semi."

"Yes, life as we knew it will be different when we get back."

"Waking at home at our leisure will be a wonderful thing."

Jason opened his eyes, turned his head toward her, and discovered Monique in a heavenly gaze.

"Why such a passionate look?" Jason asked.

"I don't know. I think it's the magic of the moment combined with how the sun's rays are tantalizing my nipples," Monique confessed.

"Oh?"

"It's like my body's warmth is being charged from the heat coming through my nipples."

"Do you want to take another dip in the water to cool off?"

"No, I'm okay. The heat makes me feel rather nasty."

"Nasty good or nasty bad?"

Monique smiled. Jason sat up, reached to his left, and filled his glass with more Mimosa. He took two decent-sized swallows, followed by a huge one, then fell to his knees and lowered his lips onto one of her nipples. *They are hot*, Jason thought.

"That's refreshing," Monique responded.

"Think it will help you cool off?" Jason asked.

Before Monique could respond, Jason used his tongue to swirl a piece of ice around her hardened nipple.

"Yes, but your method warms me in delightful ways," Monique panted.

Jason switched to the other nipple and probed it until the remaining ice dissolved.

"What do you think you're doing, Mister?" Monique asked excited by Jason's actions.

"I'm cooling you off," Jason teased.

"Not like that you aren't."

"Okay, okay. Have more Mimosa."

"Thank you...nasty person."

Monique picked up her empty glass, leaned back on the towel, and rested on one elbow as she extended the glass for a refill of the satisfying beverage. The cold drink that met her flesh felt even colder because the raging sun baked her skin oven-hot. Monique screamed. She believed that her man had lost his ever-loving mind. She sat up quickly, momentarily overtaken by the sudden chill that invaded her skin. Jason moved the cold liquid stream from her stomach and poured onto her hidden desire, where Monique now experienced two uniquely different forms of wetness.

He tilted the pitcher upside-down; the ice cubes tumbled down like tiny glaciers crashing onto her tightened stomach muscles. Jason lifted her bikini bottoms fabric and placed two rectangular ice cubes under the garment. He strategically placed one cube against her lower lips and made sure that the bikini bottom held it in place. Monique screamed from the excitement and pleasure of Jason's playfulness.

"I don't believe you," Monique announced. "What if I did you like this someday?"

"That would be fun, but not today. Today my only mission is to serve you."

"Jason," Monique moaned as his lips closed over the ice cube through the garment.

The ice was like liquid hydrogen on her as it would be on a man, thus a means to prolong her orgasm. Monique's clitoris popped up as if the tune for the Jack-in-the-Box had just ended. Jason sucked on the ice cube for a long while as he alternated the pinching of Monique's nipples. This prompted the cube to move to Monique's toy surprise.

"I feel like it's going to pop off," Monique moaned in deep passion.

"What does?" Jason asked as he paused to nibble on her inner thigh.

Monique refused to solidify Jason's rhetorical question. She couldn't answer if she wanted to; she was too far gone to formulate a reasonable answer. Jason's mouth was heaven to Monique's passion, and the pleasure pain received from the alternating nipple pinches, all but helped Monique lose her mind. The ice yielded to the constant warmth of Jason's mouth and Monique's increased body temperature. Jason sensed by the feel of it on his tongue that her clitoris had softened and his soft warm tongue had produced greater, sultrier battle cries from Monique.

Jason didn't know if it was the gentle rocking of the yacht, the ultraviolet rays that constantly bathed her skin, or his wondrous instrument, but he couldn't remember a time when Monique's hips bucked so wildly. He slid a finger between her pleasure haven and the garment, curled his finger and pulled it to the side, then dove back into her flesh with his hungry mouth. Oddly, the strangest thought materialized in his mind, *Now that's old school.*

Monique's passionate moans were more sensual and erotic than he had ever known. Like a computer building a microchip, Jason danced his tongue around, in and out of her womanhood in a poetic fashion. It was lyrical. These lyrics performed as a current and ignited the electrical circuitry that took information back to her orgasmic processor. Monique suddenly slapped both hands on the bow, rose to a sitting position, and watched Jason perform his magic. The visual of her being pleased provided the last piece of information Monique's processor needed. Monique bellowed in a gigantic climax that started with the words, "Damn you, Jason" and ended with a descending in volume series of "Oh, oh, oh's."

Monique pushed away from him at the shoulders to escape Jason's overbearing mouth. Jason wiped most of the natural juices from his face on Monique's inner thigh, and then finished the rest with a portion of the beach towel.

"Had enough?" Jason joked.

"Man if you don't get that weapon from me, I'll scream."

"My weapon as in..?"

"Dangerous," Monique interrupted. "That tongue of yours. Honey, I'm too sensitive, you need to allow a girl time to regain composure?" Monique asked with a demand disguised as a question.

"Not a problem."

Jason excused himself, returned with two more dry oversized towels, and placed them in an area near Monique.

"So what are you going to do with those?" Monique asked after noticing that Jason was still aroused.

"Well," Jason replied. "This particular weapon will disengage once I lie back down and relax."

"I see," Monique commented playfully. "One of us once stated that a hard-on was a terrible thing to waste."

"Would that one of us happen to be you?"

"I don't remember," she lied.

Monique kneeled next to Jason, placed both hands at his waist, and pulled at his swim trunks.

"What are you doing, Ms. Sensitive?"

"Trying not to be wasteful."

"You're so bad."

"Actually my love, this is going to be good...now raise your damn hips," Monique stated forcefully.

"Yes Ma'am."

After the garment was removed, Monique took a note from Jason.

"We're going to tan him for a moment," Monique stated before she dashed away with the empty pitcher.

In the short time that Monique was gone, Jason found himself enjoying the sunrays on his manhood. He touched it as if he was checking to see if it had cooked sufficiently. *Interesting*, he thought.

No sooner than the thought faded from his memory, Monique's hand squeezed his tool as if she was extracting gel from a tube. The move startled him partly because his eyes were closed while he listened to the waves splashing against the yacht, but mostly because Monique's hand was cold. Prior to her seizing Jason's tool, her hand was submerged in the pitcher with water and ice.

Monique placed her other hand in the cold water and simultaneously lowered her mouth onto him. She did this before her previously chilled hand had time to warm completely. Her hot sensual mouth elevated Jason's erotic state. He closed his eyes and felt the sun's rays try to penetrate through his eyelids. Monique had been in her position far too many times for Jason to remember, but this time, her mouth felt as soothing as the first taste of warm apple pie.

She gauged Jason's mounting excitement by the slow movement of his hips. Suddenly Monique stopped, gave him a taste of the first sensation by stroking him with the cold hand from the bucket. Another adrenaline rush consumed Jason, but when she placed a couple of ice cubes against his genitals, Jason would swear that his blood had frozen. The warmth of her mouth teased him again. Jason bathed in the sensation that was almost heavenly. He was speechless and completely inundated by her spell. The movement of a soft pleasing tongue coupled with chilled genitals couldn't be put into words. Monique continued the hot-cold treatment until her hands couldn't withstand another dunk into the freezing water. Then, she spent a long time, showing great patience enjoying her throbbing tool. Jason, on the other hand, had subdued his release for the past few minutes. If he relaxed, an explosion grander than the bomb dropped on Hiroshima would occur.

"What do you want?" Monique asked in a sultry voice.

Jason didn't respond to her inquiry. She asked the question again, immediately after her mouth left his hardness.

"I want..." Jason panted, but continued to hold his orgasm.

Monique stood tall above him, removed the hindering clothing, and straddled her joy backward in the reverse cowboy maneuver. Her cushiony haven accepted Jason slowly, willingly and uninhibited. Her hands were at the side for support as if Jason's manliness had penetrated too deeply for that position.

Jason pulled one of her arms behind her back, then the other. Monique gasped as her body fully accepted him. She wanted to scream, but she remained motionless in order to adjust to the pleasure pressure that filled her. Jason used his pinky fingernail to trace an imaginary line from between her shoulder blades, down to the center of the small of Monique's back. Monique responded with a small hip movement. Jason retraced the line once more and a similar response came from Monique. Jason traced the same line so many times that a red trail became visible on her sun-baked skin. It burned to touch, yet it aided in the sensation that Jason's manhood was giving her. However, during the process, Monique's hip movements had quickened and become a rhythmic motion that she wasn't aware of.

She wanted to buck wildly through the orgasm that swept her. Instead she oddly leaned forward and was awed that Jason's manliness extended deeper into her. She squeezed her internal muscles hard for a count of three before releasing and executing the move again. Her reward was a series of "mini-gasms," her word for the quick-ending yet pleasing orgasms.

Monique noted that with each squeeze of her muscles, Jason's tool throbbed uncontrollably. Moments after she held and released the last of her mini-ones, Jason's juices filled her, perfectly timed as though their act had been rehearsed a thousand times. Jason moaned pleasurably. His passion cry was different than most. It was filled with more exuberance and delight. Jason's wondrous sounds thrilled Monique's ears.

Monique wasn't finished. She squeezed, held it tight and slowly lifted as if she was removing him from within her. She released the muscle control just as Jason was exiting her, and then slammed herself back down deeply onto his tool. She squeezed, held the muscle control tight and began to lift her body from him.

"Uncle," Jason announced as he slapped her butt with one of his hands.

"What was that?" Monique chuckled. "You're quitting?" she asked almost in laughter.

"Just for the moment," Jason panted.

Their bodies were sweaty, aided by the sun that seemed all their own, but primarily from the secretions of the act itself. She was pleased; her man was pleased. All was good. She lay backward, her back against his hairy chest and felt a sting from the trail that Jason made on her back. Yet, she marveled in the sensation of their union as Jason's arms draped around her in a soothing embrace.

"Could it be that the Jason Jerrard was vocal when he came?" Monique joked.

Jason smiled before replying, "Not me, never."

"Today, my dear, you were loud. I loved it."

The rebuttal concerning the amount of noise Jason made continued for a small moment and concluded with Monique stating to Jason that she and the fish knew the real truth. They lay connected in the embrace for what seemed like hours, each being satisfied with the solitude.